THE HITMAN'S GUIDE
TO HOUSECLEANING

THE HITMAN'S GUIDE TO HOUSECLEANING

HALLGRIMUR HELGASON

amazon crossing

The characters and events portrayed in this book are fictitious. Any similarity to real persons, living or dead, is coincidental and not intended by the author.

Text copyright © 2008 by Hallgrimur Helgason
All rights reserved.
Printed in the United States of America.

First published by AmazonCrossing in 2012.

Published by AmazonCrossing
P.O. Box 400818
Las Vegas, NV 89140

ISBN-13: 9781611091397
ISBN-10: 161109139X
Library of Congress Control Number: 2011913741

for Barbara Taylor

CHAPTER 1
TOXIC
05.15.2006

My mother named me Tomislav, and my father was a Bokšić. After my first week in the US, I'd become Tom Boksic. Which then led to Toxic.

The thing I am today.

I often wonder if it was me who poisoned my name or the name that poisoned me. Either way, I bring danger. At least, that's what Munita says. My darling explosive, she's addicted to danger. Munita was living in Peru until her family got killed in a terrorist bombing. Then she moved to New York and found a job on Wall Street. It so happened that her first day of work was 9/11. On our first trip to Croatia together, she witnessed two killings. I have to admit that one of them was by my own hand, but the other one was totally accidental. I thought it was quite a romantic scene, actually. We were having dinner in Mirko's restaurant when the guy sitting at the table next to us got a bullet through his brain. Some of his blood splattered into Munita's glass of wine. I didn't tell her. She was having red anyway.

She's not crazy about violence, she says, but I still think she's drawn to me because of my toxic nature. Bombing is the basis of our relationship; the sex is always explosive. My Munita is a body-girl and she gets noticed. Men always look her up and down. Like many from Lazy America, she is short, and some people have called her fat, but those people haven't talked much after that. When she walks down the street I can hear her breasts moving about *Jug-jug, jug-jug.* My favorite sound in America. If she's wearing her stiff orange shirt, others can hear it too. When I first saw her I had the feeling I had seen her before. Before we get married I will ask her if she's ever acted in a porn video or if I saw her on an Internet thumbnail.

What makes my Munita Bonita perfect for me is the fact that her family is dead. There is no mother in-law, no brother in-law, no Thanksgiving dinners, kids' birthday parties, or weddings to attend, which would mean standing unprotected out on some stupid lawn, in the screaming sunshine, with fifty people at your back.

Yes, Munita Rosales is drawn to men of the gun. Before me she was dating some Talian guy from Long Island. (For us "Italian" became "Talian" after Niko accidentally shot the "I" off a sign above one of their restaurants.) His CV was much shorter than mine, but I guess he could still be called a colleague. I'm what they call in our language a *plačeni ubojica.* In New York they call it a contract killer, or a hitman. Ever since I arrived in New York six years ago, I've been keeping the funeral homes busy. I even thought about making a deal with one of them and told Dikan he should secretly buy one. That way we could make more money off our dead victims. Hit and run to the bank.

Let me tell you about my job. During the week I work as a waiter in the Zagreb Samovar, our beautiful restaurant on East 21st Street. The word "waiter" fits perfectly well since most of my time is spent waiting for the next job, which can be quite boring.

The Balkan animal, which is my soul, is always hungry for prey. I get restless if three months go by without firing a gun. My slowest year was 2002: only two hits and one miss. I still regret that one. In this business, missing the target can be deadly. You don't want some wounded psycho out there shopping around for your good-bye bullet. People tend to get a bit upset if they notice you're try-ing to kill them. But let me assure you, my miss of 2002 became my first hit of 2003. Nowadays, I never waste a bullet.

You see, I'm what they call a triple six-packer. I've been told this is a Manhattan record. Some Talian guy named Perrosi became a double six-packer back in the eighties, when John Gotti was king of Queens, but no one has ever gone triple until Toxic came along. Ac-tually, I think the Talians are not the same as they once were. When they're shooting more movies about you than you are shooting peo-ple, it means you're past the bill. In twenty years' time we will have our own show, like *The Sopranos: The Sliškos*. But then I will have become like Shaking Trigger, high on Viagra with a woman's hairdo.

I tell Munita that being a six-packer is really all about the environment. I'm an environmentalist. I don't want to add an un-necessary gunshot to the already noisy city. I told her this on our third date after she had asked me for the third time what I did for a living. It took me four weeks of phone calls and one quick break-in to get her on the fourth.

Sorry, I forget. Doing a six-pack means that six consecutive bullets produce a funeral. Six bullets, six funerals, weeping wid-ows, flowers, and all.

With a record like mine, Dikan should have promoted me long ago, but the sucker is stubborn like an ass without a hole. Fucking Fingerlicker. That's the nickname we gave him because he sucks his short, fat fingers at the end of every meal. But all he ever says is, "Toxic is good waiter. He never misses an order."

I will be pleased to follow Bilič's order when it comes and put an end to Fingerlicker.

We try to keep up our LPP, or Lowest Possible Profile, as we do our business. This means I usually try to settle the case in the privacy of the person's hotel room, his car, or his home. Preferably without any witnesses. If this doesn't work out, we often invite the victim to our restaurant. The "last supper" joke is customary. After dinner I bring him the bill for the whole table, a sum that is so high that they always prefer paying with their life. We have a special room in the back that we take them to. The Red Room, we call it, even though it's green.

As you might have guessed, there are no regular customers at the Zagreb Samovar.

By the way, the name of the place is totally stupid since a "samovar" is a Russian tea-machine and has nothing to do with *hrvatska* culture, but Dikan thinks it's really clever. "Acting stupid is best disguise," he likes to say.

Though I'm still waiting for that fucking promotion I can't really complain. The money is good and food, of course, is excellent. I have my great apartment on Wooster and Spring, a location Munita is willing to fuck for, and I love Noisy York, though I miss my fucking fatherland every fucking day. But earlier this year I struck cable gold and found I could watch *HRT* and *Hajduk Split* on my flat screen at home. My mother calls once a year to ask when I'm going back to studies. This is Croatian slang for "the money's up." As soon as I hang up, I send her $2000 through the Internet. Good for another year.

She lives alone with my fat little sister. Both my brother and father got killed in the war. I come from a family of hunters. My grandfather was Tito's personal gamekeeper. Tito was the head of my ex-fatherland, Yugoslavia. It passed away shortly after he did, like a sad old widow. Tito loved bears. Especially dead ones. I never had the chance to shoot one, but when I was a boy my father often took me boar hunting. "The wild boar is just like a woman," he said. "You have to pretend that you don't want to shoot it. So we just wait here." He was a big *waiter*. Just like me.

I see myself as a hunter. I shoot pigs for a living.

CHAPTER 2
THE FUCK-UP
05.15.2006

But now I'm in trouble. For the first time in my spotless career. I'm riding in the company car, crossing the Williamsburg Bridge, with Manhattan at my back, Munita in my ear, her body on my mind, and my eyes on driver Radovan's piggy neck-back. A bullet would have a hard time with this head. The afternoon Manhattan sun throws skyscraper shadows down on the river's surface.

"Oh, baby. I will miss you," Munita whispers from behind her desk on the twenty-sixth floor of Trump Tower. Two years ago she started on the ground floor. And yet she never did *The Apprentice.* That's my Munita. You can't dislike her. Her voice is half Hindu but the accent is all Peru. Her mother was from Bombay, and she's got that Indian olive oil skin, a softwear that can keep you going all the way to the North Pole in a golf cart with President Bush at the steering wheel.

"Me, too," I answer, one more fucking time not totally sure whether this is 100 percent perfect English that I'm speaking. But I guess I'm right. I will miss myself. I will miss my great life in the great city.

I'm going into exile. Disappearing for a while, six months at least. My plane ticket reads: New York – Frankfurt – Zagreb. Signed by Dikan. I will come crawling back under my mother's kitchen table with a gun in my mouth. I fucked up. Or somebody fucked me. Hit #66 was a miss. Don't get me wrong. I got the bullet into the guy's head safe and sound, but there was some serious aftermath. The mustached Polish guy turned out to be a mustached FBI guy. What was supposed to be a bright and sunny murder in broad daylight became a nightmare. I took him to the trash dump over in Queens and put him away in a heap of fake Levi's jeans and then covered his ugly face with an old Pepsi Max sunbrella. On my way back to the car, I noticed some friends of his had arrived too late for the coffin-free funeral. My old Croatian heart skipped from waltz to death metal, and I turned quickly around. For the next ten minutes I ran like a hurdler at the Obese Olympics through the waste of some six thousand nuclear New York families, all the time heading for the river, and finally sought shelter in a rusty old container full of ancient teddy bears that, strangely enough, smelled of grilled cheese. The Federal Bastards sealed off the area, so I ended up spending the night with them. It was a sleepless night of Manhattan skyline, cold container, and smelly bears. For the empty stomach, the smell of food is like perfume to a boner.

In the morning hours it was a bit lovely to see the rooms in the United Nations Building light up, one after the other—their reflection in the East River scrambled by the running water. It was way before sunrise. I guess every nation on earth has its own office in the building, and the lights in each room are programmed to go on at the same time the sun rises in the country it belongs to. I watched 156 sunrises that night. Before number 157 broke, I was in the river. The ice-cold stream brought me down to a different dumpsite. It was more like a Web site, actually, full of net-like lines and cables.

In the mouth of the Midtown Tunnel, I found a cab. The driver had a problem with the fact that my clothes were all wet, but I took out my gun and dried them in an instant.

Toxic is traveling under the name of Igor Illitch. I was born in Smolensk now, in 1971. I've been born all over the place. Once I held a German passport that gave me a pretty happy childhood in the then-capitol Bonn. I even made the effort, on my way through the Rhine valley, to concoct some idyllic childhood memories. Father Dieter worked as a janitor at the Russian embassy, and mother Ilse was a chef at the American embassy. Every night was cold war, with me being Berlin, a wall between my eyes. Though I'm no actor; I don't mind getting a new life once in a while. In fact, I've always enjoyed that part of my work. You get a break from yourself. Except for my weekend as a Serb back in '99. Then I really felt like killing the man I had become.

But even though they've had me born in different cities, they usually use the same year, the right one: 1971. I was born the day before Hajduk finally won the championship after some twenty years of waiting. My football-fanatic father believed I was a good-luck charm and called me "Champ."

The highway snakes its way through Brooklyn. I look at all the advertisements with almost-tears in my eyes. I just don't want to leave this town. We pass a big blue billboard: "Eyewitness News at Seven – WABC-TV New York." Three days in a row my face was there, "...*known in Mob circles simply as 'Toxic'.*" But it was never more than a flash. No big story, like the ones they do on the mass killers. Those guys become household names in one day while the honest and hardworking men and women of the assas-sination industry are only mentioned in passing. The nation that measures everything in money sucks up to amateurs instead of us professionals. I guess I will never fully understand this country. I love New York, but I don't get the rest.

The suburbs quickly thin out, and soon we enter the land of liftoffs and landings. Igor's passport sits in my breast pocket, like a Gucci bag made in China. Behind it my heart beats the drum of doubt.

"*Doviđenja,*" Radovan says outside the International Departures Terminal. I forbid him to follow me inside. His sunglasses scream for the FBI like a gay on a hot tin roof. Stupidity is no disguise for the stupid. I shaved off all my hair this morning and tried my best to dress Russian: black leather jacket, the ugliest jeans in the closet, and Puma Putin running shoes.

Before I left, I turned around in the doorway and fingerkissed my flat screen goodbye. Munita asked me if she could take care of my place while I was away, but I told her no. We don't have thrust-trust yet. The sex bomb won't tick for six months without exploding, and I don't want some Peruvian prick drying his dirty after-sex-sweat on my Prada towels.

The check-in goes smoothly. A shallow blonde with deep dimples tells me not to worry about my bags. I will see them again in Zagreb. Seems they have direct NYC-Zagreb flights for luggage only. Immigration requires self-control. I put on my Igor expression while the officer admires the Chinese handiwork. Then two over-proud security guys make me deliver phone, wallet, and dimes. Jacket, belt, and shoes. In the middle of my coincash, they spot an object that makes my heart skip from samba to rock. Turns out my ugliest jeans contain a lone bullet, a beautiful golden 9mm from the Browning Hi-Power semi-automatic that Davor presented me with on my arrival in New York.

"What is this? That's a bullet! No?" a small Long Island Latino woman in uniform asks me in her horrible mall accent.

"Oh...Yeah. That's a...That's a souvenir," I hit back.

"A souvenir?"

"Eh...Yes. It...It was removed from my brain," I say, trying to look like the thing did permanent damage to it.

She buys it and lets me go after giving me a full-body massage.

I'll never get used to this no-gun traveling thing. It's not in a man's nature to cross countries or oceans unarmed. Fucking 9/11 makes me really want to shoot bin Laden. But I can't, since I'm not allowed to carry the gun on the plane.

I'm starting to look forward to Zagreb when two Feds suddenly appear and make their way towards the people standing at the gate, tickets in hand. I'm the last in line. There is no denying it's *them*. I can smell undercover all the way from Jersey, like a dog in heat. They're sporting the usual H&M jackets and sunglasses, all stitched up in the classic FBI hairdo straight out of DC. The look is sort of "official casual," quite shiny and a bit curly, like Michael Keaton's in *Multiplicity*.

I immediately duck for cover behind waiting passengers, pick up my bag, and start walking away from the gate, in the opposite direction of the undercover agents. *Doviđenja, Zagreb*. My heart's pounding, but I do not allow myself to look back. *Don't ever look back on danger!* Mother used to say. I walk for some six fucking minutes, my shaved skull turning into a fucking fountain on the way. Airport hallways are endless. People stare at me like I was carrying Saddam's balls in my bag. Finally I spot the everyman sign and take a swift turn to the left. Inside the bathroom I catch my breath and dry my head. While they dry their hands, three businessmen look at me as if I were a Russian arms dealer waiting for a customer. Finally, I set back out on the open sea. Not clear. I immediately hurry back inside the bathroom as I spot one of the Michael Keatons. I know he didn't see me, though. He was walking by.

I go into one of the stalls and pretend to do what I'm thinking. What the hell can I do now? I can't possibly go back to my gate. Too risky. The Keatons will be waiting for me there, smiling like silly relatives. But then, what?

The answer comes to me in the shape of a belt, the tip of a belt that introduces itself from below the wall between my stall and the next. I wait for a few moments and pray to God. Finally the owner of the belt finishes and leaves his stall. As I open the cheap door, our eyes meet in the mirror over the row of sinks. God seems to have heard me: just like Igor, Belt Man is shaved to the bone. Two bald and chubby fellow travelers, they look remarkably similar, though Belt Man wears almost invisible glasses and is a bit older than Igor. But he won't get much older now. Igor puts him out with a near-silent punch in the back of his head, right in the G-spot. His glasses fall into the sink as his head hits the mirror. There is no blood. The fellow is quite heavyset, even more so than me, but still I manage to deliver him into the same stall where he dropped his final shit on this earth, and close the door behind me.

I take his pulse. No heartbeat.

The adrenaline pumping more slowly, I'm rather horrified to realize that #67 is a holy man. He's wearing a white clerical collar around his neck, plus black shirt, black jacket, black coat. White skin. I search for his ticket, passport, and wallet and *pooha!* Toxic Igor has a new name: Rev. David Friendly. Born in Vienna, Virginia, on November 8, 1965. I can go for that. I've never been an American before. Where is he going? "Reykjavik," reads the ticket. Sounds like Europe. With some difficulty I manage to remove the coat and jacket from the holy man's chubby torso and then start unbuttoning his shirt, sweat pouring off my head again and breathing like a boar. I make a quick break when I hear someone enter the bathroom and try to hide my heavy breathing under the sound of his pee. It's followed by a quick gush of water and the drying of hands.

As soon as the coast is clear, I emerge from the JFK toilets a born-again Christian, with a halo around my neck and a new mission in life: Gate 2.

CHAPTER 3
ICELANDAIR
05.15.2006

It's fucking amazing. I'm moving across the North Atlantic sky at the speed of sound and yet his soul has caught up with me. I feel restless, buried in some extra-small window seat on a plane full of blonde women and bland men. I don't know what's happening, but my legs are absolutely killing me. Mr. Friendly must have connections in heaven; an army of angels is pinching me with their pointy fingernails and strangling my throat with the clerical collar.

Holy men are the worst.

Back during the war I once was ordered to guard a church in a small village near the town of Knin. The Serbs had been using it for storing their bombs, but now we were taking control of the region. On a foggy Sunday morning, the fucking village priest suddenly appeared out of the blue and said he wanted to hold a mass. I said no way, nobody was allowed inside the church. He was an old man with a white beard and white hair around his ears. In a way he looked more like a monk than a priest. And his face was full of this peaceful fatigue. Looking into his eyes was like getting a sneak preview of the afterlife: two silent ponds in the Everwoods. It was as if he was already dead. As if he didn't care anymore. Without saying a word, he just walked past me, towards the church door. I ran after him and told him again in cut-throat-clear Croatian that *nobody* was allowed inside the church. I had my orders.

"ABSOLUTELY FUCKING NOBODY!" I screamed into his hairy ear.

He just closed his eyes for a slow moment and then made for the door. I tried to push him away with my rifle, but I couldn't really do it. I just couldn't get physical with this old man who was like the Spirit of Humanity itself or some high-brewed shit like that. In pure Sunday silence, he brought out his large key and started opening the wooden door. I had already spent four years in the war and had shot more people than were sitting in my family tree, but I was still shaking all over like the badly made cigarettes I would smoke later that day. What the hell was going on? I was being outplayed by an eighty-year-old unarmed priest! How could this be happening? As I watched him disappearing inside the church, I finally freaked out and shot him in the back. He fell on the stony floor, crucifixion-style, like the guy hanging on the opposite wall.

I shut the door and sat down with my back against it. I would have cried if the war hadn't cast all my tears in stone. So I just sat there, stone faced, cursing the whole thing: my land, his land, our land, and the whole fucking war. I sat there for some twenty cigarettes. My Sunday in hell. I had killed a holy man, and I was deadly surprised by the effect it had on me. I had killed older guys before, even one that could have been a lady, without suffering this type of moral hangover. But somehow this one was three tons more dramatic—probably about the weight of his chapel. I could feel horns breaking through my hairline, and the fast-growing tail between my buttocks made sitting painful.

It was then that I began to lose my mind. A strange feeling started growing in me. I felt like the big bang of my rifle shot was still vibrating inside the small village church, that the horrid sound was slowly filling it up, all the way up to the bell. I even heard the bloody bronze thing resonating with rage, filling my head with the same heavy-metal droning. And before I knew it, I started firing at the fucking church bell like a crazy boy shooting at chickens. It cried out into the fog like a woman in childbirth.

After some fifteen bullets had banged the bell, a different kind of shooting rang out. I threw myself in the wet grass, ducking from a blizzard of bullets blowing straight out of hell. In a split second, all the church windows were shattered to pieces. Moments later, the whole holy thing blew up in a big yellow blast. Rubble punched my back like some iron-fingered masseuse and a cornerstone dented my helmet. I was left semi-conscious.

He who kills a man of the church will be killed by a church.

I've never been inside one since. For weeks and months my young sick soul was tortured by the image of an eighty-year-old Jesus facedown on a stony floor. Every night I hammered a big iron-nail into his back and out through his heart, which exploded, painting my entire world red.

They offer *Sideways* on the plane TV, but also vintage stuff like *Seinfeld*, some rusty old reruns of weirdo hairdos. Seinfeld was typically American in that show. He was a pretty funny guy, but he had no sense of style. Tacky like a Texan tux. Tasteless dressing and tasteful jokes. That's Seinfeld for me. I would have preferred it the other way around.

The guy sitting next to me is reading some paperback monster that looks to be one of those Mob thrillers (how many volumes can they write about those Sicilian brats?). Occasionally he murmurs a yes or a no to the older gentleman sitting in the aisle seat who keeps popping some pills. They must be uppers since he can't seem to allow the poor fellow to read his book without peppering him with questions in a bizarre accent. It turns out the talking guy is Icelandic and the reading guy is a basketball player, born and bred in Boise, Idaho, but now on a transfer to the Schniefel Stickholmers or something like that—a small team in the Icelandic conference.

Oh, yeah. I forget to mention that this is a nonsmoking Icelandair flight from New York to Reykjavik, Iceland. This was the surprise that awaited me at Gate 2. My exile has taken a northern turn. By the touch of my index finger, the video screen abandons Seinfeld's hairdo for an info-map: A red airplane, the size of Britain, slowly crawls up the Atlantic, past some white thing that the talking man says is Greenland. Iceland on the other hand looks pretty green. The chatty one takes the next ten minutes to explain his theory about this mix-up: When the Norwegian Vikings discovered Iceland in some year before 1000, they found Irish monks up there, who'd already named the land *Island*, or The Land of Christ, for Jesus was *Isu* in their language. The Vikings, however, took the Savior for *ice*. I'm glad they did. Or else I'd be traveling to Christland.

"OK. Cool. What about Greenland then?" the basketball player asks.

"The first settlers wanted all of Iceland for themselves, so they named the other one Greenland, so that next wave of immigrants would go there instead. Many people say it was the first PR trick in history. It really should be the other way around. Greenland should be called Iceland and Iceland, Greenland."

Cool. I'm traveling under a pseudonym to a country with a pseudonym. Not too bad. I've heard about Iceland before.

A friend of Dikan's went there once for some arms-for-legs deal. The nights are bright and the girls are long, he said. Or was it the other way around? It's a small island (ah, well, it's two times bigger than Croatia) in the middle of the North Atlantic. The in-flight magazine shows lunar landscapes and sunny faces. Mossy rocks and fuzzy sweaters. They say Iceland is a young, hot country that's still very active, shaking from eruptions and earthquakes almost daily, with boiling water and running lava breaking up through the surface. I wonder what brings Rev. David Friendly to this remote place? That's me, that is. I have to start thinking like a priest.

Bless my soul.

Once more I try to find the right position for my aching legs. The stewardesses all have nice bodies and speak English with super confidence. Bright girls, long nights. Yeah, that's how it was. The Icelandic look seems to be a cross between Julia Stiles and Virginia Madsen. Broad faces, barren cheeks. Cold eyes, cool lips. One of them hands me a tray of food and gives me an innocent, *oh-what-a-sweet-puppy* smile. Must be the dog collar I'm wearing. I'm not a man anymore. I'm a priest.

In that way the bloody collar works. It keeps the sin away. Or keeps it all inside. My mind starts giving Munita a very long leash as I try to picture myself in bed with one of these northern nymphs. I don't succeed. Munita has the upper hand. I miss her soft skin already.

They make you pay for food. I find a few holy bills in Friendly's wallet and send him my warmest thanks. Then I find out airline food tastes no better even when you're paying for it. Maybe your taste buds stop working at five thousand feet. Suddenly the Wise Guy raises his voice as well as his glass of red wine, and, smiling, says "*skull!*" to me and the basketball player. At first I think he must be toasting my fresh hairdo, but he explains that this is the Icelandic version of "cheers!" The Vikings used to celebrate their victories by filling their victims' brain shells with booze.

I love this country already.

After dinner I try to fall asleep. I really need my after-killing nap. But I seem to be the only one who wants to shut his eyes. The Vikings scream for another skull of cognac. And then the captain starts his voice-over bit, his manly voice tuned to the max in the overhead speakers. As with all his colleagues around the world, he speaks in Airish, the incomprehensive language of the skies. Those cockpit-monologues always sound to me like some Latin prayer, asking God for permission to cross his lawn. This one is fourteen minutes long.

I keep my eyes shut. Being Friendly is an iron collar around my neck.

Behind me I can hear the stewardess take yet another drinking order from two happy Vikings. And down the aisle, a group of chubby women have drunk themselves back to their high-school days. The Icelanders seem to be related to the Russians, who can never leave their motherland without being totally hammered and would never return to it in a sober state. Makes me think of old Ivica, who used to live in our street in Split. He was so afraid of his wife that he had to soak himself in courage each time he wanted to leave the house, and never dared return unless he was deaf from booze.

"Skull!" "Skull!" I hear them say behind me, all around me. I give up on sleeping and open my priestly eyes.

Now it's selling time. They've turned the plane into a flying mall, with the stewardesses all busy running credit cards and handing out sunglasses and silky ties. I've never seen that before, not even on Aeroflot. But it seems like an effective but deadly combination: drinking and shopping. I think to myself that Macy's and Bloomingdale's should definitely consider opening bars in their men's and women's departments. Or, maybe there are no shops in Iceland?

Despite the captain's prayer, the angels keep on pinching my legs and punching a conscience I thought I'd lost. Normally my profession carries no side effects, though I do get tired after a hit. The post-slaying siesta is a close relative to the after-sex nap; though there's little physical effort (she always prefers to be on top), the inner achievement calls for a little rest.

I finally manage to tune out the drunken shopping of my fellow travelers and fall asleep with Munita on top of me—her wonder balls bouncing and her long, black hair tickling my chubby chest, like the tip of God's long white beard touching my sick soul.

CHAPTER 4
"FATHER FRIENDLY"
05.16.2006

The landing wakes me up. It's a harsh one, with the plane shaking all over, from nose to tail, long after it has touched the ground. A bright, sexy voice rings out over the system, first in the lunar language, and then in English, welcoming us to the local temperature of three degrees Celsius.

I guess Iceland is the right name after all.

The photos didn't lie. It does look like the moon. Nothing but gray rocky fields topped with moss with small blue mountains in the distance. It's lava, I guess. Lava fields. This is Volcano Island.

The stewardess gives me another platonic smile as I leave the aircraft. The walkway is made of glass. Actually, the landscape looks like a huge set design from a Star Wars movie. I attempt to enter this strange land like a regular visitor, trying hard to walk like the man I killed last night, swinging his black briefcase like a happy priest, wearing his all-black shoes, shirt, jacket, and coat plus the white collar. I kept the jeans on. I'm a modern minister.

I follow the basketball player inside the terminal. He's way too small for his profession, shorter even than six-foot me. Maybe they ship all the smallest players to the small nation leagues. Wise Guy said the Icelandic nation only counted three hundred thousand people. Is that even legal? It's like if Little Italy was a country, with its own flag and everything, a small Olympic team. They'd sure take the Gold in Restaurant Shooting.

The basketball player leads me to Passport Control, where two lines have formed in front of a glass cage housing two officers. One line is for the people of the European Union and the other is for the rest of the world. I'm trying to remember if Russia is a member of the EU when I realize that I'm American now. I'm Friendly! The line moves pretty quickly. This will be easy, I tell myself. I find the holy man's passport in the inner breast pocket of his black coat, step up to the glass booth, and hand it to the officer, a dark-browed guy with a grayish beard. He opens it and then says something in his own language. I give him a blank look. As he repeats himself I realize he's speaking Russian. The motherfucker is speaking fucking Russian.

"I'm sorry?" I say.

"You don't speak Russian?" he asks in English.

"No, I was born in the States."

He holds up my passport. "It says here that you were born in Smolensk?"

Suddenly all the veins in my neck become as thick as strings on an electric Fender bass. Fuck. I gave him the wrong passport! I gave him Igor's passport. I'm Igor now, not Friendly. Big, big *fuck*.

"Eh...Yeah. I was, actually, but we moved...my parents moved to America when...when I was six months old, so in...in my mind..."

"So you've been living in America since then?"

"Ah, yes. Yes. Exactly."

I'm relieved.

"But you speak with a Slavic accent?" the motherfucker asks. What the fuck is going on here? This guy's way too qualified for his job. Your average Russian physics professor working as a passport control officer?

"Eh...yeah, it's a kind of strange story. My...my parents...I was living alone with my parents all my childhood, deep in the woods, and I learned the language from them. And they spoke English with a very strong...very strong Russian accent."

The officer looks at me for two long seconds. Then his eyes glide down to the collar.

"You're a priest?"

His accent is difficult to decipher.

"Ah, yes. I'm Reverend...Reverend Illitch."

This is getting ridiculous.

"But it doesn't say so in the passport." Damn. He's like some super stubborn Serbian shitfucker.

He asks me to wait and leaves his glass booth. I hear restless sighs in the line behind me. I don't look back.

A minute later he's back in the booth with an older officer in a blue shirt. They look me over like a gay couple auditioning for a threesome. Finally the older one says, in an accent I recognize from Wise Guy and the stewardesses, "You are priest?"

"Yes."

"What are you doing here in Iceland? Are you here for business or...?"

Finally I find the voice of Igor. His true orthodox spirit.

"The minister's job is all pleasure, but you may call it business if you like."

The blue shirt looks impressed. He looks me over one last time, hands me the passport, and tells me, "OK. Have a good stay."

THE HITMAN'S GUIDE TO HOUSECLEANING

Shit. How could I have been so careless? How could I...Or no. Maybe it was the right thing to do. The Feds will probably have found Rev. Friendly's body by now. How long will it take them to identify it? When they do, it's better they not find out that someone is surfing the northern seas on his passport. Yeah, it was pure luck.

I follow the flow of passengers deeper inside the air terminal. There is carpet on the hallway floor. And the soft-floored silence brings out the squeaking of Mr. Friendly's leather shoes. Igor's running shoes are inside the briefcase, along with his leather jacket. I reach the main hall and wonder what to do. I go to a desk and ask for flights to Frankfurt, Berlin, London, anywhere but here. There are flights, the blonde MILF says, but they're all sold out. The next available is three days from now, to Copenhagen and then on to Zagreb. I wonder what my bags will say when no one claims them. I find Igor's VISA card and buy him a ticket to Tomislav's fatherland. Mr. Friendly looks on as Toxic signs Mr. Illitch's name. Suddenly my simple life has become quite complicated. A layer cake of IDs.

The mature blonde recommends I go into town and hands me a hotel address. "It's only forty minutes with the bus," she says and smiles. Ah, well, I guess three days in Vikingland won't hurt. Three days without a gun will be hard on Toxic, though.

An escalator carries me down one flight and I walk through the busy luggage hall. The exit gate is divided in two, for those with something to declare and not. My latest identity asks whether I shouldn't use this opportunity to declare myself guilty of sixty-seven homicides, but I wave all the angels away, like the cloud of mosquitos.

Surprise awaits me outside the exit gate. Out in the small welcoming area, a man with thinning hair and a thick-haired woman are standing, holding a sign that reads: FATHER FRIENDLY. I seem to be out of sync with myself (too many selves, I guess) for I make the huge mistake of stopping short in front of the fucking sign. And me, wearing the fucking collar! They make the obvious connection.

"Mr. Friendly?" the woman smiles out in the more and more familiar sounding accent.

I'm about to say no, when suddenly I spot two policemen standing further out in the hall, close to the exit. So, before leaving my lips, my no turns into a yes. And I'm done for. I'm grounded for the next few hours. I'm forced to be fucking Friendly.

The killer becomes his victim.

"Very nice to see you, Mr. Friendly. Did you have good trip?" the man asks me with a very strong Icelandic accent. I notice his bad teeth when he smiles.

"Yeah, yeah, it was OK." Suddenly I hate my own accent. Not very Virginian, I guess.

"I hardly recognized you! You look even younger than on your Web site," the woman says. Always a big smile.

I have a Web site?

"Oh? You...you saw me there?" I mumble.

Fuck it. I'm a hitman, not a spy.

"Yes, of course!" the woman continues. "But we have not seen your TV show."

My God. I have a TV show? I would like to see that.

"You wouldn't like to see that," I say.

"Oh? Of course! We would love to see that!" they both cry out loud like kids high on candy. They're a happy bunch. God's doing, I guess. They introduce themselves and their names are incredible. His is Goodmoondoor (must be his stage name) and her name is something like Sickreader. I wonder what their

24

American nicknames would be. Goo & Si? Even "Tomo" was too long for the Yanks. The more people, the shorter the names. The less people, the longer the names.

Suddenly Sickreader looks me down and asks:

"Don't you have any luggage, Father Friendly?"

I pause for a moment.

"No. The Word is my only luggage."

They laugh like happy cartoon hamsters. I feel like an actor who has just made an important step in the development of a new character. Hallelujah!

They bring Father Friendly past the two cops (I give them a blessing look) and out on the parking lot where it's as cold as the inside of a fridge. And me who was looking forward to the Adriatic Spring, chilling on the Riva, sipping *pivo* and watching the tightly jeaned asses sway by, with the sound of sandal-heels clicking against the white limestone tiles. Ah, the girls of Split…

But, no. Instead I'm standing out in some polar parking lot collecting goosebumps and watching the reflection of my bald new self (I could, actually, pass for a priest) in the window of a silver Land Cruiser two strangers are indicating I should enter. The vehicle has already been blessed by the presence of the great Benny Hinn, they tell me. It seems Goodmoondoor and Sick-reader are professional televangelists. They run a small, local Christian TV channel called Amen. Minutes later we're rolling through the lunar park with the Goodmoondoor at the steering wheel.

"We have many Christian TV show from America. Benny Hinn of course. And also Joyce Meyers, Jimmy Swaggart, and David Cho. And we also have our show, in Icelandic and also in English. We are on TV every night, me and my wife. Sometimes we are together and sometimes we are alone. You will see."

This is the Goodmoondoor speaking in his primitive English. His nice looking wife sits by his side and smiles to me in the back-seat. Her husband continues:

"So, what are you going to talk about tonight? What text are you going to talk from?"

"Eh…Tonight?" I ask.

"Yes. You will be special guest of my show tonight."

"On TV?"

"Yes!" he laughs with all his crooked teeth, almost like a halfwit.

"Uh…I see. I thought I…"

I'm saved by my mobile. The screen reads "Niko" and without thinking I greet him in Croatian: "*Bok.*" Niko is Dikan's personal assistant. The Number Two Man. He asks me where I am, and I tell him the inconceivable truth, stopping short of the fact that I'm sitting in a Christian All-Star vehicle on my way to my first TV mass. He tells me that me landing up here is not so bad after all (does he even know that Iceland is a country?) since things are getting serious after the big fuck-up. "You fucked up real bad, Toxic," he says. The Fed-ups, as he calls them, have already been to the restaurant, and they've also broken into my place. They even visited my mother this morning, in her small hardware shop in the heart of Split, and broke her arm. Dikan's balls are boiling, Niko says. "If you are in this fucking Iceland then stay there!" he screams. "Don't go to Zagreb or Split and don't come here! Just stay where you are and do the LPP!"

As mentioned, that's short for Lowest Possible Profile. I wonder if Goodmoondoor's TV show fits into that category.

As I hang up my mobile, Sickreader turns towards me again and asks what language I just used.

"It's Croatian," I say.

"Oh? So you speak Croatian?"

"Yes, we have some Croatian people in our church."

"Where are you from, in the beginning?" the Good Moon driver asks.

"In the beginning we were all God's children." I'm too damn good. "But if you are asking about my accent, it's an acquired one, if you can say so. I was a missionary for many years in the former republic of Yugoslavia."

"Oh, really?" they both say.

"Yes. Spreading the good word of God in a communist state. That was some tough shit, man. I mean, tough holy shit. And being American over there, man, that was plain suicide. I had to take on another name and get rid of my American accent completely. They called me Tomislav. Tomislav Bokšić. Nowadays everyone thinks I'm from over there. But no. I'm one hundred percent American. I even have Clay Aiken CDs at home. In fact, the Friendly family has been in Virginia since the twelfth century." I guessed this would be called overacting. "Excuse me, since the eighteenth century."

They take it all in with a smile. There is a beat—along with my heartbeat, straight out of some suspense film score—before the woman asks:

"How old are you, Father Friendly?"

"I'm...I was born in sixty-five. That makes me...uh...forty."

"So you have been very young when you were in...."

"In Yugoslavia? Oh, yes. I'm deeply marked by it. I had some really tough times over there."

It's a bright and early May morning. I mean, an early morning in early May, and the sun is about to rise from behind the mountains ahead. Their sky has no clouds at all, and on the left-hand side the ocean keeps the waves below its gray-green surface.

Still the scene looks just as cold as it is. The arctic May looks like a Midwest March. There are some vacant houses scattered along the coastline. "Summerhouses," my hosts inform me. OK. So they do have summer up here.

The flight lasted five hours, and the time difference is about the same: a whole night has passed from the restroom scene at JFK. Killing Friendly was my first manual murder since the mustached kid in Knin. I used my hands, a trick I learned from Comrade Prizmić, the oldest one in our platoon, the WWII veteran with the big nostrils and absent cheeks. "It's just like blowing out a candle," he used to say. "It all depends on position and speed. Man is wax. Life is flame. Blow out his light and he's dead." Good old Prizmić. They cut the breasts off his wife and made him eat them.

There is a sticker on the back of the driver's seat. It's in English. "Woe unto them that call evil good, and good evil; that put darkness for light, and light for darkness; that put bitter for sweet and sweet for bitter! (Isaiah 5:20)"

Woe, man. Finally the six o'clock sun breaks out from the sharp mountain edge. Like a bright chicken from a blue egg. The road lights up.

"We drive the road of light!" Goodmoondoor says and turns towards me with a big, happy smile. "The road of light!"

CHAPTER 5

GUNHOLDER

05.16.2006

They want me to stay in their house. "We never let our guest stay at hotel. Our home is your home," Goodmoondoor assures me. I thank him. It's a small suburban villa on two shiny floors, in a neighborhood called Guard the Beer, or something like that, situated between the city center and the airport. Therefore I still haven't seen the famous Reykjavik that I read about on the plane: "the hottest city in Europe, the capital of cool." Apparently this is where Tarantino goes if he wants to play up his celebrity status. Bad luck it wasn't him next to me in the men's room. Then I'd be entering town in a white limo, with a gold chain around my neck and his VIP passport in my pocket, waving out the window to the young girls lining up at the side of the road holding up their old *Pulp Fiction* posters. Instead, I'm offered a seat in a silent suburban kitchen with no chicks in sight.

Sickreader prepares a wonderful breakfast table with coffee, toast, and two boiled eggs that instantly make me think of Dikan's balls. What the hell do they mean it was my fault? *My* fuck-up? I killed the right guy. Then it turns out he was FBI. That's not my fault. *I* should be mad *at them.*

"If you will be so kind, Father Friendly? We always ask the guest to say the table prayer," Goodmoondoor says when we are seated.

"Yes. Of course."

Again I have to regret not having killed Tarantino instead of this priest guy. But then again, it wouldn't have been easy to mess with the writer of *Kill Bill.* Yeah, I guess I was lucky. At least the clergyman looked a bit like me. At least they believe I am him. That's pretty low profile, I guess.

OK. Here we go. Table prayer. I bow my head and close my eyes.

"Dear God, dear beloved God. Thank you for this…for those eggs. Thank you for…thank you for having Friendly… friendly people around here. Thanks for sending me up here to this beautiful island and meeting those beautiful…those good and kind people. Thank you for giving me safe harbor in the sea of trouble. And breakfast as well. Amen."

Not too bad. They murmur their "amen," and then it's smiling time again.

"Do you have many people in your organization, Father Friendly?"

I lose my grip on the situation here. Accidentally it's Toxic who answers. "About forty."

"Forty thousand?"

"Forty thousand? Oh, yes, about forty thousand. Forty thousand registered members. But we have millions of people tuning in each week."

I remind myself to ask for the latest ratings report the next time I meet my program producer.

After breakfast they show me to my room on the upper floor. I'm back to Catholic school. A crucifix hangs over the bed and two studio photos of Jesus Christ are on the opposite wall. White linen, white curtains, white rug.

They tell me I must be tired from the long flight. I say you bet and then use the opportunity to tell Goodmoondoor that I cannot possibly go on TV tonight.

"I'm sorry, but I just have to be totally relaxed when I go on TV. If God is to speak through me, I have to be totally empty inside."

I pause briefly, regretting using the wrong words. He looks at me like a freshly cuckolded llama. Big eyes, long teeth, hairy neck. His wife whispers something about my jet lag before I continue:

"I mean, I'm just saying that nothing can be in the way, so that his word can travel through me. No tiredness, no nothing…I always have to be in super shape for TV."

"But," he finally says, "I said on my show that you will come tonight and talk to the people."

"Oh? You did?"

"Yes. I cannot cheat my promise to them. They are very faithful people."

Poor guy. He looks heartbroken. But I have to think of my LPP.

"How many people watch the show?"

I guess, for the small time TV-man, this question is a no-no. He gets all tangled up in his face, like a politician faced with a difficult question, and comes out with an excusing laugh.

"We have many people watching."

I see. He only has ten viewers.

"OK. We'll see. You just call me, in the afternoon."

I don't know what in the hell I'm doing. I give him my NYC number. The priest gives his colleague a hitman's number.

"OK, that's good," the Good Man says. His smile is back but a bit dented from the shock I just gave him. "You can stay here today and get a rest. Just be like in your home. We have to go to work now. In the TV station."

From my window I watch them board the fancy SUV. The believers always seem to have the best cars. God knows how to reward his people. Of course he knows you do need an SUV to reach heaven. The preacher's wife wears a skirt and has lovely legs. If she were the only woman in our platoon and we were stuck in the mountains for a month, I'd start dreaming about her on Day 12.

I'm left alone in the house. Despite the glacial spring outside, the rooms are warm like a July midnight in Memphis. That's where I carried out a rather clumsy operation under an ugly bridge. When it comes to killing, I'm no racist, but shooting black people has never been my favorite. There's nothing fresh about that.

I strip to my true self, happy to get away from God's collar, Friendly's shirt, and Igor's jeans, and crawl into bed. How soft, how cozy. And how incredibly quiet. It's almost too much. It's the loudest silence I've heard. I realize that I've been living in a disco for a decade or so and now, finally, I have stepped outside. I'm not kidding. *There is absolutely no sound to be heard.* It's as silent as the Serbian skull my mother keeps on the shelf above her bed.

Then suddenly the room is flooded by sunlight. White room, bright sun. If I were to wake up here, in this sunny silence, lying in this soft eiderdown bed with crispy, clean sheets, and the signed picture of the Lord on the opposite wall, I would think I was dead and gone to heaven. But of course I'll never go there. I'm stuck in traffic on the highway to hell.

Damn. It's so fucking silent I can't sleep. For a man who's lived in the noise all his life, being sung to sleep by Chetnik bombs and SoHo manholes, this is hard to take.

I give up and go downstairs, roaming around the house with my piggy belly sticking out over my Calvin Klein black boxers. The beautiful mountain morning fills every window, the light harsh and cold and very strong. Ice-sun. And I get this touristy feeling: the stupid surprise you experience when you realize that the same sun has also been rising here for the past million years. Also here, in this north-of-all-nuts city, people have been waking up and going to sleep for centuries. I remember when I first came back to Split after four years in NYC and was shocked to see that my mother had aged. I was almost angry at her, as if she had betrayed me, and started talking to her about moisturizing and masturbation techniques. I guess I was just not made to travel. I'm a One Place Man.

I never should have left Split. But when you've fought so hard for something, you can't really *enjoy* it. I guess I'd still be in Croatia if it wasn't called Croatia.

The house is full of fancy stuff and this kind of furniture-store-furniture. A big black sofa full of pillows fills the TV-corner, the dining set shines like a piece of porcelain, and every windowsill is crowded with vases and statues. A small St. Bernard looks me in the eye, a wine barrel hanging around its neck, to be broken in case of emergency if God deserts you. The walls sport real paintings (some lunar landscapes in golden frames) and all kinds of stuff made for hanging on nails—a small Jesus, some dried roses, and this colorful Japanese thing that I don't know the word for but is used for creating wind where there is no breeze. Still, the living room looks as if no one lives here. It could well be an installation at The Icelandic Museum of Modern Living. Plus, I find it all a bit too luxurious for devout followers of Christ. I doubt that any of the apostles possessed such a big flat screen. But at least it's all as clean as the Savior's conscience.

I turn on the bathtub, for my jet lag, and the TV, for the sound of it. The screen shows ten thousand people singing in Christian unison in some overblown indoor sports arena down south. *"Our God Is an Awesome God!"* Pretty awesome, I have to admit. Born-again people are so energetic. Screaming like newborns. I switch to *The Bold and the Beautiful* and try reading the subtitles. Looks like Hungarian to me.

In the kitchen I spot some letters addressed to *Guðmundur Engilbertsson* and *Sigríður Ingibjörg Sigurhjartardóttir*. It takes about two minutes to read each name. And back in the living room I find some family photos standing in frames on a big cabinet. They seem to have two kids. A girl and a boy. The little snow-haired girl looks a bit like her mother. Still the house seems totally kid-free. Maybe they store them away at some papal prep school. Or they donated them to missionary work down in Mozambique. There is a nice photo showing the whole family in America: Four holy smiles at some outdoor rodeo mass. Somehow it reminds me of hit #43. The fat man outside the church in Atlanta. My bullet traveled the incredible distance of two city blocks before entering his head. One of my master hits. He was wearing a white cowboy hat made out of felt—the kind of material that absorbs liquid. By the time I drove past the scene it all looked quite wonderful, so calm and innocent: A fat man had fallen on the sidewalk, nothing more. A fat man in a beautiful red hat.

The water in the tub is crazy hot. Volcano water. I have to cool it down before adding my body to it. I lie there for an hour while my mind travels the bushy regions of the sweet old republic of Munita. The dark forest reeks of clit extract; drops thick with lust run down heavy leaves in very slow motion. Down by the harbor I come across my mother standing outside her little shop, in her horrible communist skirt and Marilyn Monroe blouse, with a white cast on her right arm, and a fist on her left, pounding the air and shouting at me:

"This tandoori woman is all pleasure and no partner! When you pick a wife you must have conference between heart and brain. But you don't talk to any of them and let your dick decide! I loved your father for forty-two years. He loved me for forty. The first two years he was still fucking Gordana, the Serbian whore. But then he got bored with her and kept his dick at home after that. You are lucky to be born after his sex life was over! Or else you would have been a Serb and your brother would have killed you in the war. Let me tell you, lust don't last! Only love does! You break my heart, you break my arm, and you break all your promises. Tell me, Tomo, when are you going back to your studies?"

I studied architectural landscaping for a year and a half in the wonderful town of Hanover, Germany. There I met Niko Nevolja (Naughty Niko) who introduced me to the science of the con. It all started with a couple of small-time cocaine deals. Then we got on to drug and gun smuggling and finally, we were introduced to the art of game-fixing. Every Friday night we dined with a different soccer referee from one of the lower German Bundesligas. They were not the most fun dinner partners ("I always iron my jersey the night before the match") but watching them perform the day after was nothing less than addictive. Giveaway penalties and excellent goals denied. Angry players and a crowd gone mad. And it was all our work. Architectural landscaping was out, social landscaping was in. We being Croatian added an extra kick to it. No matter if the fucking Germans won the international games against us, we won all the games in their Bundesligas. And then we collected the money from the Fußball-Lotto. We were doing it for the fatherland. The Sauerkraut Suckers destroyed half of my grandfather's generation.

I'm sitting with the pillows on the sofa, with a white Christian towel around my waist, browsing the local TV channels, when suddenly the front door bangs open and a super-blonde girl in her twenties rushes inside. Without noticing the hitman of her dreams, she beelines for the kitchen and starts opening every one of the drawers. She seems to be in a big hurry, flinging curses inside each drawer before closing it with a bang. "Shit!" Finally, there is silence. She must then have heard the TV, for seconds later she stands in the doorway and asks me something that sounds like:

"Queer air thew."

"Excuse me?"

She switches to pretty professional English:

"Who are you? What are you doing here?"

"I'm To—I'm Father Friendly. I just got in this morning. From New York. They, Goodmoondoor and Sickreader, they told me—"

"Aha," she sighs with disinterest and disappears back into the kitchen. On the screen some balding carpenter-type is reading from a book that must be the Bible. The set looks like he built it himself. This must be their channel. Right. The letter A shines in the upper corner. They should call it "Omen" rather than "Amen." This is one-camera TV: the still-life style of it, the dead plant in the background, the carpenter's Polish suit, the way he only looks up from the book every three pages (as if he's checking the red REC light of the camera). It all makes North Korean State TV look like MTV. Poor guys. Dikan's position as the big boss can't possibly be hurt by me appearing on this drab channel. Judging from the expression on the carpenter's face, he knows he's not talking to more than ten viewers.

I get up from the sofa, make sure the towel is tight around my waist, and head for the kitchen. I comfort my shy belly—it always withdraws at the sight of serious girls—before appearing in the doorway like a freshly updated and slightly inflated version of Adonis. The girl is still searching the kitchen like a burglar on speed.

"Are you looking for something?" I ask her. Tone is hymn-like, voice is gym-like.

"Yeah. My keys," she murmurs into a cupboard.

Her body is slim, with small breasts and a tight ass, firm as a fully inflated airbag. If she was the only woman in our platoon and we were stuck in the mountains for a month, I'd start dreaming about her on Day 1.

"Your keys? You live here?"

This priest is turning into a moron, or a Mormon, or whatever.

She turns her head and looks at me for a while. Belly instantly ducks for cover, crawling all the way up into my rib cage. Poor little thing. The girl seems to feel sorry for the belly and can't help but look for it, letting her eyes travel to my middle, probably wondering whether her software supports the updated version of Adonis. I'm almost out of breath when she's finally done.

But it does give me time to examine her.

Her hair is more than blonde. It has the color of butter fresh from the fridge, before it gets all soft and yellow. Her skin looks incredibly smooth, as white as Philadelphia cream cheese, untouched in the box. The nose is small, with an upward tip that looks like the top of an ice-cream cone, that last bit coming out of the machine that you put in your mouth first. Her eyes are ice-blue like Gatorade Frost and her thick lips glisten like straw-berry sorbet.

Oooh. My stomach comes out of hiding and starts whining like a kid for candy. Man. She's not just a Day 1 Girl; she's a Day-break Girl.

"No, I don't live here," she finally says with a heavy sigh full of irritation. "I'm their daughter. I lost my keys. I can't get into my apartment. Argh! I have to be at work at ten and I can't go like this!"

She's the preachers' daughter though she speaks like a pagan prom queen, or a porn queen, for that matter. Her English is straight from MTV, and she wiggles her head along with her words in an imitation of black n' bitchy. She belongs to a tattooed generation of waxing masters brought up on thong songs, intent on making the stomach "the new boobs." This particular one is crowned with a pierced navel and proudly bares itself between a tight thin blouse and some deadly cool jeans. The tips of her black shoes are shaped like their high heels, and she cuts the air with her long white fingernails while she talks.

"Are the keys supposed to be here?" I ask in a fatherly way.

"Yeah. Mom said she had an extra key but I can't fucking find it."

She already said "shit" and here comes the F-word. The holy couple have produced a ho.

"Why don't you call her?" I ask her.

"They're taping her show now. Her phone's on silent."

She seems pained by her mother's TV fame. I feel pity for the poor girl and say:

"Maybe I can help you to get into your place."

"You mean, without a key? Are you going to use the cross?"

"We might try that. A cross and a quick blessing," I say in a tone that is perfectly Friendly.

I have the priest under my skin by now. Even naked I can appear to be a man of the cloth. She looks at me with surprise in her *Gatorade* eyes while I enter the kitchen and start searching the drawers for a knife that resembles the tiny Swiss wonder that I've kept in my pocket since Comrade Prizmić gave it to me on his deathbed, a shaky kitchen table in some bombed-out house in All Dead Village, ADV. Thanks to bin Laden, I had to leave it behind in NYC. *Ah ha!* I find a suitable substitute.

It's not until we're outside, sitting in her well-used Škoda Fabia with me freshly dressed in my holy outfit, that I ask for her name.

"Gunholder," she answers and darts off down the street.

CHAPTER 6
LILLIPUT ISLAND
05.16.2006

Gunholder drives over two hills, scarcely planted with low and ugly buildings, and approaches the city of Reykjavik. The name sounds like Dubrovnik, but it's more like entering Split, with all its highways and billboards plus the occasional sports field. (I notice that the stands are hardly bigger than the bench.) Like my hometown, this city seems to have a split personality: a historical center with hysterical suburbs.

They seem to have had their share of communism up here as well. Concrete housing projects line the side of the road and salute my Titolitarian past. We used to live in one of those gray monsters close to the stadium before we moved downtown, into a building older than New York City itself. I remember we had to leave our car behind since the narrow streets in the old town don't support any gas-related traffic, but every Sunday father took me and my older brother Dario to visit our good old Yugo, where it still held its parking space in our ugly old neighborhood.

Gunholder lives downtown, close to The Pond, a small swan lake close to the harbor. Here we're back with the bourgeoisie:

houses with gabled roofs and French windows fill the slopes around the water, gazing out at it, like over-proud guests at a New Year's ball standing around an empty dance floor. But we're not there yet. The girl is still driving a highway called Killing My Rabbit or something close to that. Icelanders seem to have a Native American taste in naming people and places. Gunholder tells me we just drove through a town called Cop War.

"But this is Reykjavik?" Father Friendly asks her, adjusting the stiff collar to his thick neck with one hand while pointing out the windshield with the other.

"Yeah, now we're in Reykjavik."

"They say it's a Tarantino town?" Oops. This sounds a bit too cool for the churchman. I quickly add, "I mean, Tarantino's favorite city?"

She quickly looks me over—wondering whether she's sitting in a car with some famous Scientology pastor, a man who spends his holidays playing golf with Tom Cruise and John Travolta—before saying:

"Yeah. He was here for New Year's Eve. My girlfriend knows him. He's OK."

I'm glad I didn't kill him.

Across an islanded bay, a long mountain guards the city to the north. It has the shape of a giant whale stranded ashore. Further north and out east, more mountains surround the city, lying out along the horizon like blue leopards dotted with white snowdrifts. Though they are as far away as the Hamptons from Harlem, I can see them as clearly as the tips of my shoes, for the air is as clean as a Trump Tower window. The ocean is a strong blue, and I can see waves forming and breaking as far as the eye can fly. Everything around here is crystal-clear. Like in the mind of a cold-blooded killer.

The car radio delivers Justin Timberlake. The streets are buzzing with traffic, but the sidewalks are totally empty. Kind of reminds me of Sarajevo during the curfew. Excellent conditions for roof-to-sidewalk hits. The cars are mostly Japanese or European, and all of them look brand new. These people have money. Every other one is an SUV, and many of them are driven by butter-blonde ice-queens like Gunholder. Where are all their husbands?

"Did you have a war recently?" I ask.

"A war? No. We don't even have an army."

Tell me another one.

"Why do you ask?" she asks.

"I just wonder where all the men are. I only see single women driving those cars."

"Most people have two cars. One for him, one for her."

I look at the black Range Rover in the lane next to us. One of those Virginia Madsen types is at the wheel.

"I see. But that's not exactly a lady's car?"

Gunholder gives me a fierce look.

"In Iceland women are equal to men."

I look at her for a moment, and judging from the determined tilt of her ice-cream nose, I should at least try to believe her. Equal to men. No shit.

She is clearly pissed at me and only gives the shortest possible answers to my following questions. Yes, five degrees is a bit cold for this time of year. Ten degrees is normal(!). Yes, she was partying last night. And yes, Justin Timberlake is quite big in Iceland. (I seem to have decided that Father Friendly is a pretty boring guy.)

Gunholder enters the old town. Here the trees are taller and the streets more narrow. She parks her Škoda on a steep side street, outside a small green house with a rusty red roof. Like the other downtown houses, this one is covered in curly-waved iron on all sides, dressed to kill in a suit of armor. Actually, we could have used this back home: bulletproof vests for buildings.

Gunholder lives on the second floor. Father Friendly does the sign of the cross in front of her door before unlocking it with a small kitchen knife from her mother's collection. The girl looks at him as if she just witnessed a miracle.

"Here you go," I say in the most blessed way and open the door for her. She tells me to wait and disappears inside. Her place is the total opposite of her face; it's a complete mess. I notice a tower of empty pizza boxes on the kitchen worktop; underwear, jeans, and jerseys on the floor; a half-used lipstick and a half-eaten sandwich. The smell of beer that has been sitting open for a week. Yet, in some strange way, this apartment seems much closer to Christ than her parents' place. It's much more believable as an apostle's den.

Gunholder works in a café downtown. She's a fellow waiter. She offers to drive the miracle man back to the holy house, but I can't stomach going back to Silence Grove. Anyway, she's already late for her shift. I walk her to work. The priest and the preacher's daughter. She walks like a nutty New Yorker, and Father Friendly needs all his energy to keep up with her. Before I know it, we pass the American Embassy; a building as long as Laura Bush's smile, and as white as her teeth. The front is decorated with six surveillance cameras. Some duck-eyed imbecile in uniform guards the entrance. I lower my head and shift sides, passing the embassy with Gunholder as a human shield, LPP style. She voices her surprise at my sudden move, and her sweet fucking face brings out my own fucking self: I accidentally murmur a "fuck." She hears it.

"A priest that says 'fuck'?"

"Sure," I say, "we can say it. We just can't do it."

She slows down a bit.

"Oh, right. So you've never…you're a virgin?"

"That's for me to know and you to find out." Her café turns out to be a pretty cool bistro in the heart of town called Café Paris. It looks like a three-star Starbucks with a smoking section, but I'm happy to be inside, wringing my hands like it was January. They're not kidding about the arctic spring. Gunholder puts on her apron and brings me an All Icelandic Latte with a double shot of irritation. Despite all his miracle-working, she still seems to hate Father Friendly and his deflatable stomach. He gives her a stupid holy smile.

"Does your father keep a gun in the house?"

"A gun? That's a strange question."

"Yes. In the States we all keep a gun in the house. You never know. Especially if you're a priest."

She rolls her great eyes.

"Nobody has a gun in Iceland. It's a safe country."

Safe country, my ass. I make a few calls and within a week it'll be a Croatian colony.

It's 10:30 AM on a Wednesday morning and there are three of us in the café. I count two people out on the street. If this is downtown, no wonder the suburbs are silent. Cars sail by in slow motion. I can't get over all these driving ladies that look like millionaires' wives or daughters, with Prada sunglasses, Barbie hair, and airbag lips. On my scale, they all range from Day 2 to Day 4.

It reminds me of my week in Switzerland, when my architectural studies took me to a small village in the Alps to research a brand-new skiing area. The week felt like a month. It was even calmer than the fucking Belarus. The only people out were some totally unfucked housewives with Gucci hairdos doing hundred-dollar lunches in the village restaurant. Their husbands spent their days in the city, locked up in their bank safes. They reminded me of the queen of Spain, these ladies in fur and heels, as they slowly passed the jewelry stores (rich people always walk slowly, because of the deep pockets, I guess). They were all Day 26 types, but by the fifth day, I was on the brink of a mass rape. I pictured the headline in the *International Herald Tribune*: "Student Fucks Fifteen, Then Self."

I finish my coffee and put it on Igor's card. Gunholder doesn't seem to notice. I ask her for things for the Friendly tourist to do. She points out the window.

"It's all there: the cathedral, the parliament, the statue of John Secretson, our national hero…"

She must be joking. The cathedral is the size of God's dog house (I imagine he has a tricolor Chihuahua), and the parliament building is no bigger than my grandfather's country house in Gorski Kotar. I'm on Lilliput Island.

I try to dive into the downtown area, but it's only three blocks square. It's easier to lose it than get lost in it. How am I to keep up my LPP in this town?

I drift past a hunter's shopping paradise, and the sight of a rifle tempts me inside. The clerk is a kind-looking gentleman with the soft eyes of a prey animal. I ask for a handgun, shotgun, whatever. Just something that's good for mailing bullets. He looks at me for a moment before telling me, in a wannabe British accent, that they only sell rifles for hunting, no handguns.

"OK. Can you tell me where I can buy a pistol in this town?"

"I'm sorry, you can't. Not in a shop at least."

What is it with these Icelanders? No army. No guns. No nothing. Only gorgeous women driving luxury jeeps, roaming around Big Chill City in their pussy-warm wagons, hoping to pick up a professional killer posing as a priest.

Since I can't get a gun, I settle for a Swiss army knife, similar to my old one.

I wonder if Father Friendly is Catholic, or does he have a wife? Kids? Actually, I don't know why the hell I'm thinking about this. Usually I don't want to know anything about my victims. It's like back in the war. I kill strangers. I don't feel for them. They're just another head to swamp my bullet into. I don't even want to know *why* they deserve to die. Usually they have refused to pay their tithe, failed to deliver for Dikan, or they show up with the same tie as he at the Mafia Oscars. But I have to admit that killing Father Friendly was different. It wasn't professional, it was emotional. I had to kill him to save my own ass. It was *assemotional.*

As I walk I notice the people of Reykjavik move quickly about, as if they believe this were New York and not the smallest capital in history. As if they were all late for a job interview at Merrill Lynch. It must be the cold. The only fellows warming the benches are too drunk to feel it.

All around me the Icelandic national face: round, with a small nose, like a snowball with a pebble in it. I guess every nation has its one distinctive facial feature. We, the Slavs, have the nose, that big strong dog's snout that enables us to smell trouble all the way back to the twelfth century. The Africans have the lips, the Arabs, the brows, the Americans, the jaw, the Germans, the mustache, the English, the teeth, and the Talians, the hair. The Icelanders seem to have picked the cheeks. Some of these faces are just two cheeks with a hole and two eyes pressed between them.

But for the most part they speak better English than I do. I talk to three of them before I find the city library. Here you have 470,000 books at your disposal, all in Icelandic. (The guy from the plane said writing was one of the basic industries in Iceland.) And here you have Internet access. A bookish bearded guy hands me a code. I punch in the numbers on a keyboard, and the big world opens up for me. Reverend David Friendly is the minister of the Westmoro Baptist Church down in Richmond, Virginia. Sorry, *was* minister. Plus, he had his own TV show, "*The Friendly Hour*," on CBN, The Christian Broadcasting Network, owned by crazy man Pat Robertson, the former presidential candidate and the eternal opponent of abortion and gay rights. In a photo, Rev. Friendly appears as his fat, full self: a round bald head with a big smile and small glasses. He's surrounded by happy children, all white, plus the customary black one. On a Web site he voices his stance against "same-sex blessings." Father Friendly was a homophobe. He deserved to die, I guess.

I try googling his name along with different keywords like "murdered," "killed," and "death" without any serious results. He hasn't made the news yet. They still haven't identified his body, even though I left the fatty gay-basher wearing his own smelly socks, pants, and underpants, sleeping in the men's room. The lone result to my last search contains a Friendly interview where he voices "an understanding for the people like senator Coburn who favor the death penalty for abortionists and other people who take life."

Reverend Friendly wants me dead.

47

CHAPTER 7
FATHER FURY
05.16.2006

I'm sitting in Café Bahrain. Yeah. I think it's called Café Bahrain. Nothing Arabic about it, though. Just a nice little old-timer with squeaky chairs and Day 3 Girls. Some people are smoking. I haven't been to a smoky bar in years, and it's a bit hard on my eyes. I understand the smoking ban is on its way up here, in a sunny sailboat named the *Al Gore*. On the other hand, Croatia is more likely to see another war than quit smoking. Only when you've had some fifty warless years do you start worrying about things like air quality in bars.

I'm celebrating my first day in exile. With beer number five. It's almost eight o'clock in the evening, but it's still morning outside. The sun refuses to set here, they say. "It's up all night, and so are we." "They" are Ziggy and Hell G, two scruffy local barflies with broken wings.

"The Reykjavik nightlife only has two nights, basically. One is bright and lasts from April to September. And the other one is dark and lasts from October to March," they tell me.

"And which one is more fun?"

"The bright one of course. Icelandic girls don't like to do it in the dark," they say with a laugh.

They're younger, thinner, and hairier than me, smoke like machines, and find it "so freaky, man" to be drinking with a priest. The clergyman asks them about the gay situation up here, the abortion issue, and whether Iceland honors the death penalty? No. Apparently Iceland is a gun-free, abortion crazy, gay paradise with no death sentence. Father Friendly has come to the right place.

"Our Gay Pride Festival is even bigger than that of the seventeenth of June, our Independence Day."

Father Friendly takes it all in stride. I try to sit on his gay-bashing, death-dooming self. He only nods his head and adjusts the collar around his neck.

Actually, I wonder why the hell I'm still wearing this stupid collar. I guess I could forget Father Friendly altogether, go back to my toxic self and check into a hotel. No. Not wise. I think it's better to keep the sucker alive. Otherwise my preacher friends would contact the police and the police would contact his family and all hell would break loose.

"What about murders? How many homocides have you got each year?" I ask them.

"*Homocides?*" they ask, with bewildered eyes.

"Yeah. How many gays are killed each year in this country?"

"Gays? None, I guess," Hell G says, a bit shocked by the harshness of the vicar's words.

"Oh? But how many homicides then? How many regular people are killed?" Friendly continues.

"Sometimes one, sometimes none," Ziggy says.

Seems my intuition this morning was right. I'm in heaven. No army, no guns, no murders... They don't even have a red-light district. It's a ho-free city, they tell me.

"There are no prostitutes in Iceland, but we'll be forced to have some when we join the European Union," they tell me with another laugh.

Sex is still free, but the beer costs a bear. Igor's card bleeds with each glass. I've drunk an iPod's worth of alcohol since stumbling into this place some hours ago, recommended to me by this horribly charming bookstore clerk, a Day 5 type. Two beers later I found out that Café Bahrain is the most famous bar in the land, heavily featured in some hip movie years back. So much for my LPP. How can you lay low in Lilliput Island?

"So what do you do then if you can't buy sex and don't do murders? You have drugs?"

There is a beat. This pastor is something else, they seem to be thinking.

"Yeah. Sure," Ziggy tells the stranger with an even stranger pride. "We, we have a lot of drugs."

And his friend adds, "We also have a lot of murders in *books*. In the last years we have many good crime novel writers here in Iceland, like Arnaldur Indridason for example. Also Ævar Orn Josephsson, Viktor Arnar Ingolfsson, Yrsa Sigurdardottir, and Arni Thorarinsson."

Icelandic names are like Scud missiles. Their trails linger in the air long after they've reached their target. Still, these guys have my respect. Being a crime writer in the land of no murders can't be easy. It seems you need the creative powers of a genius just to be able to provide your murderer with a gun. I close my ears, but keep my Friendly smile on, as the two barflies go on about their country, trying hard to convince the clergyman that it's no Sunday school.

I'm pretty spaced out. I feel the alcohol searching out my jet lag and amplifying it. Jesus. I wonder what my holy hosts are up to. They must be on TV already. Goodmoondoor never called. I sure hope the embassy bastards didn't catch my face on camera. There must be a poster of me on every one of their bedroom walls. I killed one of *their* men. In fact, I have exactly sixty-seven crosses in American graveyards to my credit, so they would have a good reason to put my face on the sidewalk. But not all sixty-seven were happy-go-lucky greencarders. Some were Talians, some Russians, quite a few Serbs, and one Swedish or Norwegian guy, if I remember it right. It was the strangest accent I have put to rest. But most of them were square-faced, burger-butted Marshmallow Men. With that many dead Americans to my credit, I could probably get an honorary membership in Al-Qaeda.

Yes. I'm on the most wanted list. Yes. I have to remember that this is exile. Yes. I have to maintain LPP. And yes. My name is David Friendly.

Suddenly I hear a familiar voice.

"So there you are!" Gunholder is back in a party outfit, dressed to thrill, and spots me in the corner. "What the hell are you doing *here*? My dad's been looking for you! He called me like twice. You're supposed to be on TV!"

"He never called me," I say in a drunken drawl.

"He didn't? You have your phone with you?"

I search my coat and jacket. No mobile. The butter-blonde looks down at me like a mother at a child who has lost his school bag. Ziggy and Hell G watch her in silence, like two skinny puffins on freeze-frame.

"OK," she says. "I will call him."

Half a beer later, the Good Moon himself walks into the bar, looking very much like a reindeer entering Macy's on Christmas Eve, with horns blinking and eyes glowing. Still, he puts on the smile as he spots his fellow preacher half fallen into the depths of hell. He holds out his hand. I grab it.

"Hello, Father Friendly. I'm glad I found you." Always the happy one. "Gunholder told me that you have helped her in this morning."

"Yes. Our true faith can open any door there is," I say with a drunken smile.

"But you forgot the phone. It was in the house. I was calling it and I heard it ringing upstairs!"

He laughs like a happy child. I have to laugh too. This guy's just too damn Good. Either you have to shoot him in the face point-blank or you just *go along* with him. And I have no gun.

"We have to be quick. We begin after twenty minutes," he says.

"OK. I'm really sorry."

I wonder if he notices I'm drunk. Does he really want me on his show? I watch him say good-bye to his beautiful blonde daughter who has joined her girlfriend (a Day 2 brunette that probably has Tarantino's name on her done-list) at a nearby table. He pauses for a brief second as he watches her suck on the cigarette in her left hand, ready with her white wine in the right. I spot a small movement of Goodmoondoor's lips, a tiny signal that betrays a willingness to smash his daughter in the head with a large-format, hardcover edition of the King James Bible. He bites his tongue and begs her farewell in Icelandic. Then she finally looks up and blows smoke into his face, with cold eyes, and says in the most chilling voice: "Bless, Pappy."

Clearly it can only mean "Bye, Dad" but the hateful tone of it breaks a hitman's heart.

We go outside. The ice-cold evening is as bright as an opened fridge. If this is the hottest city in Europe, I guess we can cool it about this global warming thing. The Good Man drives out of old town on a freshly built highway that takes us past some spruced-up commie projects. Those white-spotted leopards surrounding the city are bathed in sunlight, and seagulls flutter from one light pole to another. The small, grey clouds drift against a light-blue sky. Most look like human sperm to me, others like small whales that swim slowly across town. I try to give sober answers to the holy man's questions.

"I was totally stranded because I didn't have your address and I forgot to get your daughter's phone number. So I just ended up sitting in this café. Talking to some Icelanders. It was OK, actually."

"Yes, but the coffeehouses in Reykjavik can be dangerous place," he says with a smile and starts laughing.

His laughter seems to indicate that he himself once had a drinking problem, before God dried him up and gave him a TV station, but the longer it lasts, it becomes clear that he's trying to cover up the pain caused by the sight of his daughter sitting in a dark demon's den, smoking and drinking, dressed for action. I must be under the good spell of Father Friendly, for I have to admit that it was quite a horrible sight. For a brief second, she really looked like the Devil's daughter, with eyes of fire and a mouth full of smoke. I try to laugh with him.

"Like it says in Luke: 21, the day will come over you like snare, if you spend it drinking and surfeiting," the preacher says as he turns left from the highway into a short Brooklyn-ish boulevard with three floored houses on each side. Is he talking about me? As he parks behind one of the buildings, I can feel the clerical collar turning into a snare around my neck.

"Do you know Brother Branham?" Goodmoondoor asks as we walk from car to building.

"Yes, of course," Father Friendly says with drunken determination.

His Icelandic colleague stops dead in his tracks and gets all agitated:

"Do you know his theories?"

"Yes, I think I can say so."

"Do you remember when he said that Los Angeles will sink under water and sharks will swim on the streets?"

"Eh…yes."

"It's very interesting, because I was dreaming last night. I was dreaming that I was driving in my car. This car," he says and points towards his silver Land Cruiser. "I was driving here in Reykjavik and then suddenly a very big whale was swimming beside me. He was swimming fast, and he even went before me. He was on the street. Just like a car. And when he was beside me, he looked at me and he said something. But I could not hear it, because I was in the car and the window was not down."

Goodmoondoor looks at Father Friendly as if he was hoping for his American brother to interpret the dream as a major event in the history of Christianity.

"Wow," I say and look to the sky for advice. The shark-like clouds pass overhead. I suddenly feel that I'm stuck in some underwater cartoon for kids, doing the voice of "Marty the Monkfish."

"That's amazing, man," I say. "You should maybe call him and tell him? Maybe he can tell you what it means."

"You know that brother Branham died in 1965."

Fuck.

"Sure. I'm not talking about a phone call. I'm talking about a *soul* call," I say.

"A soul call?"

"Yes. We do that all the time, in our congregation down in Richmond. Every Tuesday night people come in and speak with their dead relatives. It's very popular. People really like it. I turn myself into a human switchboard and make the connection through the Lord."

He starts to laugh. I stress out.

"I don't know the Baptist Church very well, but in my church we never talk to the dead. We say it's a hairy sea," he says.

A hairy sea.

"Yeah, I know. But it's like, you know, we don't call them. They call *us*."

The temperature must be close to thirty-three degrees Fahrenheit, and here we are, on a sunny spring night, standing out in some backdoor parking lot in the middle of the North Atlantic, me and him, Father Friendly and Father Fury, two complete strangers drunk on beer and God, talking complete nonsense. Exile is a hairy sea.

"We are living the last days. I am saying this on my TV for over fourteen years. We are living the last days. But now I have the feeling that there are not so many days left," Goodmoondoor says and burns his eyes into my face in that crazy preacher way, not letting go until he's one hundred percent sure I have received the message.

Looking away is like turning my face away from a bonfire.

CHAPTER 8
GODFELLAS
05.16.2006

"Good evening, dear friends, and welcome to our program. I am very happy to tell you that tonight we have a dear guest with us, and this is the reason we are speaking in English tonight. This is Father Friendly, visiting from our friends at CBN in America. He is a good friend of Pat Robertson, that you have seen here on Amen and the Sermon Channel. He has a very popular TV show in America. And he is one of the best known preachers in many states. A true Christian brother in the faith of the living God, Reverend David Friendly from Richmond, Virginia. Father Friendly, welcome."

"Thank you, Brother Goodmoondoor. It's a pleasure to be with you here."

"I have to tell you that Father Friendly has a Yugoslavia... What do you call it?"

"Accent."

"Yes. He has a Yugoslavia accent because he was teaching the word of Jesus over there in the time when they were Communist. *Hallelujah!*"

He almost hits me in the head as he throws his hands in the air, but I manage to step aside. We are standing behind a white lectern, with a blue curtain behind us and a messy TV studio in front of us. I count five people in the room. One man is standing behind a camera, a smiling Sickreader stands in a doorway, and an audience of three pious people is waiting for me to save their souls.

"Communists don't believe in God, Father Friendly?"

"No. You're absolutely right about that, brother Goodmoondoor. And this is the reason why they don't exist anymore."

"Well. You can find some of them even today," my preacher friend says with the funniest smile. It's the smile of someone not too clever showing off his cleverness. It's quite hilarious. I need all my strength not to laugh as I carry on:

"Indeed. But they are in hiding! They are hiding in the darkness of their godless existence!" I try to speak with the preacherman's blind faith. "For they do not dare to come out into the light! The light of God. The light of Godness. The light of Goodness! The good of the light! We are here in Iceland, in the island of light, where God lets it shine long into the night. He lights up the night. He makes the night bright. I have to say: You are very fortunate, you are fortunate people. You live in God's land. The land of the living God. *Hallelujah!*"

What in the hell am I saying?

"Yes, Father Friendly. Maybe you can tell us about your work in Yugoslavia. Was it before the war?"

"It was before the war, when Comrade Tito was president of all Yugoslavia, of all the countries that we now know as Croatia, Slovenia, Bosnia, and Herzegovina and others."

What the fuck am I saying? Friendly must have been all of fifteen when Tito died.

"This was the time of oppression and imprisonments. My father...My father the Lord guided me through the dark streets of dictatorship, to seek out the souls willing to open their hearts for the light of God. We had to be very careful with our conviction and sometimes we had to betray with our tongue the faith we kept sacred in our hearts, just in order to survive. In that sense we were almost like secret agents, like James Bond or...Ray Liotta in the movie *Goodfellas...*"

I'm falling out of character here.

"Or like the first followers of Jesus Christ," the host helps me out.

"Yes! Exactly. Thank you, Brother Goodmoondoor. We were just like the apostles. We had to hide. We had to be careful. But we were never doubtful. God was showing us the way. He was...He was the searchlight that we needed, so that we were able to walk the dark street of dictatorship."

"And then you were a young American boy?"

"Yes. Yes, exactly. I was young David. David Friendly, a... young boy from Vienna, Virginia. What the hell was I doing over there, in old Europe? I was sent there as a missionary. I...I had been...Back home, I was what they call a...a teenage dirtbag, a bad boy. A very bad boy. Instead of doing my homework I was out stealing and fucking girls."

I can feel the smile freeze on Goodmoondoor's face. Better watch my language.

"But I always did it in the missionary position."

Fuck it. I'm still drunk. I even allow myself to smile a bit. The old lady in the front row closes her eyes for two seconds.

"Sorry. But here is the story. I was once robbing a local church with two friends of mine. We were running away with some candlesticks, chalices, and stuff, and I was the last one out, because I was then, just like I am now, a little bit on the chubby side."

I can see that Sickreader laughs in her sweet and discrete way.

"So, my friends were already outside when all of a sudden the light came on and I heard this great voice. 'You can carry away all the silver you want, Brother Judas, but it will never save your soul!' I didn't even dare to look back. I just stopped for a second before I ran to the door and threw myself out in the dark. I did escape, but I could not escape those words. They came back to me again and again. Maybe because I didn't know who it was who spoke them. The voice was very deep, a very deep man's voice, and in my mind it was the voice of God himself. 'But it will never save your soul!' For days my soul was totally tortured by those words. Finally, I went back to the church with all the stuff I had stolen. I put it on a bench inside the church and I was about to run outside when I heard the voice again. It was the rector. We had a long talk. And half a year later, I found myself on the streets of Sarajevo spreading the word of God. With a searchlight."

I smile. This one is right on target. Father Friendly would be proud of this performance.

"Hallelujah! Holy brother. Hallelujah," my Icelandic colleague calls out. "You are like Paul the Postuli, Paul the Apostle, St. Paul. You had same experience like him. Did you also be blind?"

"What?"

"Did you also be blind when the light came?"

"In the church, you mean? Yes, absolutely. Absolutely. I was totally blinded by the light. That's why I had to stop."

Goodmoondoor has that reindeer expression again. He looks at me as if I just parted the Atlantic Ocean all the way down to the Canary Islands for his people to go on vacation. He puts his hand on the top of my head as if he was baptizing me, and suddenly his English improves:

"Blessed be your soul, holy brother. Hallelujah! Amen. The force of the living God is with us. Hallelujah! Blessed be your soul, Father Friendly. For you are anointed. Your soul is saved." He then removes his hand from my bald skull and faces the camera. "For let it be heard: The Story of the Postuli, Chapter Nine, that is Acts Nine in the English Bible…It tells the story of Saul, of Levitan Saul, this ordinary man from Tarsus, this simple man working as an executioner for the Roman government. And they sent him to Damascus, so that he could carry the Christians in robes…"

"In ropes," I quickly correct him, suddenly sounding like a Bible expert.

"…So he could put them in ropes and carry them to Jerusalem. But on his way, before he came to Damascus, he saw a great light and a voice spoke to him: 'Saul, Saul, why you persecute me?' And Saul said, 'Who are you?' And the voice said, 'I am the Lord.' And the Lord told him to stop working against the Christians, and Saul was blind for many days, until the Lord sent Ananias to him. And Ananias came to him and told him to see again. And Saul became Paul. The executioner became number two in God's Church on earth. Jesus was number one, and Paul was number two. Hallelujah! And he wrote a big part of this book!"

Goodmoondoor holds the black Bible in the air.

"He wrote a big part of the holy book, the book of books, the Word of God. His soul was saved. He became a holy man. A holy man. Hallelujah!"

"Hallelujah!" I repeat after him. I really do. Must be the beer.

CHAPTER 9
TORTURE
05.19.2006

The best thing about the war was sleeping outside. In the Dinara Mountains. The cuckoo was our alarm clock. I never saw him, but he always got us up before dawn, *for the land was on our side.* The Serbs were still asleep, behind the hill and the next. Lazy bastards. Never started fighting before eight. I guess we can thank them for those beautiful mornings. Sunny silent mornings with the best breakfast in the world: a woodcutter's coffee and *povitica* bread. We ate in silence, watching the first morning rays deal with the butter still cold from the night.

One of those early dawns, Andro, the crazy boy from Pula, suddenly started talking about the morning dew. In a little while he was shouting about:

"We are fighting for dew! We can't let the Serbs have the dew! We want more dew! Stupid war! Fighting for dew!"

Then he sprang to his feet and started running around the hill pointing to different spots on the ground.

"Croatian dew! Serbian dew! No-ownership dew!"

Javor, our commander, pulled out his handgun and shot him in the back of his head. Andro fell in the grass like a dead calf.

"Now you can drink it, you stupid son of the ugliest whore in Pula!" the lava-faced Javor spit out of his mouth.

Piti rosu, to drink the dew, became our phrase for dying. I felt a bit sorry for Andro. Among all the members of our squad, I probably had the biggest tolerance for his nuttiness. I owed him.

Andro was a big Madonna fan and even named his rifle after the American pop star. Every now and then he would burst out with "...*like a virgin*," in his Morrissey voice. And he always carried a small crucifix in the breast pocket of his uniform. The mini-Jesus was white, but his cross was sort of brown, thus blending in with the dark green of the uniform. The effect was that the small Messiah always stuck out of the pocket as if waving his hands, saying: "Hey guys, listen!" Maybe Andro did, because from time to time he would start philosophizing about the pointlessness of war, not really the type of thing a soldier needs to hear. And every now and then he would do something crazy, like running naked through the enemy line and back, or now, screaming about dew. He was unstable, and Javor was absolutely right to kill him.

But me and Andro once spent a whole night together, drinking and singing out in the open. We had lost our group and spent all our bullets when we stumbled upon a blown-up Chetnik tank. Inside it we found a bottle of *rakjia* that quickly released our singing spirits. It was the most stupid thing we could do, singing Croatian songs in the heart of a Serbian night. A bullet could have silenced us any minute. But you have to understand that fighting in a war is like playing Russian roulette 24/7. Every breath could be your last. It's a dreadful thought, but it slowly becomes a thrilling one; you kind of get addicted to it. You even start teasing the limits. We were young and fearless, tired from killing, and couldn't care less.

Luckily, we were singing the Yugoslavian winner of the 1989 European Song Contest when a dead-drunk Serbian soldier suddenly appeared in front of us, in full army gear. Could he join us? he asked, did we have booze? Apparently he thought we were his countrymen, as we were sitting on top of a Serbian tank and singing a Yugoslavian song. Only after the first sip did he realize that we were the enemy, when he spotted the *Hrvatska* emblems on my uniform. There was this long moment of suspense as he stared at it and we looked at his rifle. Ours were lying on the ground below us, devoid of all ammunition. Then, Andro saved the night by picking up the song again, and the Serbian guy joined in. Together we screamed like a trio of alley cats, all three of us: "*Rock me baby! Nije vazno šta je. Rock me baby! Samo neka traje.*"

Eurovision saved my life. Andro saved my life.

At the end of our bottle, Andro came out with the truth. He was gay. He wanted to kiss me. Andro was a handsome kid. Black hair, fair skin, thick lips. I guess he was a Day 156 type, and the war had already lasted half a year and…Okay, I *almost* wanted to kiss him. (War either makes you a fascist or a fag.) But I just couldn't, not for the memory of my Serb-fucking father. But we all got excited, and pants went down. Andro jerked us off, me and the Serb. It was the strangest image I have from that fucking war. The crazy gay boy from Pula jerking us off in the deep Dalmatian night, with a prick in each hand: one Serbian, one Croatian.

If we had gay nations, there would be less wars.

I wake up with war shadows fluttering about the bright white room. My dark past tries to balance out my life here in the bright, silent island, where you go to sleep in broad daylight and wake up in screaming sunshine at six in the morning. It's hard to sleep. I feel like I'm in a hospital. A neon-bright, deadly-silent, no-one-wears-shoes-indoors hospital. Goodmoondoor even walks around his own house wearing only his socks. It's disgusting.

And this peaceful land has never seen war. Not in a thousand years. Must be the island thing. No extra dew to fight for.

Was it necessary for all those people to die just so that we could claim Knin as a Croatian town? I still ask myself that question. Shortly after the war, I drove through it, this insignificant town of fifteen thousand people. The sight of our flag flying above those broken roofs made me sick to my stomach. I actually had to stop the car and puke. I puked on the land that we had claimed, the land I had been willing to give up my life for. Yet we had to do it. We had to. Don't ask me why. We just fucking had to.

Every man belongs to a nation, a thing greater than himself. A nation is the sum of our strengths, as well as of our collective stupidity. War makes the former obey the latter.

I get up and go to the bathroom. It's so freaky clean. This is where the angels shit. I have a holy hangover. Not only from the beer, but also from all the hallelujahs I said on TV. Goodmoondoor was very happy with my performance. His American colleague didn't let him down.

I wonder if they have a TV guard at the US embassy, some pimpled wacko whose job it is to watch all the local programs and check if they contain some blow-Bush or fuck-the-FBI messages. And then, in the middle of the night, he suddenly would have seen me on the screen, the bald round face that matches the America's Most Wanted poster on the wall beside the TV set. The Croatian clitsucker that killed the FBI agent in Queens last week, posing as the priest they found dead in a JFK bathroom last Tuesday. I've been waiting all night long for the SWAT team to show up, waking up every half an hour. At 4.00 AM I called my love, Munita. No answer.

The holy couple gets up at 7:00. Morning prayer starts at 7:30. Father Friendly has to show up. "Dear God. Save me from my sins."

After breakfast they take me sightseeing. There the president lives, there the shopping mall is, there they store the volcano water. Here they make the world famous dairy product called Scare, and the swimming pool over there is one of the world's best. In fact, they do their best to convince me that their country is the "best in the world." They go on and on about the longest life, the happiest people, the cleanest air, etc. I really want to tell them that a country devoid of brothels and gun shops can't even think of claiming such a title, but instead the Friendly one nods his head, slowly but persistently, like a Texas oil drill.

Goodmoondoor drops his wife off at the TV station to tape her show and we drive on, though he feels the need to explain.

"I don't think woman should work outside the house, but my wife is doing her work for God and that is different, I think."

"She's working in the house of God," I have Mr. Friendly say.

Goodmoondoor is pleased with the answer and laughs a bit before asking a rather tricky question:

"What about your wife? She work outside the home?"

Oops. I have a wife.

"She? No, she prefers housework. And I'm very pleased with that."

"I was very sad when I heard about her accident."

Oh? My wife was in a car crash? Hope she's OK.

"Yeah. Thank you," I say with sorrowful eyes, like a bad actor in a stupid commercial.

"You must miss her very much."

Oops, there went my wife. This is like watching a thriller movie backwards.

"Yeah, you bet. It's hard being alone."

"And you don't have any children with her?"

Wow. That's a tough one.

"Eh...No, I don't think so." Fuck. That was terrible. "I mean, no. Not technically." Don't ask me what I mean by this. I have no idea.

He drives on in silence. He doesn't ask any more questions. It's quite uncomfortable. Does he suspect anything? I break the silence by going back to the start of the conversation, women and work.

"But Gunholder, she works in a café?"

"Yeah. I am giving her time. She has time to think. When I was thirty year old, I was on the street. I was drinking. I didn't see the light. When the wine goes in, the brain goes out."

I take a good hard look at him. Not so holy after all.

We visit his friend's church in the neighboring town of Cop War. It looks more like an aerobics gym than a regular church, and the smell of sweat fills the air. His friend's name is shorter than either of my hosts,' but it's much harder to say. Written as *Thordur,* it sounds like "Torture" when they try helping me out. He has a round face with round glasses and a full, biblical beard. The only modern thing about him is his long hair that he anoints with blessed gel. Actually, he reminds me a bit of my broad-faced father, bless his soul. Goodmoondoor tells me that Torture appears on his TV channel every day. It shows: His speech is loud and clear, as if he were still on camera. He doesn't let go of the Bible the entire thirty minutes, holding it in his hand like a holy hammer. Once or twice he pounds it into the air as if he were nailing his theses to the front door of his church. His views are unorthodox and extreme, his language more colorful than most.

"People sometimes ask me if you need to be circumcised to enter into heaven. I tell them no. There is no need to. It's not about the genitals, but the heart. The question is: are you ready to open up the foreskin of your heart and let in the light of the living God?"

The fire of homophobia rages in his eyes. When I look deeply into them I see, through the flames, a skinny gay fellow nailed to a cross belting out "I Will Survive." Father Friendly adds fuel to this fire, while Toxic remembers his night with Andro.

"We used to have this gay guy at our congregation in Virginia," I say. "But after I ripped the ring out of his earlobe with pincers, he went from GAY to OK."

Goodmoondoor looks at his bearded friend like a small boy, and Torture laughs like the devil himself, answering in his fine English:

"*Heh, heh.* That's the way to do it. Brand them by the balls!"

Friendly gets carried away. "Or use them as fire extinguishers. I once had an altar boy who looked way too feminine for his age. I had to teach him a lesson. So I used him for putting out candles. With his mouth. I used to tell him, 'Better to blow the light of the Lord than the dick of darkness!'"

They both stare at me for a moment before they start laughing like two middle-aged fraternity brothers having a chance meeting in a hotel lobby forty years later. "The dick of darkness! Ha ha!"

"Father Friendly was very good on TV last night. Did you see him?" Goodmoondoor asks his friend.

"Yes, I saw him. He's an excellent footman in the army of God," Torture says and puts his right hand on my shoulder. The arm of fire.

CHAPTER 10
MOJA ŠTIKLA
05.20.2006

The days go by. I slowly adapt to exile existence. It's going OK. I'm getting used to the silence and the brightness, as well as the sterility of the house, but the cold is more difficult to handle. It's the coldest May of my life. Still, everywhere they talk of the loveliest spring.

"We are happy if we get ten degrees here in Iceland," Sickreader explains.

Poor guys. I'm happy if I only get ten more minutes up here.

In the morning Father Friendly visits various churches and volunteer organizations where they treat him like the pope on tour, fill him with coffee and cookies, and load him up with booklets and brochures that show off their good work. They're building a kindergarten in Kenya, a primary school in India. The priests are all men, the volunteers all women. I make my objections to Goodmoondoor once we're in the car.

"I'm worried to see all those women working outside their homes," I say.

"It's all right because they are not paid," he answers and winks at me in the funniest way.

My afternoons are usually my own. I walk around the city LPP-style, moving slowly down Liquor Vicar, the main street, women-watching and window-shopping, forever seeking the gun of my dreams. I follow my weight all the way down the hill, to the main square, which looks more like an empty parking lot than a city plaza. In a warm bookstore near the square, you can buy *Handgun Magazine*, the hitman's favorite. Seems Smith & Wesson has a new model out. "Easy on your hand, easy on your target." Pretty close to the "guilt-free gun" that we hangmen have been dreaming about for six hundred years. I wrap my scarf around the collar before paying for the mag at the cash register. One more local wonder girl, a Day 3 type, hands me the receipt. It's a well-known fact that Croatia has the most beautiful women in the world, but Iceland might be a close runner-up. They are very different, though, those butter-blondes from our dark-haired *ljepotice*. From a bench by the big pond behind the cathedral, I watch the ducks and swans sail about. It's a beautiful setting, really, perfect for a cigarette. But I won't break my five-year abstinence from tobacco, even though I guess I've got good excuses to do so. Have to take care of my health. Instead I read about this innovation called NSK (No Spill Kill) made possible by the new, revolutionary bullet from Eagle Eye "big enough to ice your victim instantly, but so small that it won't spill any blood at all." Only in the most God-fearing, Christian country on the planet would they allow such a publication. Who's buying it up here, on Gun-Free Island? I throw it in the garbage before entering Café Paris. The butter-blonde is on duty. I suck in my stomach and pick one of her tables.

The priest is worried about her relationship with her dad and asks her if she dislikes him.

"I think my father is more interested in God than his own children," Gunholder strikes back, unusually hostile, while she cleans the table with a wet rag, head wagging like a sistah.

"Well, we are all God's children. Sons and daughters of the Holy Father," I respond, all Friendly.

"Holy Father, holy shit. Where is the holy mother then? She's a virgin. Wow. Great. The church is good only for stupid white men," she spits out. She leaves with her cloth and tray. I have to say that I'm pretty impressed, but Father Friendly thinks otherwise. When she returns with his latte, he says, "Your parents are holy people and I think they deserve your respect."

"They're not holy. Not committing sins for some years doesn't make you holy. An inactive alcoholic is just as much an alcoholic as the one who's drinking."

Wow, this one is way too deep for me. I concentrate on her lips instead. Behind the heavy church gates of my priestly exterior, I keep a crazy Croatian army dog. Sooner or later he will break out of this fucking dog collar and start licking those glistening strawberry lips.

I'm supposed to be back at the holy house by six. I usually travel by cab, even though I could fly from New York to Boston for the same amount. Igor can afford it. Money's never an issue in our game, though Friendly's American Express Gold card probably has a higher limit. But using his pious plastic would be like sending an invitation to the Feds.

At 6:30 PM we eat a modest meal prepared by Sickreader. Her food always makes me think of Jerry Seinfeld. The table setting is very tasteful, but the food has almost no taste at all. By 8.00 PM we're at the studio. Sickreader lends some of her own makeup to the two gentlemen who start their broadcast at 8:30. The funny thing is that I'm getting into it. I'm starting to like it. I'm almost looking forward to it. I even bought a copy of the King James Bible. Preaching makes you powerful.

"For I am his Word! His Word is me! Word up!"

I almost regret that we take Saturday off. "It's because Eurovision," Goodmoondoor says. The annual European Song Contest will be on tonight, with Iceland taking part for the twentieth year, Croatia for the eleventh. Apparently this is *the* TV event of the year. "It has no purpose to be preaching tonight. Ninety-nine *prósent* of all the people are watching Eurovision. The streets are empty when it is. We will just have some old show in the air tonight." And it's also family reunion time; Gunholder and her brother Truster are both coming for dinner. Sounds like Thanksgiving.

Truster is quite different from his sister. If she's a swan, he's a sparrow: A shy-eyed, thick-breasted fellow who is small and round, though one would call him strong rather than fat. He's got working man's hands and his strong fingers dwarf the needle and thread. His face is smooth save for white down that covers his upper lip. Still, he must be around twenty-six or twenty-seven years old. He hardly says a word and never looks up from his meal, but still I find his mere presence strangely soothing. I realize I would have a hard time following orders if they told me to take him out.

"Truster is the name of a very nice Icelandic bird. He brings the spring," says the woman of the house as she passes me the white, and very holy-looking, sauce.

"It's not Icelandic," her daughter protests with heavy eyelids.

"What do you mean? Truster?" Sickreader says with a big surprise. "It's one of the most Icelandic birds. We even have a poem about him."

"Yeah, but Mom, it doesn't mean it's Icelandic. The bird's only here for the summer. Most of the year it's in France or Spain. Doesn't that make it more Spanish than Icelandic?"

"Spanish? How can you say such a thing? Truster is the most Icelandic bird we have."

"It spends more of its time in Spain."

"But his…his kids are born in Iceland. They are Icelandic citizens, and he must also be. He was also born in Iceland!"

"Icelandic citizens? You speak like a racist, Mom," Gunholder says.

It's hard to tell whether her parents understand the word, but her mother closes her eyes and purses her lips. Goodmoondoor rises from the table and walks over to a bookshelf and pulls out a volume. Sickreader tries to smooth things over by turning to Father Friendly:

"I don't know what you call this bird in English, but…"

"It is 'redwing,'" her good husband calls out, looking up from a slim dictionary.

She thanks him and explains to me that the redwing is a "travel bird." Gunholder rolls her eyes, but Truster just sits there, like a deaf sailor the family found on the beach this morning. His virgin cheeks are stained with a soft blush, as if they are trying to help me picture a redwing.

"Or is it *traveling bird*?" Sickreader continues. "What do you say? What do you call the bird that lives in two…"

"I don't know. Migration bird?" is my wild guess.

Gunholder picks up on it with evil-eyed sarcasm: "Immigration bird."

We eat in silence. Truster has finished his meal and our eyes meet. Poor guy. When his parents introduced him to me they had strangely added that he was in love, like he was a retard.

"Oh? And who's the lucky one?" I asked.

"Yes. She's very lucky. And we also," came the answer.

I have to admit that all day long I've been looking forward to watching that stupid Eurovison Song Contest. It's been six whole years since I've been able to see the program that saved my life. We gather on the big corner sofa, and Goodmoondoor turns on his flat screen. It's live from Athens, Greece, and the atmosphere is not unlike that of a televangelist mega-mass: ten thousand people screaming with joy at the end of every song. Except after the Icelandic one. A trashy girl in a hooker's outfit gets nothing but heavy booing. The song seemed OK, but her arrogance is definitely not going down with the Greeks. Actually, she reminds me a bit of Gunholder. I look at my hosts. Of all the secular acts, this one was probably the least godly, the singer wearing a devilish grin, as if she'd just slept with the producer of the show. Goodmoondoor looks at me with a complicated smile, as if he were a UN delegate and his prime minister had just peed at the podium.

"It's just a joke," Gunholder explains. "This singer…She's just making fun of the whole fucking thing."

The f-word quietly explodes in the room, like a silent but serious fart. Her father kindly reminds her that such a word is not accepted in his house, and even Toxic is thrown off guard, remembering how "the fucking thing" saved his life.

We go through ten or so more songs—most of them falling into the Slavic techno category, or Technoslavic as we say—until my dear Croatia appears. Good old *Hrvatska*. Tomo almost pees in his underpants as he watches the national goddess walk on stage. It's Severina. Good old Severina. Severina Vučkovič. To the boys of Split she was the most beautiful girl in the world. She was four years older than me, and I didn't even dare *dreaming* about her. I once saw her walking down Marmontova with her mom, and got those terrible heart-hiccups. Though I haven't seen her in years—not since her sex tape went viral on the Internet and got every Croat peeing tears for a week—but she still looks like the most beautiful woman in the world. She's wearing a long red dress, open at the front, showing off her perfect legs. She's backed by some funked-up folk band. *"Jer još trava nija nikla."* I get all homesick; I feel it in my stomach. Ah, this is terrible. *"Tamo gdje je stala moja štikla."* Man, this is too much for me. I can't help it, but watching her dance on the screen creates a deep feeling inside me. It's like seeing your parents' foreplay, the prelude to your conception, the very reason for your existence.

I get a very homesick hard-on.

And somewhere deep inside, I feel like crying. But my tears of stone won't return to liquid form. They should make Viagra for crying. I hope they don't notice my misty eyes, my sad mouth, or my heavy-duty hard-on saluting my homeland. It's my language. The girl of my childhood dreams…It hits the lonely man in exile like a man being run over by a NYC truck full of tabloids (with Tony fucking Danza on the front page). Oh. *Moja voljena domovina…*

They look at me. I must look like a lone puppy longing for his mother. I have to say something.

"It's the memories…," I manage to stammer. "…of Yugoslavia."

They turn their heads back to the screen, ignoring the heart-broken priest sitting on their sofa. Severina keeps on screaming: *"Moja štikla! Moja štikla!"* That would be "My high heel! My high heel!" Suddenly the doorbell rings. It has the sound of church bells. Goodmoondoor goes to the door, and I hear two men talking to him.

This is my cue.

I excuse myself and get up, pretending to go to the bathroom, but continue through the dining room, all the way to the back of the house. I open the door out on to the veranda and hesitate for a very brief moment. The icy spring air in my face, I face the fact that I'm not wearing any shoes, only my NYC socks. In the background, Severina howls on about her stilettos. I let them be my shoes as I step out on the cold veranda and quickly close the door behind me. Then I run like a crazy man out in the garden and through the next.

CHAPTER 11
TADEUSZ
05.20.2006

Running on Icelandic asphalt in summer-thin American socks is hard on Croatian feet. Still I'm not going to cry about that. I'm a hitman, not a priest.

I let the cold be my whip as I run up the street, heading deeper into this suburb of mini-mansions. Luckily no one sees me. Everybody's watching Severina's *štikla* dance. High heels are the woman's pedestal. You just have to worship the girl who wears them. In fact, you can measure a woman by her shoes. The more feminine she is, the higher her heel. Severina's heels are usually as long as the barrel of a 9mm. One of our friends said he spent a night with her on his father's boat, right in the harbor. "Making waves until the morning light." We didn't believe him, but of course we couldn't prove him wrong either. True or false, he built his whole reputation on the story and ended up in fucking Parliament. Every time his face pops up on *HRT*, I automatically reach for my gun.

I don't see any police cars around. No SWAT teams or secret agents with woolen caps jumping over hedges. I think the two men spoke to Goodmoondoor in Icelandic. The local police department is working for the Feds. All small nations suck up to the USA. Everybody wants their Hollywood moment. I wonder if the Icelandic police would ever do the same for the Iranian equivalent of the FBI.

I turn right at the next intersection, spotting a small delivery van from Domino's Pizza. The engine is running. I duck behind the car. The pizza boy is standing on the porch of a nearby house, with his back turned towards me, delivering his hot pies to some hot chick with naked shoulders, a Day 6 type. I jump in the car and drive off. He comes running out on the street as I drive away. I see him waving goodbye to me in the rearview mirror. Icelanders are polite people.

I do some fast-as-a-bullet thinking as I drive the empty streets. I must not go far. The pizza van is like a bell around a bull's neck. And Javor always told us:

"When you need to hide, you shall hide in the heart of the enemy. It's the one place he will not search."

All the mansions come with a double garage. Some of them are almost as big as the house itself. And in front of each one there's parked a huge SUV beside a smaller one: his and hers. A Super Duty Ford Truck next to a Porsche Cayenne. Those people keep cars like the Bedouins keep camels. They all look brand new, their roofs shining in the white spring night. Yet those vehicles are never put inside the garage, the holy couple told me the other day. The flatroofers are only built as shrines to the golden calves resting in front of them. Goodmoondoor told me his neighbor polishes his Lexus every other week. He probably makes love to it the other week. At least many of those SUVs have been tricked out, with huge tires, putting their exhaust pipe at the ideal height for such an operation.

One of the houses has no cars in front of its double garage. I drive past it and five other houses. Then I stop, park the pizza lemon, jump out, lock it, and throw the keys into the next yard, before making a quick run for the empty-looking house. (You would probably like to see this in slow motion: the chubby priest running sock-footed on the sidewalk, like a lottery-addict too late to buy his ticket.) There is no light in the windows. At least no visible light. It's quite hard to tell, though, since the night is bright as a prom in hell. I walk the short walkway and up three steps to the front door. I ring the bell. A dog barks in the distance. I wait a good while in the freezing cold, catching my breath. I ring again. The doorbell seems to be connected to a dog some two blocks away. Otherwise it's dead silent. The whole neighborhood is glued to the TV. Even the trees stand motionless with excitement. I wonder if Severina will win?

A car can be heard on a nearby street. The FB-eyes must be on their way. I bring out my knife and open the door to find the barking dog inside the house. I find some slippers in the entryway and take a quick tour of my new home. Two hundred square meters of pretty square people. An unused fireplace and some more of those lunar paintings, heavy duty stuff in heavy golden frames. Some obese sofas and a treadmill. The dog seems to be in the basement. I find the staircase and let my ears lead me to the laundry room. Once I'm inside it, I find a small, hairy dog that we used to call "a walking wig" back home in Split. The small barking machine goes into a fit until I unplug it with a quick turn of its neck. It's as easy as breaking a chicken leg at the joint.

On the clothesline I find some silly pants, a tacky shirt, and freshly washed man's underwear. The holy man strips and donates the collar to his fellow dog—his fellow *dead* dog—and says goodbye for good to Father Friendly. I put on the funny pants and shirt and quickly find my way to the no-cars-allowed garage where I begin looking for a can of paint or something close. In a messy corner, I do find some house paint. I open the can with my army knife and smear some of the white paint on my clothes and in my face. This is pure genius. I get all excited. My heartbeat goes from Bolero to Bossa Nova. I bring the open can with me inside the house and find some newspapers in the kitchen. I spread them on the floor in the hallway—some sixteen photos of the trashy girl singing for Iceland—and put the can on top. In the kitchen I find a radio and turn it on. Phil Collins screams he's been waiting for this moment, all his life. I used to cry out loud with him when my Hanover girlfriend dumped me like an empty paper cup in a garbage can. It's a great breakup song.

I'm just about done with everything, and completely wet with head-sweat, when the doorbell finally rings. I wait a minute and let it ring again. The sound is very luxurious, as if designed to remind the owners about their money. I then go to the door and open it. Heartbeat is Disco now. Two policemen are standing out on the porch. Black jackets, white hats.

"Hallo," they say in pure Icelandic.

"Hchello," I say with a thick Slavic accent.

"Oh, sorry. Do you speak English?"

"Hchyes...a little."

"Is Christian home?"

Is this a Christian household? That's a strange question. Maybe they're not the police. Maybe they're just two priests on hood patrol. "Hchyes, I think is Christian home. But I no live here..." I say in my best immigrant English.

"Can we speak to him?"

"Hchim?"

"Yes. We want to speak to Christian."

Their accent is strong, like a wrestler on cocaine.

"Ah, I see. No. Christian no home now. No."

"Who are you?"

"I am Tadeusz."

"Polish?"

"Hchyes. I work in hchouse. Christian no home," I say with wet white paint on my nose.

"Okay. We are looking for a bald man in priest clothes. Have you seen anyone running around here?"

"No. Zorry. A bald priest?"

"Yes. He has no hair on his head and is wearing a priest uniform. He is a very dangerous man. A criminal. We are looking for him."

"Criminal priest?" I ask them, remembering Dikan and his "Stupidity is the best disguise."

"Yes. He is wanted in America."

"I think they hchad enough criminal priest in America?" I say.

The two Icelandic policemen give away gentle smiles, beg me good-bye, and wish me luck with my painting job.

CHAPTER 12
MR. MAACK
05.20.2006 – 05.21.2006

I have never lived in such a big house. I quite like it, I have to say. Suddenly exile is excellent. Escaping the holy house was a big relief. Now I don't need to put on a stupid smile in the morning or walk the shiny floors like Christ on water. Getting Friendly off my back was like dumping a loud girlfriend with a Texan accent and a cell-phone addiction.

I spend the rest of Saturday night home alone, enjoying the European Song Contest 2006 on my big new surround-sound flat screen, which looks more like a fat screen, actually. The counting of the votes was always my favorite. Some screaming Finns in Halloween costumes take home the trophy. Bosnia & Herzegovina comes in third. Severina finishes at number thirteen with only fifty-six votes, all of them coming from the former republic of Yugoslavia. Even the Serbs feel bad enough to give us ten points. Or it was their dicks voting. Apparently the rest of Europe hasn't seen Severina's sex tape. If we are ever to win this fucking thing again, we need to create more Balkan states.

The fridge is full of food. I make a late-night omelet for the hungry hitman in hiding. I take it in the billiard room downstairs, trying to keep low profile and lights off. My landlords are Kristján Þ. Maack and Helena Ingólfsdóttir, and it seems they've been enduring these names for about sixty years. The photo albums show a happy mustached couple smiling in all the right places from Florida to Slovenia. They seem to travel for a living. The kitchen calendar shows March in Kenya, April in Bulgaria. Probably thinking of me, Helena has marked this weekend: London, London, London, London. They're due back on Monday.

After a long and eventful day, I'm happy to go to their bed. It's big as a boxing arena, with his and her corners. I can't find the gloves, but I can see that she's reading some Italian cookbook and he's reading *Cosa Nostra: A History of the Sicilian Mafia.* Fucking Talians all the time. How about some press for the honest and hard-working men of the Croatian Mafia? How about some books, some films, some fame? Fuck it. Even some ugly-named nobody on Gun-Free Island is reading about the pasta-poopers. I sleep on her side, reserving my last waking minutes for a survey of my strange situation. What's next? I could either kill them when they return and stay here until the fridge is empty, or use the ticket Igor bought me at the airport. I don't see any other possibilities.

I spend Sunday at home, enjoying a long and luxurious breakfast, trying hard to read the article that accompanies my photo on the back page of the newspaper that came through the front door late last night. The headline reads: *Mafíumorðingi á Íslandi?* Sounds like Mafia something in Iceland. The question mark is reassuring. There is a mention of Father Friendly and Goodmoondoor's Christian TV station, along with some words from the preacher himself. I can picture his big-eyed llama-face on a long hairy neck in front of the reporter: "We are in big shock. We didn't suspect anything. He was very friendly. We consider ourselves lucky to be alive."

Igor's name is not mentioned. He's my only hope now.

I try to call Munita, using the Maacks' house phone. I know it's not the wisest move, but I just can't resist. I have to talk to her. I call her mobile and her machine. "So please leave me a massage after the beep." You got to love that voice. That soft, oily, hairy world that sucks you in like the mother of life itself. Even her speaking mistakes are sexy. She doesn't answer. And she doesn't call back. I wonder if she's OK? Violent death runs in her family.

I take a long hot bath in the biggest tub east of Vegas, letting bubbles bounce my belly for fifty minutes, then enjoy a naked walk of the house with a cold beer in hand, taking all possible advantage of the extraordinary feeling of being out of sight, out of time. I live in an empty house. I'm the no one who's at home. I do not exist. I'm just that invisible force that moves a small green can of Heineken beer around this big house, slowly sucking away its contents.

As I go back inside the bathroom, I'm unpleasantly surprised to see my face in the mirror. For a split second I see Father Friendly. I'm reminded of our quick eye contact in the mirror at JFK and my heart skips a beat. Mr. Friendly is stubborn like a stud on steroids. He just won't let go. He keeps calling me from his grave like an angry senior complaining about his coffin. I even dreamt him last night. At some open-air gathering of long white gowns and tall green trees, he came over to me and kissed me on the forehead. His lips felt big, thick, and warm. As if he was black. And when he backed away, I saw that in fact he looked like Louis Armstrong, the good old trumpet man.

I don't get it. Sixty-six pigs have gone down, without the slightest twinge of conscience, and then all of a sudden: a bald priest killed in an airport bathroom keeps following me around like a retarded girl in love. Maybe he wasn't just a holyman but a holy man? Like Louis Armstrong.

The beer makes my brain swim inside my head, like a whale trapped in an undersized aquarium, and I get all confused. I look at myself in the mirror, look *for* myself in the mirror. Somehow I'm not there. I'm faced with a babushka doll with the face of an American TV preacher. Inside him there is the charming polish housepainter Tadeusz Boksiwic. Inside him is the Russian arms-muggler Igor Illitch. Inside him: Toxic the hitman. Inside him: The fresh-off-the-boat Tom Boksic. And finally, inside him, there is "Champ," the tiny little Tomo-boy from Split, Croatia.

Instead of getting depressed about the number and sizes of all my different selves, I add yet another one to the wooden doll: I walk out of the house as Mr. Maack, the successful business man of Guard the Beer, Iceland. I'm wearing a long light brown winter coat, a dark gray hat, and a red scarf around my neck. Shoes from Lloyds, London. On top of it all, I'm holding a brown leather briefcase containing my Russian sneakers and some clean underwear. I must look totally ridiculous, like a royal hitman on his way to a late night job.

Still, I try to walk like a business man: with a straight back and belly out front. A man who's got all his successes behind him now doing his victory walk. As if he was not moving his feet himself, but was being pushed down the road by the steady growing interests of his investments. This means that I walk rather slowly along the sidewalk. I'm the only one to do so here in the country of no streetwalkers. It makes me a bit nervous. Every fucking car is full of eyes. Apparently they've never seen a walking man before. It's like being on stage to a full house at the HNK. But this is the only way. Stealing a car wouldn't be Mr. Maack's style, and a taxi was too risky.

The light is on as ever. At 10:33 the sun is still burning on the horizon like an orange lantern at an outdoor Chinese restaurant in Brooklyn. It's a beautiful evening, actually, with completely calm seas and the customary ten degrees.

Damn it. Now I sound like a British gentleman. Must be the hat.

CHAPTER 13
MURDER & KILLING INC.
05.21.2006

I didn't feel like killing Maack the couple. Their dog was enough. I'm still without my habitual working tool, and to tell the truth, I didn't fancy another *assemotional* one. I don't need two more Friendlys on my back. I also came to the conclusion that Igor was no longer an option.

I used to think my mistake of presenting myself as Igor at the gates of this country, instead of being Father Friendly all the way from JFK, was a bit of dumb luck, but now I'm not so sure. The fact that Mr. Friendly was traveling on the Icelandair flight that night, but then never showed up in Iceland, must have triggered suspicion in some high places. And when they identified the dead body in the airport bathroom as Friendly's, they made the easy calculation: his killer was traveling on his ticket that night. They will have then checked the list of passengers and identified them all as guilt-free, glacier-loving tourists except for this one guy. And then the passport controller's report that night must have given Igor away as a potential Friendly-killer. So leaving Iceland in Igor-disguise is a risk I won't take. I don't want to spend the next thirty years eating thirty-two-cent meatloaves and listening to Snoop Dogg thumping out from the next cell. I'm a Creed fan, for crying out loud. I'd rather stay here nameless, gunless, and aimless in The Land of the Ten Degrees.

The walk from Guard the Beer to Reykjavik is almost one hour long. A white police car goes by. I keep my cool. It's like walking a tightrope. I have to maintain my concentration all the time. One look to the left and I might fall. Into federal hands.

I walk the same route that Gunholder drove me on day one. I'm going to her house. The butter-blonde is my only hope now. I didn't dare calling her. Her phone must be bugged by now. I have no reason to believe that she'll be waiting for me with balloons and brownies, but somehow my Balkan animal instinct tells me she will show me something else than the door.

I stroll down the barren sidewalk along the *Miklabraut*. Here I meet the first passerby of the night. A thin gray-haired man comes jogging towards me in a red T-shirt stained with sweat. His face is filled with horrible pain, as if he was playing Christ on the cross. It's only a matter of years until jogging will be banned along with smoking. I had five jogger friends in NYC. We used to meet in Central Park four times a week, just to keep in shape for the honeys. I managed to quit after six months, but they couldn't kick the habit. Three years later, three of them had lost all their weight. Well, I have to admit that for a very good reason one of them became my #32, a sad story really, but the other two both died from jogging-related conditions.

As the tortured jogger passes me, I manage to cover my face by pretending to lift my hat in greeting, like some old-school movie man. I have to be careful. I'm a household face in Iceland now. My picture was even on the TV news earlier tonight. It was the same photo they had in the paper, a terrible mug shot from the early

Toxic days in Germany. I look different now, more cheeks and no hair, but a clever face-reader would identify me on the spot.

The sun seems to be setting at last as I enter the old town. Still there is no sign of darkness. It's bright as a morgue at midnight. Here the cars are all still, parked outside the small houses, but there are also some passersby to stay clear of. I get lost for a good while, but finally I find Gunholder's bulletproof house. She's not home. I use my Swiss knife to get inside.

In the days since Wednesday, she has only added to the mess in her apartment. How can she live like this? Even an old foot-man from the Homeland War wouldn't survive for three days in this dump. All the ashtrays are overflowing, and the situation has called for extreme measures: A small frying pan is sitting on top of the TV, filled with ash and broken butts. Clothes are everywhere, covering floor and furniture like a colorful snowfall. Here and there an empty beer can stands like a tombstone in the snow, a memorial to a long dead party. The bedroom looks to be growing dirty linen, and it smells like a gym. I spot two mags lying at my feet. One is called *Dazed & Confused,* the other one is *Slut Magazine.* What did I tell you? The holy couple have produced a ho.

I take off my coat, hat, and scarf, and start emptying the ashtrays and picking up clothes. In forty minutes' time, the place looks like it could be photographed for *The Hitman's Guide to Housecleaning.* I've just fallen into an armchair, the one facing the kitchen and the front door, when Gunholder opens it. I suck in my stomach. She screams a silent "what!" and then closes the door.

"What are you doing here?"

If I was still Father Friendly she would have said: "What the FUCK are you doing here?" The killer has a bit more appeal than the clergyman.

"What...I don't...Who are you anyway?! And how did you get...So that's why you could open the door the other day?"

She's a bit drunk. Her beauty is slightly out of focus. Only now she notices the neatness.

"What? Was Mom here as well?"

After some more unanswered questions, she settles for a cigarette and lets herself fall down on the sofa.

"Who are you? What's your name? What are you doing? Did you really kill the priest? At the airport? Why?"

There is a touch of admiration in her voice. A hint of a smile on her delicious lips. I tell her my life story minus the sixty-seven homicides, my two years with Munita and my night with Andro. She smokes and listens and looks for an ashtray.

"Where did you put all the ashtrays?" she asks.

"There is one right there, in front of you."

Apparently she has never seen an empty ashtray before. The Icelandic slut. She smells like a New Jersey Devils' banner that's been hanging in the dim corner of a seedy Newark lounge for the past twenty years. I really want to vacuum her with my nose.

"Oh, thanks," she says and puts the ashtray to use.

"You should stop smoking. It can kill you," I say.

"Are you telling *me* about killing?" she says with an offended smile.

"Yeah. Why not?"

"You just killed a priest didn't you? Plus you're wanted for another murder."

I see. They've made the connection between the dead man in the airport and the dead man in the dumpsite. Good job.

"You think the killer doesn't care about life? You think he doesn't care about health or keeping a clean house?" I say and point to the tidy room.

"Very nice," she says.

"The killer is a human being like everyone else. He has his rights."

"Right. I'm sorry."

"It's OK."

"So you're the…the sensitive type of a killer, then?"

"I don't know. I just hate it when people discriminate against me, only because I…kill people."

Oops. Shouldn't have said that. She stops in mid-smoke.

"What do you mean? You've killed more people?"

I'm in trouble. Never show your gun on a first date. But she already knows I killed two guys, plus this is not a date, right? I'm here looking for her help. I'm in trouble.

"Some people just have to die," is my solution.

"And my father's friend had to die?"

"Well. He had to be killed. Or else I would be in jail right now, being raped in the shower every morning by black Hulks with limp hose-dicks."

She looks surprised by my vocabulary. I am as well.

"But what do you mean by: Some people have to die?" she asks.

"Just, you know. There are people who deserve to die."

"Why?"

"Because they're evil. Evil people who do evil things. People who do the wrong thing. Or refuse to do the right thing. Then they have to be taken away."

"Wow. You speak like my dad's friend, Þórður."

"Torture?"

"You call him that? *Ha ha*. Fits him well. Are you religious, or…?"

"I'm Catholic."

"OK. How can I be sure you're not some crazy TV preacher who was Father Friendly's competitor and wanted him dead?"

"Because I'm not."

"OK. But you say you're a Catholic?"

"Yeah, but I'm a Croatian Catholic. There's nothing religious about that. It only means you go to church two times in your life. When you marry and when you die."

"That's nice. And how often have you been? Once?"

I have to smile at this one.

"No."

She hesitates for a second before extinguishing her cigarette in the ashtray. Then she says:

"Who are you then? Just another loser murderer who shot an FBI agent by some mistake and had to flee the fucking States?"

Well. Fuck her.

"I'm not a 'loser murderer,' I'm a…. "

"Yeah? What?"

This is going too far.

"I'm a…professional."

"A professional?"

"Yep. I'm a professional killer. I've killed over one hundred people."

This is just great. I'm in bed with her by now.

"Come on. ONE HUNDRED PEOPLE?!"

I guess the exact number would be something like 125. In the Midwest I used to drive through towns with a sign saying: POP. 125. I always stopped for gas, imagining this was my own personal ADV.

"Yeah. On the whole. I killed about fifty or sixty as a soldier in the Croatian army defending the land of my father and mother. And since then I have killed exactly sixty-six motherfuckers from various countries in my work as a hitman for the national organization. Father Friendly was my first and only 'amateur' murder."

She is speechless and remains so, like the Catholic priest in his confession booth.

"The national organization?" she finally asks.

"Yeah, the Mafia."

"The Mafia? You're in the Mafia?"

"Yeah. The *Croatian* Mafia, that is. Not the Talian shit."

She stares at me for some good ten seconds, suddenly look- ing totally sober. The Mafia. In my early New York days I used to think this was my magic word. I thought every girl in Manhattan dreamt about a real and authentic Mob man with a foreign accent and expert humping style. I always dropped it on the first date, right after the main course. They all reacted in the same way; they politely excused themselves, went to the bathroom, and never came back. Oh, the girls of Manhattan, this whole dating army of mystic blondes and loud brunettes, with their moneytoring eyes, hair smelling of TV soap, and the fame-detector buried deep in their purses. Some even left their purses with me, and twice I went looking for them in the ladies room, but there was no trace of them. Yes, "the Mob" are magic words.

I slowly learned not to discuss my profession with my bubbly dinner partners, feeling very much like the AIDS-infected dater. I kept that info like a secret weapon, saving it for dumping pur- poses only, or SOS situations. If I was, for example, stuck on a first date and the food was better than the girl (a Day 3 Girl who was turning into a Day 20 type in the middle of her lecture on the American voting system and how some Nader guy was "our only hope"), all I had to do then was to drop the magic word and *bang!*—I could reset my radar.

The reaction is a bit different here. The ice-girl weighs her options until she asks:

"You're like a...mass murderer then?"

"No."

"What do you mean, *no?*"

"I'm not a murderer. I'm a killer."

"OK."

"There is a big difference between murder and killing."

"Oh?" she asks, raising her eyebrows.

"Yes. It's like the difference between a hobby and a job."

"What do you mean?"

"Murder is something you choose to do. It may be wrong. Killing is something you have to do, or you die yourself. That's not wrong."

"Bullshit."

"Bullshit?"

"Yeah. You think your victims will feel the difference? 'Oh, I'm so happy I was killed and not murdered! It's so much better!' Fucking bullshit. One hundred people? What kind of a monster are you *eiginlega?*"

This last word must be Icelandic. She's too agitated to have full control of her brain. I'm a bit worked up as well:

"Hey. What do you know about war? You've never even HAD war in this...this cold and silent land. You've never had to live outside, in the mountains in the middle of winter, without any tents or any real food for days, and then you see your father dead and they tell you your brother was killed and then they have those people lined up in front of you and they tell you to shoot. And you shoot, and you don't know how many you shoot, and you don't want to know how many you shoot, but still you want to shoot as many as possible. Because..."

I can feel that somewhere inside me tears are being manufactured for the first time in years.

"Because war is shit and we're all deep inside it. No one can say that this is right and this is wrong, because it's either ALL WRONG or ALL RIGHT. And..."

Tears have left the factory. The order has been placed. They're on their way. But it's a long haul.

"And you still don't know. You still don't fucking know. Fucking fifteen years later you still don't know if it was wrong or if it was right. It was just..."

I pause before my speech dies out in a lone, soft, final word: "...shit."

We sit for a while. The bright night entering through the windows fills the room almost sarcastically. This should be a dark scene. Tears have yet to arrive.

She looks at her hands. They're resting on her knees. She has long nails, freaky long. They're painted light pink. I remember the hand from the mass grave in ADV. It was a girl's hand, the hand of a teenage girl, and it had those same long nails. And as we were trying to finish the grave, it always stuck out from the dirt. We tried hammering it with our shovels and jumping on top of it, with no success. It always popped up again—this chubby, white girl's hand with long green nails. And it looked so ridiculous. It did not fit the circumstances; it just didn't belong in a mass grave. A mass grave was a thing of the past, something that you associated with World War Two or whatever. People in mass graves were old women with dirty headscarves and poor peasant kids dressed in worn out clothes and wooden shoes. And here was this hand, waving to us from the goddamn grave, that was more like a graveyard, really, and it was so fucking modern. It was so very much a *today's hand*. You could almost see that two hours ago it had been pushing the Play button on a Walkman with a Michael Jackson tape inside it.

Out of respect, I had started humming *"You Are Not Alone,"* the perfect psalm for a mass grave. Still, I couldn't sing the hand to rest. And after trying for the tenth time to get the fucking palm into the ground, I totally freaked and pulled out my knife, chopped the hand off with some effort, and then threw it away. And this was one of my worst war moments: as I was working on it with my knife, I thought I heard something beneath my feet. Something like a girl's cry muffled by dirt.

"Nice nails," I finally say, looking at Gunholder's hands.

She looks at me as if she wants to bury them. In my face.

CHAPTER 14
FROG ON A COLD RED ROOF
05.22.2006

My Balkan animal instinct was right. Instead of showing me the door, the preacher's daughter put me up for the night, up in the attic. It's pretty cold, but her sleeping bag is warm, plus the loft is a bit darker than the rest of the country. It only has two small windows: one in my corner and a rusty skylight in the middle of the roof. Sleeping up here is not only the preacher's daughter's way of punishing me for all my sins. I had to go up here because her brother Truster is her roommate for the time being. I wonder where he sleeps? In the birdhouse, maybe, out in the garden. We came to an agreement that despite his name he should be kept out of this. So I forbid myself to make a sound while he's in the house. From midnight till dawn I play dead. "He's working like crazy. He only comes home for sleeping," his sister tells me. The perfect roommate. He works as a crane operator at some construction site.

"He doesn't say much, does he?" I ask.

"Yeah. I know. He's always been like that. And then it's also his job...I mean, he's used to spending the whole day in the air, alone, two hundred feet above ground. Plus all his co-workers are from Poland or Lithuania."

Once Truster is back in the air, I'm allowed downstairs for some toilet work and breakfast. This type of exile is actually more fun than Friendly's, because this is real exile: a hitman hiding in the hot girl's attic. The best thing is that I don't have to do any more acting shit. No more American priests or Polish painters. Though my body is not allowed out of this small house, I feel more free here than when I was running around town with a cler-gyman's collar on God's leash.

I'm Anne Frank online. Gunholder lends me her laptop so I can surf the digital seas. I spend the day digging up my past, looking for and reading war stories by my fellow soldiers. Darko Radović is the heftiest blogger of them all, probably because he left both his legs in Knin. In our brigade we lost five lives, six legs, three arms, and some fingers. It's sad to say, but my one-legged brothers still have to keep fighting for their lives. You can see them stumbling on their crutches through the streets of Zagreb or Split, asking for a *kuna* in their cup. Our government has for-gotten all about them, and still its power rests on their dead legs. I was lucky not to lose any limbs to the Chetniks, but sometimes I ask myself if I would rather have lost both my legs instead of my father and brother. Wartime poses questions that peacetime can-not answer. So we'll always have a new war.

On Darko's weblog I find a photograph of myself in full gear, a smiling lunatic with an AK-47, on top of a captured Serbian tank back in '95. The happy face of a murderer in the making. I really look stupid. I always hated the "Kodak Moment." This all-American happy-go-lucky thing that forces you to smile into the eyes of the future that can only take you for an innocent imbecile who doesn't know anything about anything, who only has killed two or three people, and yet he's smiling like he just won an Olympic medal. Looks more like the Special Olympics to me.

I prefer mug shots.

I search too for Senka, my ex-girlfriend, the missing chapter of my life. Ever since the war ended I've been trying to track her down, without success. I owe her an *oprosti*.

Gunholder's shift at the café starts at ten. "Have a nice day," she says and leaves me with a smile that I keep warm until she comes back. At first I thought I heard her say, "Have an ice day." But even she thinks ten in the morning is too early for sarcasm. My ice machine. The slut of my sleepless dreams. My prison guard, my priest. In the afternoons she works for the local music festival called Airways or Airwaves, doing phone calls and other type of secretary work. She's on speaking terms with tons of popstars, some world famous celebrities you've never heard of.

"You ever had Creed up here?"

"Greed?"

Forget it. This is never going to work out.

She usually returns around seven or eight, always equipped with food, usually some Thai or Chinese takeout that she has to pay for. After dinner she usually puts on some Icelandic weirdo music, doing her best in introducing me to people like *Mugison, Gus Gus* or the black sounding *Lay Low*. I tell her that if she could arrange a gun for me, I could do wonders to the promotion of Icelandic music. Her laugh is slightly offended. But her curiosity is piqued. I watch her smoke while she keeps the questions coming like an intern in the Oval Office. "If some of your victims belonged to other 'organizations' they must have tried to kill you, right?" Right. "Have you ever known any of them, your victims?" You bet. She's fascinated by my job. I finally have a fan.

"And do you remember them all, your victims, I mean?"

"The professional ones, yes."

"But not the war ones?"

"No. The soldiers are all blurred, but I'm really proud of my hitman work. I always try to do a good job. 'Victim first' is my motto. I try to make it as easy for them as possible. Nearly all of them have died instantly. No time for regrets or anger or anything. It's just *biff!* and you're gone. Like turning off a machine. No pain, no nothing. They couldn't have asked for a better service. I always prepare everything perfectly: the timing, the place, the angle, everything. And I've studied the human body like a doctor. Where to aim for the quickest result and stuff like that. If this were a category at the Olympics, I'd be the Mark Spitz of the killing world."

"And what's the most difficult thing about it?"

"To hit, of course. To hit the guy in the head, the heart, or the butt, if you find yourself in that position. But in that case you have to make sure the bullet travels straight up his spine. Butt shots are really angle-sensitive. It's like playing pool."

"So you have to like…practice?"

"Sure. You have to be in good shape. I had to give up cocaine because of it. You need a steady heart for this kind of work."

"Wow. And you keep count of them? The dead ones?" she says with big blue eyes. I got her in perfect Lewinsky mode.

"Yeah. Well. I don't really count them. You sort of remember them. It's a bit like, I mean, you remember all the guys you've slept with, right?"

"Well, I've tried to forget some of them," she says with a sexy grin.

I can't resist.

"How many in all?"

"I don't know. I mean, I don't count them. Forty maybe."

Slut.

"Forty?"

"You think that's a lot? My friend has done a hundred and forty or something."

There we have it. Tarantino has 139 fuck-in-laws in Iceland. He better update his Christmas card list.

"And you've done sixty-seven?" she continues.

"Girls? No, you mean hits? Yes. Sixty-seven. Sixty-seven suckers down. Sixty-seven pigs in the oven."

"And you really remember all of them?"

"I try to keep their memories alive."

"And you think about them?"

"No. Never."

"You don't feel bad about any of them?"

"No."

"How is that possible? You have no conscience?"

"It's frozen, I guess. You feel bad about any of your…?"

"My bedfellows?" she says with an icy grin. "No."

"No? You've had forty people between your legs and you don't feel bad about any of them?"

"I can't allow myself to. I see them all the time."

Give me a fucking spring break.

"You're still seeing them? Forty guys?"

"Not 'seeing' them. I just, you know, meet them in the street and stuff. It's a small town. They come into the café all the time."

"OK. So, that's why they hired you?"

She switches from Lewinsky to Britney.

"Hey. Shut the fuck up, will you! We're talking about dead people here, and yet you make ME look like the guilty one. As if you can compare killing people to making love with them?"

"Love and death. Equally important in life."

"Love and death? It's not about love. It's only about sex!"

"Even more serious."

She jumps up from the sofa, screaming at me: "OH! Fuck you!" before leaving the room. But she's back in no time, looking like she just realized that this is her place and not mine. "I don't know why the hell I'm keeping you here! I really should call the police or Torture or something, but…Argh! Get up! Go upstairs! Get away from me! And shut the fuck up!"

"Sorry. I'm really sorry."

"Fuck you!"

"Yes, I'll…I'll do it later. Please, sit down."

She goes into the kitchen and stays there for a cigarette's worth of time. I use those minutes for spanking my green-eyed monkey.

Jealousy is the old and ever-caring aunt that never forgets to show up at my dates. It has long been the driving force in my life, ever since my Hanover girlfriend, the optician's daughter, dumped me Prussian style. Hildegaard was a Day 8 Girl (as a freshly landed foreigner who spoke little German my chances were limited) who wore turtlenecks half the time, played the violin with an angel's face, and never used a dirty word, but told me, at the moment of her parting, that she had cheated on me with seventeen men. Seventeen fucking Germans. Ponytail, mustache, and all. It was supposed to make me feel better, she said.

"You should only be happy to get rid of a…"

"…slut like you?"

It took me seven years to bury the bastards in the hard soil of my soul. They've hardly bothered me since, but they did turn my mind into a suspicious one forever. As God only knows too well, I've a hard time *enjoying* relationships. I'm always like some fucking secret agent trying to prove that my partner is a counterspy. And when it comes to love I'm like the referee at a soccer match, totally unable to enjoy the game, but always ready with the yellow card.

And here I go again. Aunt Jealousy has ordered Gunholder out in the kitchen. So the old hatch did make it all the way up to Iceland. Still, this should hardly qualify as a date. It's more like a crash course in the business of shooting people. Killing 101. We're at the end of our first lesson. The teacher waits for the student to return from her smoking break. In a while she does. Gunholder reappears in the doorway, with red eyes and angry cheeks. She crawls back onto the sofa and lights another cigarette. I watch her inhale and exhale for a while. She makes a small windy sound each time the smoke leaves her mouth.

"How did your parents react when the police came and Father Friendly was gone?" I finally ask her.

"They were in big shock, of course. I mean, they totally believed in you," she says with a modest laugh.

"Was he angry, your dad?"

"I would say more shocked than angry. And then he started reassuring the police, putting his hand on their shoulders and telling them: 'God will find him. He will not escape the waking eye of the Lord.'"

She laughs some more. I try to laugh with her. Then all of a sudden we hear the downstairs door open and her smile disappears. She kills her cigarette, stands up, grabs my dish and brings it to the kitchen. I run up the primitive staircase and then pull it up behind me. It comes with a hatch that closes behind it, once the staircase is all up in the attic. I crawl across the splintered floor and get inside my noisy North Face hide. I listen to Truster trot inside the apartment, the poor horse. He's home early. I hear them exchange the smallest hellos followed by some toilet sounds. He then says something that my wild guess would have as: "Some food left?" She says *nay*. That's Icelandic for "no." She has taught me some phrases already. *Tugthúslimur* is "good morning" and *glæpamaður* is "good night."

Then we have sibling-silence for three hours. They don't even watch TV together. No music playing, either. What the hell are they doing? Neither of them leaves the house. Are they playing cards? Reading? At midnight there are some toilet sounds again, followed by the sweet sounds of silky underpants gliding down soft white legs. The war gave me a cat's hearing.

At three in the morning I dial Niko's number in NYC. I speak with the voice of a dormer mouse, explaining my situation. He listens for a while, but when he finally talks back, he acts like a wannabe Talian on TV: "You callin' me? Why you callin' me? Who gave you my number?" Then he hangs up. He hangs up on me. My good old Niko. Niko Nevolja. This is really bad news. Some really, really bad news. I should consider myself dead. At least I should never even think of going back to NYC. Or even Croatia. Fuck. Fucking fucked-up fuck.

I fall asleep at five.

I'm woken at seven by some loud knocking and soft voices downstairs. I'm prepared for this one: Sleeping in my (or Mr. Maack's) clothes, I pocket my phone and put on my running shoes in less than a second. Two such later and I have thrown the sleeping bag into a dim corner and put away the mattress beneath a box of books. I hear Gunholder acting crazy downstairs.

"QUARY GONGI?!"

Her voice follows me up through the skylight, the small rusty one in the middle of the steep bulletproof roof. It's freaking cold outside. Gray skies, green trees, and the colorful roofs of Reykjavik. This one is rusty red. I quickly close the window and climb the steep roof. I can spot the white hood of a police car parked on the street below, and I hear the voice of a masculine officer traveling from street to garden. I jump on the other side of the roof, hanging on the ridge by the total sum of eight fingers. Through my belly I can hear the suckers already up in the attic, looking for the hiding man's hide. Moments later I hear one of them open the fucking skylight. I can't see him, but he can possibly see my cold white fingertips. I have to let go of the ridge. I do so. I let go. I slide down the roof in a very slow, slow motion, floating down the cold iron on my big Croatian belly. I stretch out my arms and feet, trying to stop myself with my sticky shoes and clammy palms without making a single sound. Two inches later I stop. I fucking stop. I'm spread out on the steep red roof like a gigantic frog.

CHAPTER 15
ICELANDIC ARMS
05.22.2006

I should write a thank you letter to the Icelandic police force. How they managed not to find a six-foot, 240-pound frog on the roof of the house they searched is a big mystery to me. The FBI should do some deep thinking before signing another deal of collaboration with them. I did the frozen frog for a freezing hour or so before returning down through the attic. The hatch in the floor was open. I kneeled before it like a ballet dancer in front of an imaginary lake, center stage, and was about to put my head down into it when I was suddenly faced with another head, containing two lusty lips. She was equally surprised to see me, and after a short sigh of relief we kissed.

It was an unusually long kiss considering the fact that it was our first one. It was a kiss brought to us by the Feds. And their white-hatted assistants. Once it was over, I invited her up to my loft space, and in a matter of minutes we were making our first love atop the North Face sleeping bag, me thus becoming her #41. She turned out to be all the ice cream I had been longing for. *Warm* ice cream. She was incredible. My boner was steel-hard

and she got very excited as well, screaming like an angry femi-
nist protesting against a rapist being brought from car to justice.
I even had to cover her mouth with my hand, fearing the police
would show up again. She bit me. The arctic animal. I got a bit
intimidated. Still she seemed to enjoy my shaky performance,
her body shaking all over like an old man's hand with Parkinson's
disease—or maybe it was just something she picked up in *Slut
Magazine*. Afterwards we lay like two naked criminals at large,
resting and talking.

"You're so beautiful."

That's me talking, of course.

"And you're so…."

"Fat?"

"You're so strange."

"Strange?"

"Yes, you're so strange. I've never…You come from another
world. I've never…."

"You've never been with a killer before?"

"No. Yeah. Never," she says with a short laugh. "A Mafia
guy…."

I should maybe thank the Talians here. They've really done
the image work for us mobsters. Though the girls of Manhattan
may treat us like second-class citizens, we're still king overseas.

"You didn't like me when I was playing the priest."

"No. That's right."

"Well. I'm a bad actor."

"No, it was because you're such a good actor, I guess."

"You hate your dad?"

"No. I don't hate him," she says with a soft voice. "But it's hard
being brought up in a church. I wasn't even allowed to dye my
hair. 'We have to respect God's original design, blah, blah, blah…'

I mean, I just had enough. I had to break away. And that was pretty tough. Like coming out as a lesbian or something. When Dad found out about me smoking, he had his friend Torture come by the house to exorcise the evil spirits from my body. It was insane, really."

"And he didn't succeed?"

"Well, in a way. I went from Winstons to Winston Lights."

I get pregnant with laughter.

"So you don't have much contact with your parents then?"

"No. The least possible. I only go there two times a year. For Christmas and Eurovision."

"What about Truster?"

"Truster?" she laughs. "You always call him Truster. It's Þröstur. Like 'thrush,' you know, the bird. 'Thrush' and then T, U, R. It's not that hard."

"OK. Sorry. But what about your dad and him?"

"Oh? They're OK. Dad likes him. He's quiet, handy, and helpful. He's done tons of work for him at the TV station. Without getting paid at all. 'The Lord will pay him in heaven, blah, blah…' You get it? My parents are just impossible people, really."

Then she goes to fetch her post-orgasm cigarette. Because of the low ceiling, she's forced to walk like a hunchback towards the open hatch. Her small breasts stay put (I mean, there is no flopping around) as she bows over the opening in the floor, but shake a bit as she descends the staircase. Moments later she's back with her packet—polished pink nails tiptoeing across the rough floor—and lays herself beside me. Her butter-blonde hair is combed back in a small bun at the back of her head. I gently stroke it from forehead to bun. It feels kind of hard and sort of reminds me of the helmety hairdo of my black NY-doorman, though I've never dreamed of touching that wonder of nature.

I let my eyes travel along her white, healthy body, from toes to cigarette, with short stopovers at her trimmed triangle and the pierced navel. She sucks on the slim stick of poison.

"How do you say 'love,' in Icelandic?"

"*Kynlíf.*"

"Queen Leaf?"

"No, *kynlíf.*"

She's fucking playing with me. Those bloody Icelanders can never be honest, apart from the ones that God has ordered to. They always have to be cool. Must be the cold.

"What's it in Croatian?" she asks.

"*Ljubav.*"

"That's like 'love' with a B."

"Yes, it's love to be. Yours is with a Q or a K…"

"I was joking. *Kynlíf* means sex. Love is *ást.*"

"Wow. That's harsh. How do you spell it?"

"A with hat, S, and T."

"AST? That's Ax and Saw Treatment in our language."

"What does that mean?" she asks.

I don't answer. Munita suddenly breaks into my brain and fills it like a balloon. Munita, my love. Sorry. I have slept with another woman behind your butt. But it's not my fault, really. If there's someone to blame it must be the local police. Had they found me, this would never have happened. Gunholder tells me it's common knowledge that the White Hats are hopeless and that Iceland has its own SWAT team called The Viking Squad, but they're not available all the time.

"There is only one squad. They must be busy now."

I feel a bit offended, jealous even. How could they possibly have found a more serious assignment on Gun-Free Island than capturing the *triple six-pack* killer of an FBI agent and a world-famous priest?

"What could that be?"

"I don't know. They do all kinds of things. Maybe some president's in town, or they're monitoring a high school dance up north."

"A high school dance? The kids have guns?"

"No, but Icelandic kids, when they get drunk, they go nuts."

So, guns against nuts. I count myself lucky to have stumbled upon Rev. Friendly at the JFK toilets. I could have killed someone with a ticket to Baghdad. Iceland is a Gangster's Paradise. No army, no guns, no murders, and almost no police. Only gorgeous women with groovy names.

"It's not Gunholder. It's *Gunnhildur*," she says.

"Goonhilda?"

"No. *Gunn*! You start with *Gunn*, and then *hildur*. *Gunnhildur!*"

"Gunhilda?"

"Æ, whatever. I'll just call you *Tott*."

"What does that mean?"

"You don't want to know."

"You never had a nickname?"

"When we lived in the States, the kids always called me *Gunn* and my dad still calls me that sometimes."

"Gun?"

"No. *Gunn!*"

"You're my Gun. The one I've been looking for ever since I came up here."

Her lips vibrate with joyful irritation as she exhales her last draw of smoke.

"A smoking Gun," I add while taking a good look at her.

She's the total opposite of my Munita. The butter-blonde ice queen and my tandoori tarantula. I lean in for a kiss and fall into her Icelandic arms.

CHAPTER 16
LOVE IS IN THE FRIDGE
05.22.2006

I've finished my first week in exile. Even though I've not killed anyone for the past seven days, except one small dog, this has to count as one of the most interesting weeks of my life. For seven days and seven nights the sun has not set. I've had five different nationalities and held down two jobs. I've appeared on live television. I watched the European Song Contest for the first time in six years. I broke into two apartments, stole one car, three beers, some bread and bacon and six eggs. I also find myself in love with two different girls. One Icelandic and one Indian-Peruvian.

To avoid further police visits, I have the blonde buy me a new phone, equipped with a virgin number. I then call the dark one. I call her all morning, all afternoon. I call her cell, I call her at work, I call her at home. I send messages. I leave messages. And massages.

I finally decide to call the doorman of my building in SoHo, the one with the freaky hairdo. Just hearing his deep voice gives me a warm feeling mixed with a dash of homesickness. But it mixes badly in my stomach.

He says Munita came by a few days ago, accompanied by a Talian looking stud. They went upstairs. She told the doorman she had keys to my apartment. This is a lie. I never gave her any keys. But the doorman had to believe her, he saw her enter the building with me all the time. The Talian guy came downstairs a few fucking hours later, but she has not left the building since. The bitch.

I thank him and speedily finish the phone call before dialing my own apartment. There's no answer. Of course not. The horny bitch. Fucking Talians all over my bathroom tiles! I should call Interflora and order a bouquet of poisonous lilies to be delivered to my door in NYC. Why couldn't she just have done it at her place? Why did she have to smear my white leather couch with Talian sweat?

I call the doorman again—suddenly getting the feeling that he's the only person I know in the Big Apple. (I know I killed most of my New York contacts, but still, this fact is pretty sad. Six years have been erased from my life.) I ask him to call my apartment and if there is no answer, call the police or something. Someone has to enter the goddamn door and bring the fucking woman to the fist-fucking phone.

"You have the key to my apartment, right?"

"Yes, of course I have your key," the doorman says.

He tells me to call him back in an hour.

In an hour...Well, fuck my fuck. In a fucking hour the fucking Truster is back home and I can't possibly talk on the phone now. I have to remain completely still and silent up here in the cold, cold attic. In the cold, cold Atlantic. Poor me. I shouldn't have taken #66 to the dumpsite. I should have finished him in his car. Then his friends never would have gotten near me with their zoom lenses. It was just that his car was so fucking great. It looked so expensive. (I sometimes inflated my fee by giving the victim's car to Radovan's guy out in Jackson Heights, a much used used-cars salesman named Ivo.)

Fucking Radovan. The fountain of all my troubles.

I listen to Truster and Gunholder watch the evening news. Lilliput Island seems to have enough of political scandals and fucked-up celebrities to fill a daily news-hour. Or they're just saying that nothing happened today. No murders, no war, no nothing. Aw, fuck it. I call anyway. I can't possibly wait until morning. Gently I turn my body around, dive into the sleeping bag head first, butt upwards, and whisper to my good old doorman:

"It's Tod again. Did you call her?"

"Yes."

"And what?"

"There was no answer. So, I went upstairs."

"And…? Was she there?"

"The apartment was empty."

"Empty?"

"Yeah. But there was this strange smell. A very strong smell."

"What kind of a smell? Body-smell? Sweat?"

"A kind of like, body-smell, yes."

"Well, fuck her," I try not to shout into my brand new Icelandic phone, shaking with wrath inside the loud sleeping bag.

"So I checked all the rooms, sir," he continues.

"Ah ha?"

"I checked all the rooms, sir…The bathroom, the kitchen…"

"Uh-huh?"

"All the windows were closed. I checked all the windows. They were all closed."

"OK."

"Finally…I don't know why really…I opened the fridge."

"The fridge?"

"Yes. I opened the fridge, and…"

"Some food gone bad? I left some food?"

"I'm sorry sir, but I don't really know how to tell you this."

His deep baritone voice turns even more serious than normal.

"What?" I ask, trembling with excitement.

"Her head was there, sir."

"Her head? In the fridge?"

"Yes, sir. Her head stood there, on a plate. The…the face was all swollen, yellow, and blue. But…"

"But?"

"But it was her. I recognized her. It was your friend."

"On a plate?"

"Yes, sir. In the fridge. It was rather…"

"Only her head?"

As I say this, it dawns upon me that *Munita is dead.*

"Yes, sir. Only her head. I couldn't find her body."

"But you could smell it?"

"Yes, I guess so. It might be there somewhere."

"What kind of a body-smell was it?"

"What kind?"

"Yes. Was it pussy? Pussy-smell?"

What the hell am I saying? My sick old Croatian mind. I deserve to die. Oh, Munita. Why did you have to cheat on me with a mobster? I cheated on you with a nice little ice-mouse. I guess I should cry now. Your head in the fridge! Those lovely lips turned cold. Those eyes with a frozen glaze. Your hair like cold noodles. What about your body? They ate that already? And now your soul, your beheaded soul, is hugging its limbless parents in heaven. Oh, Bonita…

"Yes. I guess you can say that, sir. Pussy…but very strong," my doorman says into my right ear.

CHAPTER 17
THE HOWLING HITMAN
05.23.2006

I come downstairs. I don't care anymore. I open the hatch and bring down the staircase. They wake up of course. Truster comes at me with a flying fist, as if I was a simple burglar. I stop his blow in mid-air, holding his arm in my hand. He's pretty strong, but of course he was never a soldier. The girl cools her brother down and asks me what the hell I'm doing?

"I don't care anymore."

She looks at me with a frozen face and Truster looks at her, even more bewildered.

"You know him?" he asks her in Icelandic, which must mean I don't look like a priest anymore.

She doesn't answer. He's naked except for some crazy underpants. Homer Simpson looks at me out from his crotch, a tongue in cheek. She wears a dark blue T-shirt that says "Sorry" in white. I'm fully dressed. I got my running shoes on. Igor's running shoes. Gun follows me out of the apartment and down the staircase asking all kinds of questions that I do not answer. And I avoid looking at her face. It would spur the wrong thoughts.

I don't care anymore. I go outside. Bye.

It's very early. The streets are even more silent than during the day. They're beyond silence. Reminds me of All Dead Village. It's bright as hell, but cloudy. One big massive and foggy cloud hangs low over the city like a lid on a saucepan. It seems to be sinking lower and lower. It has the light-gray color of ice. As ever, the temperature is that of a refrigerator.

A fucking fridge.

I'm looking for a plate to put my head on.

I walk down the street. I haven't got the faintest idea where I'm going or what I'm doing. I just have to go somewhere. When your head turns dead, your feet take over. I'm a walking headless chicken spurting blood from my sore, sore throat.

Between the houses I can make out The Pond. A silly looking swan sails slowly between a roof and a light pole. They put her head on a plate. Why the fuck did they do that? To scare me? The more I think of it, the more it smells like Talian cooking. In their language your girlfriend's head in the fridge translates into heavy shit. Why can't they just come find me and kill me right away? Cut the fucking poetry!

I can't believe she's dead. My girl, Munita. And such a shameless, tasteless violent death. All according to family tradition. They took the head off her body...That holy body...Last night she was the hottest girl on the planet, today she's in the fridge.

As am I.

I guess this is my punishment, being locked inside this icy land. I guess I deserve it. I cheated on her. But at least my head is still connected to my body. She must have cheated ten times harder, ten times more often. Gave up her head for the head she gave. I knew it. I fucking knew it. The Hindu-Hispanic wonder was not to be trusted. I know they say that no human is to be trusted completely, except for Jesus Christ and Laura Bush, but you can always hope that your partner has at least applied for a trial membership of their holy club.

I remember once when we were coming from a dinner at a classy restaurant on the Upper East Side and the soft breeze was as warm as the air from an exhaust pipe. She walked slowly out on to the pavement, rearranging the strap of her purse on her shoulder, and I could feel her great thighs rubbing against each other beneath her noisy red satin dress. (Munita was one of those rare women who wear dresses half the time.) It had this triangular opening at the back (one of those things I don't know the English word for), going almost all the way down to her butt. And as the yellow cabs rushed by her great voluptuous body wrapped in red, my sick mind was hiding in the darkness inside her dress, right there up in the triangular opening, on the border of butt and thighs, contemplating whether she'd had another man that week, that day, that year…

Inside the restaurant we'd been talking about relationships in general and making fun of the square SWAP or WASP (or whatever you call it) couple three tables away. "She must have a zipper cunt," Munita whispered over her spoon full of Thai soup. I'd never heard that one before. A zipper cunt? The two words instantly unzipped my hard love for her. This woman was the girl of all my difficult dreams. I paid the bill with a hard-on and decided to tell her that I loved her once we were outside.

It would have been the first time I'd have told her.

But as we came out on the street, and my mind was hiding in her private shadows, I suddenly saw this hand between her thighs, a grown man's hand with hair on its back, fingering its way up her leg. One of the fingers wore a thick golden wedding ring. It was just a vision, quick as a flash of light.

She turned her royal sweetness around, flipping my eyes from rear to front, and smiled her sweet smile, with closed juicy lips: that sexy grin of hers.

"Thanks for dinner, honey. It was great."

A kiss. And the sound of a fire engine some ten blocks down.

"Is he married?"

"Who?"

"The guy."

"What guy? In the restaurant? Yeah. They must be married."

"No, the guy you're…"

Her sweet exotic face, like a sunflower set against the busy twilight traffic. And her sudden expression of pain, as if someone just pinched her in the back.

"The guy I'm what?"

"They guy you're seeing."

"The guy I'm seeing? I'm seeing a guy?"

"Yeah. Is he married?"

"No. No, why do you say that?"

Her voice full of innocence. But then the wrong words:

"Tod, you know I'd never do a married man…"

Eyes blinking from blunder. Lips full of regret. And then a hurried monologue full of don't get me wrongs.

I replayed that fucking sentence seven times a day for the next few months. I fucking studied that sentence like an archeologist studies the brim of a broken glass found deep inside the hills of Mount Ararat. What the hell did it mean? "I'd never do a married man." I checked the dictionaries, searched the Internet, listened in on countless conversations in the subway, watched a lot of daytime TV, and yet I couldn't quite figure it out. My English wasn't up to the task. Not then. I wasn't familiar with all the nuances of this mother of languages. And yet I had come here a year earlier than she. But of course she was "doing" all those men, learning English through pillow talk and taking lessons well into the weenie hours of the morning, while all my dates went straight to the bathroom after the main course and flushed themselves down the toilet, kamikaze style.

In the end, when this-all-too-casual sentence had flown across my Manhattan sky, for three whole weeks, I swallowed my pride and enrolled in an English class at some immigrant friendly evening school down in Tribeca. A seedy neon-lit room with scruffy plastic chairs was filled with dead-happy Day 15 Girls from the Philippines and a few Al-Qaeda members of the male sex, plus the Finnish-born teacher Kaari, a bony ugly-beauty with long blonde hair, that I could never decide was a Day 5 or a Day 25 type. At the end of the semester, I'd finally worked up my courage and raised my hand to ask the teacher if say…a certain man had been dating a certain woman for a certain period of time and at a certain moment she would reassure him that she'd never do married men…

"It means that you should stop dating her," went the verdict.

And the class erupted. They fucking erupted with laughter, all the ever-smiling Filipinas and the bin Laden brothers as well. I strongly considered bringing my Uzi to the next lesson, but I guess I was just too thankful to this Kaari woman, who had raised my English level by twenty floors in three months. Seeing all her students die would probably have made her depressed.

I owe my English to Aunt Jealousy. She helped me rise above my situation. Dikan and Co. are still stuck on ground level with their command of the English language. *"Take me to car."* It did put me in a bit of an awkward situation (you don't want to look this much more clever than your boss) and I tried to downplay my skills half the time. But Dikan saw through me and started using me as his interpreter in some of his bigger deals. I always got this bad feeling in my stomach when the Fingerlicker sat beside me in the Zagreb Samovar, sucking on his dead cigar and staring at me, while I explained our case to the Polish boys from Chicago. Dikan always seemed a bit suspicious of my rapid progress and acted like I learned English by secretly dating one of the Bush twins, spending my hit-free weekends in the West Wing, dining with the Head and Mrs. Head of the FBI.

Little did he know it was only the result of my relentless research into Munita's love life, a procedure that included some spy work as well, that brought no results, I'm ashamed to say.

But by saying she would never do married men, Munita indicated that she was in fact "doing" *unmarried* men, and her use of the terrible do-word told me that she was doing them by the numbers. Munita was a dick grinder, "heading" for the top of the Trump Tower, equipped with look-at-me! jugs and a clipper cunt.

I never mentioned any of this to her. And yes, I did keep on seeing her. I let her do me. I did her. But love was kept at bay, like a huge white cruise ship that's too big to enter the harbor. Until now, I guess. And I don't quite get it. She's dead and suddenly I'm getting all sentimental about her. I should be happy to see her get the punishment she deserved. She simply went too far, all the way into my great apartment. Onto my fucking bathroom tiles.

But probably she was forced to by the Talian Mobthrob. Her "punishment" was only meant to punish me. It was a TJ thing—Taliation Job. Done in the name of my sixty-six hits. Which one or ones? Doesn't matter. It was bound to happen sooner or later. The master hitman of Manhattan, the triple six-packer, the cruel Croat, the one and only Toxic, had to be taken down. Or was it maybe one of our own? Niko? The why-you-callin'-me Niko? The doorman said Munita went upstairs with "some Italian looking guy." He could just as well have been a Croat.

I get it.

They killed her. My friends and employers killed my girl. And now I have to mourn her. I didn't know how much she meant to me, until now. She was not the worst, really. She brought me flowers almost every time she came over. She gave me the massage of my life. And every other week she would cook me her favorite dishes from her childhood in Lima—a shark or a sea bass *ceviche* or the simple and honest *anticuchos*, the Peruvian brochette, that always reminded me of our *ćevapi*.

I fucking miss her.

I can see now that her infamous sentence wasn't so brutal after all. "You know I'd never do a married man," only means that she would not do him *if* the opportunity arrived. She was using the future if-sense or whatever it's called. But then again... if the opportunity arrived she *would* probably do an unmarried man....

Aw. Fuck it. She's dead now.

I walk down the street, and suddenly I can see her inside that car, that Japanese car parked over there at the other side, in the neon bright Icelandic night. She waves and smiles, just like she always did when she came to pick me up in her small Honda. What about the car? Her apartment? Her job? She has no relatives. I should probably call her friend Wendy and tell her...

Suddenly the big damp cloud over Reykjavik reaches my eyes. They fill up like a woolen sweater with blood from a shot wound, and suddenly I'm crying as if it was a heart attack or something. I can't fucking control it. It just comes. I haven't cried since we lost that game in the semifinals against France, in Paris '98. Fucking Thuram scored twice. I have to rest against a small SUV that sits silently in its parking space and bears with my breakdown like a white army horse.

An elderly lady comes walking around the corner with her old dog on a long leash. It's that early morning stroll. I look up and our eyes meet. I must look like a bum weeping for his bottle. Still, she looks at me as if she was used to seeing New York mobsters sobbing on her street at five in the morning. She's a Day 365 Girl, wearing a tight turtleneck and some slim-fitting pants. Gray hair, white Nikes. She makes me think of the Manhattan ladies you see on the Upper East Side, going from breakfast to lunch, with the *final* hair-do on their heads while wearing brand new *kid's shoes* on their feet. As if they wanted their bodies to represent their life's story, from childhood to coffin.

I don't know what I'm doing, but my hand does: Suddenly it goes up. My right hand raises itself, clearly trying to stop the woman. She won't stop, but her dog does. It scuttles out between two cars and out on the street, over to my side of the white SUV. The slim, almost athletic lady remains on the pavement pulling back the long leash that must be tangled up in the bumper by now. Her gray hair shakes as she orders the dog back, but the little one is a sucker for sadness: it sniffs my tears, the dark wet spots in the asphalt, like some crazy addict in rehab spotting cocaine on his daily walk in the woods. I look up and before I know it I've asked its owner a question that surprises me even more than my gesture.

"Excuse me. Do you know if there is a church around here?"

CHAPTER 18
MORNING OF THE DEAD
05.23.2006

Church is closed. It stands right on The Pond, dressed in armor and painted green. Swans and ducks sail about the still water. Some seem to be sleeping, with their heads hidden beneath a wing.

Quack, quack.

I take a seat on the church steps. A few seagulls fly overhead, hurling abuse at me like drunken angels. Gun calls my new cell two times. I don't answer. When mourning your spouse, the mistress can't help. A sleepy-eyed city worker comes driving along the pavement in a small orange machine with a disco light spinning on top. The loud monster is equipped with rotating brooms and an elephant's trunk he uses for sucking up litter: it all looks like a loud animal feeding on trash. The driver passes without looking at me. Oh, man. If you could only clean up the path of my life.

It's a fucking graveyard. Since finishing school I haven't been doing much else except adding crosses to it. There is a stone in my conscience, like the one people get in their kidneys, a stone the size of a kidney. I get up and start walking. I walk into the city center, following the trash-monster.

I met Munita in Arturo's Restaurant, the coal oven cabin on Houston and Thompson. She waited on me. I waited for her. I came back seven times before she allowed me to put a smile on her face. So much for Mrs. Dick Grinder. I had to order seven different pizzas before I could figure out the code of her heart. It was black olives, red onion, and arugula. Arugula. For months I ate nothing but arugula burgers and arugula pasta. Three months later we had our first kiss. It was a slow process, like passing a heavy bill across Capitol Hill. Not really my hunting style.

I still don't get why she played so hard-to-get with me, while the unmarried guys at Trump Tower only had to push the elevator button. Every three or four weeks she moved up a floor. No. She didn't do *The Apprentice*. But she did everybody else.

I'm standing on the main square in Iceland at 5:02 AM, like a death row criminal waiting for his executioner to arrive, plus the angry mob. But nobody's here. Nothing but the low simmer of the orange animal disappearing down the street. And a lone raven that barks from the top of the small clock standing in the middle of the square. The whale mountain across the bay is buried in gray fog down to its fair blue ankles. I head in its direction.

A small gray car is sitting at the next corner, waiting for the green light. It's driven by a chubby blonde, a Day 16 type. Must be on her way to work. How often have I found myself in her position, waiting at a red light at four in the morning, deep in the heart of Nowhere City, the only car in sight, and Willie Nelson singing on every waveband to all the girls he's loved before. I guess more than half of my sixty-six were laid out before noon. Morning is for murder. Nobody expects a bullet for breakfast.

I walk along the shore. A protective wall made of huge stones runs along the shoreline, protecting you from the beast that rests beneath the ocean's mirror-like surface. My crazy colleague. The paved walking path runs between the wall and an empty boulevard. Munita's half blue head appears in front of me, floating in the air like a huge and hairy spider. I walk along the shore, talking to her and myself. I'm stuck on Fridge Island, with no one to talk to but all my sins and losses.

Hit #42 was an unlucky business man from Winnipeg, Canada, who owed Dikan some money. I had to go up forty-five floors for this job and ghost myself into his small hotel room. As I entered, he was doing some crazy yoga shit on top of the double bed—legs in the air, ass in my face. He didn't see death coming until I sent the bullet down his rectum. It was too fucking funny not to give it a try. But he didn't die right away. I spent about forty seconds agonizing over my next move. I absolutely didn't want to waste another bullet. I was only two bullets away from my triple six-pack. So I just stood there stroking my gun. Luckily he seemed to understand my situation. He was cooperative. I would totally mention him in my thank-you speech at the Mafia Oscars.

With enormous effort he managed to turn back around and crawl across the bloody bed towards the table. The bullet seemed to have traveled up his colon, through stomach and lungs, making its exit on the border of chest and neck. Blood kept gushing out from under the chin. I rushed over, thinking he must keep a gun in the drawer. But he only reached for his wallet and spent his last breaths looking at photographs of his wife and three kids. Four Canadian faces frozen in fun. Then he drowned in his own blood dripping from his nose. Once the big one got him, I sat on the bed beside him. I sat there for half an hour and finally decided to throw myself out the window, down onto Sixth Avenue. But I couldn't open the fucking window. Modern hotels.

Then I figured out I could use my own piece, of course. But ambition ruled over depression.

Soon after, on my next date with Munita, I mentioned the idea of us having kids, becoming a family. Mary Lou and Bobby Boksic. I wanted some happy faces in my wallet. But she said she wanted to wait until she had reached the twentieth floor at work. She had five to go. Five unmarried suckers.

The walking path takes me away from the shoreline, following the boulevard into some Belarus neighborhood. Low-rises to my left, higher ones to the right. Reminds me of my week in Minsk. Me and Niko waiting in a hotel room for five days for that briefcase to arrive. Watching every single game of The World Women's Handball Championship. The Norway girls were hot.

There are some cars now. The morning traffic is picking up, most of it coming toward my face, heading downtown. I have no travel plan. I just follow Munita's frozen head, appearing in front of me every seven minutes, while hoping for a police car to appear. I've reached the moment that arrives, sooner or later, in every killer's career: When he gets noose-sick. When he starts shouting to his fellow citizens, Please, come get me!

The walk takes me past a cinema (showing some Talian Mob shit) and the local IKEA painted in yellow and blue. The morning is well underway now. Cars come flying like rhymes from a rapper's mouth. But I'm the only pedestrian around. No other passersby. No wonder the pavement then suddenly comes to an end. I carry on along the road, walking the dirty grass next to the asphalt. There is a concrete mess ahead, all hoops and loops, buzzing with traffic. The car people look at me as if I was Hannibal Lecter on his way to breakfast.

I'm dead sick of dead people. It's as if my head was a freezer full of goods and now that the plug's been pulled, it all comes thawing like brooks in spring. A bit like our first day in ADV. In the morning everything was so calm and peaceful, everything was covered in beautiful white snow, after the crazy night of relentless shooting. But by noon the snow had melted and all the bodies came to light.

Hit #51 was the Jersey thing. The family house. The fat little cheeseburger with the mustache who'd been hiding in his home out in the Jersey woods for more than a month. I sat in my car for two hours, until his wife and kids had left. Once he was on the floor, coloring the carpet with urine and blood, his wife came back. She'd forgotten something. "It's me!" her voice rang out. She went straight for the kitchen, and I quickly ducked behind a sofa. While she ransacked cupboards and drawers, I managed to crawl over to the window, hiding behind the thick floor-length curtains. I didn't want to kill her as well. Kids waiting out in the car and stuff. In fact, I've never killed a woman. (Well, except for the two old hags in ADV, but they had long ceased being women.)

Then I heard the woman enter the living room: "Hi, honey, I just..." And then some big time screaming.

I had to stand there for a fucking hour before I managed to escape. She screamed for half an hour and then just sat there for another, paralyzed, before she finally called the cops. I should have gunned her down as well. She might have been better off. Instead I ended up going to the fucking funeral, mostly to check out the widow. She was hot. Which was good. Beautiful women are quicker to recover from those things. This one looked like she could be on *America's Freshest Widow,* and seeing that at least six handsome bachelors had shown up at the funeral made me feel better. Maybe I had just found the perfect ending for her cheating game.

My head's full of heads. Screaming heads and silent ones. Munita's hairy one appears again, always some ten feet ahead of me, making me walk a bit faster. I have to admit that there were times when I did actually ask for her head on a silver plate. And here it is. She breaks into a quirky smile, and suddenly I want to kiss her cold purple lips. But she keeps her distance, crossing the slip road ahead. I follow her. A big band of car horns plays me an angry tune.

Hit #56 was the Robert Redford look-alike, a muscular guy with a yellow tie, strong jaw, and gray hair. He took several minutes to die, in the back of our restaurant. I really felt like I had achieved something, taking down such an all-American face.

Hit #59 was the Polish porn producer out in Queens. An April day of low sun and long shadows. I had to wear a mask, as his girlfriend was there.

I walk up a small steep hill of grass at the side of the road. It takes me up on the overpass, the small concrete bridge that crosses the boulevard I've been walking the past hour. The cars drive faster up here.

Hit #63 was the small, shy Chinese guy on Canal Street. He seemed so lonely that he was more than happy to open the door to death.

Hit #68 is when I jump off the fucking bridge, saying a quick good-bye to Split.

CHAPTER 19
THE AFTERLIFE
05.23.2006

I'm almost crawling as I finally reach the fucking house. Yes, it's their house. I recognize the silver Land Cruiser. That must mean they're home. I'm the only one who walks in this country. The bleeding seems to have stopped. But the tooth's still missing. I must look like I've been hanging on a cross for a day or two. I'm out of breath when I ring the bell.

When I ring the fucking church bells.

Sickreader comes to the door and immediately slams it back on my broken nose. More church bells. Goodmoondoor's face shows itself in the vertical window beside the door. The good old llama head with the long front teeth. As someone who has hitch-hiked to the core of his own soul, he's able to cut through the blood, sweat, and tears. He recognizes me and opens the door. We face each other: the toothbrushed and the toothcrushed.

"What is…What is to see you?" he asks. Must be some local phrase. "What happen to you? You are all in blood."

"Hih…."

Talking hurts like hell. The tiny word burns my throat and cracks my skull. So I let my eyes do the talking. (They must look like two tiny wells in a mud pit.) I'm so fucking happy to see them! I even lose my balance and fall on my knees at their golden threshold. I reach out for his pants, but he moves back a little, his wife standing behind him. My sore, swollen hand touches his sock-covered toes, and I start wailing like a walrus with a broken fang.

"Goodmooh..." I can't say more. The pain is too great. I have to put him through to my soul and let it finish for me. Its voice is deep and inaudible, like Barry White speaking under water. I hardly understand it myself, but it sounds something like: "...pleashe helph me."

This is getting interesting. My soul is counting on good old Llama Face.

I'm almost lying on the hallway floor now, spreading my dirty sins on their white tiles. Take a good look at them, dear pastor. Take a good look at the filthy mess. Take it all and burn it in hell, or bring it to the cleaners in your beloved heaven.

There is some tiptoeing around the matter—I think I hear them whispering above my head—but finally I can sense that Mr. Good reaches out over my head and closes the door. He then helps me to my feet and leads me into the nearby bathroom. I can barely walk.

Sickreader washes my aching head and swollen face. I try not to look in the mirror, but it whispers to me that I look like the Elephant Man. I can hardly see with my left eye. My nose has doubled its size. Must be broken. As is the tooth next to the front teeth, on my left. Upper lip looks African. Still, most of the bleeding has come from the forehead. There is a cut above my left eye, going all the way up to the hairline. As Sickreader rinses the wound, it shines again. My right arm is deaf from the ache in my shoulder, and I wouldn't be surprised to see some broken ribs if they had an X-ray camera in the house. Every breath brings pain. My right ankle feels twisted, like a semi-wet towel that somebody's trying to wring with no success.

"Did you land in an accident?" the preacher asks.

"Uh-huh."

It's like talking to the dentist with your mouth full of fingers.

"Where?"

"Ah cah…." I mumble through broken teeth and swollen lips.

"In car accident? That is terrible. We have to go to the doctor…to the hospital."

"But we have to clean him first and stop the bleeding. We cannot go with him like this in the car," Sickreader says like a trained nurse, while carefully washing my forehead with a small towel.

"Noh," I protest. "No ospitah."

"No hospital? Why? It is clean. We have a very good health system. It's the best in the world. Or, is it maybe against the laws of your church?" Goodmoondoor asks while raising his brows.

"You know he's *not* Father Friendly anymore. This man *killed* Father Friendly. He's a MURDERER," his wife says with the face of Margaret Thatcher and the hands of Florence Nightingale.

Her less-intelligent husband pauses for a moment.

"Oh, yes. You are a criminal. We have to take you to the police also," he then says.

I turn away from Sickreader and her towel to face the judge of my days.

"Pleahse. Shave me."

He looks at me and then looks at his wife and then at me again. His face is one big indecision. Maybe he really thinks I'm asking for a shave. And I might actually need one. I try helping him out by suddenly leaning my ugly head against his breast (I can hear his pink shirt and blue tie scream out loud as my bloody forehead contacts them), folding my arms around him. He steps back a little, but I won't let go, pressing my arms even harder around him. The most untoxic thing to do.

"Pleahse," I wail into his womb, forgetting my pain for a minute. "They will khill me. Pleahse, I bheg you."

I can feel that wife and husband exchange meaningful looks, two soldiers of kindness faced with the defeated evil. For a while they speak in Icelandic. I do the LPP, clinging to the preacher's body like a newborn monkey to his mother. I watch two tears mixed with blood fall from face to floor. Each one forms a tiny pond on the white tiles, a crystal-clear pond full of blood-red streaks that are constantly moving about in it like some micro-whips.

Without informing me about any further decisions, they wrap me with bandages, turning me into a mummy, and then take me upstairs to my old bed. Sickreader places a cold cloth on my nose. She tells me to relax, and they then leave the room.

Mom and Dad.

I try to get some rest. I try to get my soul some rest. The physical pain is there, but coming from so many sources it has now meddled into one big general pain, a loud buzz in my system, that I can actually ignore from time to time, like the one who's living next to a construction site finally stops hearing all the drilling.

I jumped too late. I was too fucking late. I miscalculated the time needed for my big fat body to fall down fifteen feet. I had aimed for a big, white delivery van that was supposed to give me the fatal blow with its solid black bumper. Instead, the van was already half way under the bridge when I finally made contact. I landed on its roof, immediately bouncing off its back into the concrete wall underneath the bridge hitting it with the left half of my face, before falling onto the hard shoulder with my aching one. I lay there KO'd for some minutes, but no one seemed to have noticed me bounce, like a bag of dirty laundry from an unknown army hospital. And nobody seemed to have noticed the dead boar lying in the roadside under the bridge. Still, there was some slowing of cars as a I came to my senses and crawled to my feet. But everybody must have figured out that I was the monster who lives under the bridge.

I continued my walk. Half-conscious I continued away from the crossing, heading in the same direction as I was going before my unsuccessful date with death. I walked the broad green island of traffic between the double-laned roads. I walked with a twisted ankle and a bloody face. People stared at me from behind their wheels of good fortune but no one stopped. Fucking makeup ladies and plastic surgeons all of them. Then it started raining, and from then on I was invisible to them.

So I continued walking. Like the wounded polar bear who automatically heads for the North Pole to die, I kept walking the island of traffic. It seemed endless, but I just kept on walking, without having the faintest idea where I was going. The overhead signs told me I was heading for the airport. *Keflavik* they said, with a picture of a plane seen from above. Of course I could always try to escape this country as Igor and start my third new life as an undertaker in Smolensk, Russia.

I passed under seven bridges, past a Pizza Hut and some funky spaceship of a mall that I remembered having seen before. The traffic island disappeared and made me take my aching shoulder to the hard one. Then suddenly, to my right, in between some new office buildings, I spotted the big blue cross painted on the big white gable of Torture's church, the one I had visited with Goodmoondoor the week before. It gave me an idea. It gave me hope. I knew that Silence Grove was not far ahead. I knew that Gun's parents were my only hope. The good people. And here I am, lying in my good old bed like a lost son.

Goodmoondoor opens the door. His expression is fatherly and stern. Red face, white hair. He probably owes the facial color to his demon days. He grabs a chair and sits by the bed. His shirt is light blue now. Tie is pink.

"Look. We have been talking about it…about you. And there is two possibilities. Number one is that we tell the police about you. Number two is that we take care of you. But this is very difficult."

He takes a pause, sighs, and strokes his long face with his right hand.

"It is dangerous for us."

"Uh-huh…" I mumble from under the wet cloth.

"I also called my friend Þórður."

"Uh-huh?"

"And he says he can maybe help you also."

A beat.

"Do you want our help? Do you want us to help you?"

"Uh-huh," I nod with pain.

"But we can only do this if you do one thing."

"Uh-huh, uh-huh?"

"You have to confess your faith in Jesus Christ and join our church of the living God."

Tod nods.

CHAPTER 20
TORTURE THERAPY
05.24.2006 – 05.30.2006

If sleep is a broadcast from heaven, there is too much static on my radio. I can't sleep. Too many things in my thawing, aching head. The unsuccessful suicide mourns the death he did not get. I have delivery trucks coming at me by the minute. One moment I'm making love to Munita in the middle of the road, the next her lips are frozen and a bumper hits me in the back of my head. One moment I'm going through hit #23 and the next I'm decorating my funeral home in Smolensk. I better rent a nice street-front space and cover the windows with big letters, American style: "YOUR FAVORITE UNDERTAKER — *Death's Best Friend.*" And maybe add some recommendations from satisfied customers. *"Excellent coffin and solid manicure. Thanks to Igor, I will rest in peace. —Vladimir Fedorov (1932–2006)."*

I do the mummy, lying on my back, totally still, like Fedorov in his grave. Every small movement brings pain. When Goodmoondoor drops by, I ask him for some aspirin.

"A spring?"

"No, aspirin. Medicine. Painkillers."

"Oh, I understand. No, I'm sorry. We don't have it. The Lord is our painkiller."

And then once again that stupid smile of his. I'm in Amishland.

They didn't dare touch my jeans, so I wear them to bed. My cell phone is still in the right pocket and from time to time I can hear Gun calling. The phone's vibrations have a strong appeal to its neighbor, at the other side of the pocket wall, but I'm too weak to be able to bring it out and even if I could, I wouldn't want to answer. I don't want her to see me now.

It's probably afternoon when Torture arrives. He enters the white room like a doctor, with a small briefcase. The combed back hair and the thick Lennon glasses are in place. He looks me straight in the eye and speaks to me in the most commanding voice of God himself.

"You are the sinner of sinners. You must know that. You have killed the messenger of God's holy scripture, the holy bringer of the living Word. You have committed the worst of crimes. Are we in agreement on this? Do you admit to your crime and sin?"

The mummy nods.

"Could you please put your holy confession on your satanic tongue?"

"Yes. Yes, I confess. I am sinner," the Elephant Man weakly issues through his thick rubber lips.

"And a killer."

"Yes. Killer."

"You are the true murderer of Father Friendly, our beloved brother and savior of millions, so help me God?"

"Yes. I killed Father Friendly. It was…not good."

"It was NOT GOOD? No, you were not even worthy of being in the same room as he. My dear friends here, Guðmundur and

Sigríður, are risking a lot for saving your lost soul. And me as well. We are all taking a great risk. You should know that. They risk their jobs and they risk their reputation, their TV station, their house, their car, their everything."

The good couple is standing behind him, with big eyes and proud lips.

"But saving one soul into the Kingdom of heaven…Saving one soul, even though it's the most sinful one, as yours truly is… Saving one soul is worth every jeep, every house, every job. Like true believers in the faith of the living God, they do believe in love and forgiveness of the highest kind. Following the good example of Jesus Christ, they're willing to offer their love and forgiveness, even in the face of their most vicious enemy. So you should know that you owe your life to them for the rest of your days and for the rest of all time. For heaven knows that kindness offered in the face of evil, at the risk of one's life, is a gift that lasts forever, for all time. A gift that cannot be returned, so help me God. Let us pray."

They pray for me and my lost soul. To claim it back I have to lie here for seven days and seven nights, and during this time I must fast. I'm allowed one glass of holy water per day. Only by removing the needs of the body will the soul come forth, Torture assures me as he stitches up the cut on my forehead with a knitting needle and heavy string. It reminds me of when my father stitched my small leg wound in the back of an old school bus our first night of the war. The same silent and forceful concentration on the broad, bearded face. Goodmoondoor helps Sickreader keep the bleeding away from their church-white linen.

"For he opened up his wounds and let the blood of Christ, his Savior the Lord, flow from the heavens and into his flesh…" Torture murmurs as he ties the knot on my forehead.

Fasting would be OK if I didn't smell their cooking down-stairs. It's the story of the perfume and the boner all over again. I take small sips from my glass of water, trying to make it last throughout the day. Torture is a tyrant. There is absolutely noth-ing left in my stomach except the broken tooth, gnawing away at my guilt.

Thanks to that, my Torture Therapy is going pretty good. I've had time to peek through every hole that I've made in people's lives. In my mind I have followed all my bullets down people's throats, into people's heads, and up people's rectums. And fueled with regret, I've played them all in reverse, making them return to source. By making a hundred holes in my head, I've made it a showerhead: all my deadly sins come hissing out, mixed with blood and urine, puke and poop.

The week of cleansing.

On day seven Gun shows up at her parents' house. You can't fail to notice. Some hefty arguing between her and her parents is followed by a sour howling that somehow seems to be a part of a phone call. There must be a crisis in Sibling Town. She would never come here without a reason. Or maybe I'm the reason. After a long mother-daughter conversation downstairs, I hear them come up the stairs.

Super slowly, Sickreader opens the door to my room and lets the red-eyed beauty inside. Out of habit I suck in my stomach, though there's not much need to, I guess. It hasn't been filled for a week now, plus the eiderdown bed sheet is pretty thick. Gunholder snails over to my bed, looking a bit surprised by my mummy disguise. Her face fills my eyes, my dead hungry eyes that haven't seen anything delicious for a week now. I really want to eat her. Her mom remains by the door with a stern face telling me that she's not being nice to me: this is no visiting hour. It looks like she's using me for fixing the broken bond between Gun and her. Letting the girl in on their big secret will possibly help restoring her lost respect for her parents. The fact that you're secretly nursing a broken-nosed cop-killer wanted in various countries around the world can only make you more exciting. And that's fine with me. I can be their Savior. Wow. Therapy seems to be working a bit too well.

The house phone rings downstairs, and Sickreader disappears for a while. We're left alone. Me and my teary Gun.

"Hi," she whispers in a weak voice. It's the tone that people use when they enter their deserted house after the hurricane.

"Hi."

"I've been calling you."

"I know."

My talking ability has been somewhat restored.

"How are you?" she asks.

"Hungry."

She smiles.

"Why did you leave our house? What happened?"

"I…I got some bad news."

"What news?"

"They killed my girlfriend."

"Your girlfriend? Who?"

"The Mafia. Either us or the Talians."

"No, I mean…You have a girlfriend?"

"Had. They killed her."

"OK. Yeah. Good for you."

"Good for me?"

"Yes, that you had a girlfriend. I didn't know that."

"Neither did I."

"What do you mean?"

"We were just, you know…dating."

"For how long?"

"A year and a half."

"That would qualify as a marriage in this country. For how long can you be 'dating' in America?"

"Forever, I guess, but it does become a bit more serious in the thirty-fifth year, when you get inheritance rights…"

She laughs a bit.

"What was her name?"

"My girlfriend's? Munita."

"Munita? What was she like?"

"She was…meaty."

That's the tooth in my stomach speaking.

"Meaty?"

"Yes. She…she was like a…a main course."

The butter-blonde looks at me as if my problems are not only physical. I tell my tooth to shut up.

"OK," she says, wetting her sorbet lips with her strawberry tongue.

"But somebody ate her. They ate her body but left the head in the fridge. For me."

A short silence here, and then she asks like a doctor who's testing the sanity of his patient's:

"And you loved her?"

"No. Not then. But I do now, I guess."

Death is a love drug. I didn't know I loved my father until after he was dead.

Gun remains silent for a while until she leans over and places her medium rare lips on mine, creating one of the strangest feelings of my life. In record time I need to arrange some round-table negotiations between penis and stomach. The hungry bastards both claim the kiss as theirs. Before the incredible thing is over, I manage to force them to an agreement—standing between them like Bill Clinton out on the sunny White House lawn, presiding over the famous handshake of Rabin and Aarafat. I wonder which one is playing the penis?

She rearranges the bandage on my nose.

"My parents have this big plan for you. They're very excited about it. It's almost as if you are *the* challenge of their lives."

"OK. I better not let them down."

"No. At least don't kill them."

I like this girl.

"What about you and Truster?"

"We had a fight. It's been a crazy week."

"OK."

"I'm sleeping here tonight. In my old room, for the first time in six years or something. Þórður is coming tomorrow."

"Oh? Torture time?"

She laughs.

"Yeah. He's gonna take you to his church."

"Oh?"

"Yeah. You have to pass through the Gates of Hell or something, my dad says."

Holy shit.

CHAPTER 21
THE GATES OF HELL
05.31.2006

It's Torture Therapy: Step 2.

I'm standing on the carpeted floor in the bearded man's church, with a big Band-Aid on my forehead and one tooth missing. But the swelling is gone, my ankle is bearable, and the right shoulder only shrieks a little. I must have lost twenty pounds. For the shy stomach, fasting works like psychotherapy.

They made me lie in the trunk for the drive up here. Those guys have my total respect. I don't get it, really, why they're going to these lengths for their friend's killer. Why don't they just send me straight to hell? Or maybe this is it?

"The Gates of Hell."

The church is empty. Mr. T went to his office. He comes back in a funny white robe, plus he's barefooted. Around his waist he wears a black belt, and as he comes closer I can see that this is actually a karate—karaoke?—outfit. Something Japanese at least. It has that gung-ho gay feel to it. A barefooted fighter wearing a lady's robe.

Torture tells me to follow him out in the lobby. To the right of the entrance there is a dark red door. We enter a square room about fifteen feet square. At least the ceiling is high and the walls are white, with small windows on top. A solid white, squared column stands in the middle of the room. The floor is covered in mattresses with dark red plastic covers. The air smells of old sweat.

"Take off your shoes, shirt, and pants," he says, while locking the door and turning on the lights.

I'm in for a manly rape, Japanese style.

"As you must have heard, the world is divided in two: heaven and hell. Separating the two is The Great Wall of Fire. It runs all the way from Eden to our present day, from the depths of the darkest coal mine to the fingertips of the Universe. No bird can fly over it. No fish can swim under it. NO SOUL CAN PASS THROUGH IT!" he suddenly shouts, before whispering: "But there is a gate."

He walks in a big circle around the column, breathing heavily, looking very much like some movie madman. I take off most of my clothes and put them away in a corner. Even I can smell the underpants I've been wearing for days; some black-and-white Joe Boxers from Mr. Maack's great collection. Torture picks up his speech:

"Now, you know THE GOLDEN GATE, right? People think they can enter The Golden Gate. Even the sinner of all sinners thinks he can enter the Golden Gate. Not so," he says, waving his index finger in the air. He's walking pretty fast now, circling the room and me. "Not so. People think they go to heaven or hell when they die. Not right. THEY ARE THERE ALREADY! You are there already. Either you are in heaven or you are in hell. There is nothing in between. There is no fumbling about. There is no compromise! And you, my friend, YOU ARE IN HELL!!! And now that you want to go to heaven, you first have to leave hell. To be able to enter The Golden Gate, you first have to exit THE GATES OF HELL!"

Suddenly he turns fatherly:

"Tell me, Tomislav...my dear friend Tomislav...Tell me why all the fancy entrances, like the ones you see in banks and churches, like the one out here for example...Why they all have TWO DOORS? Why are they all built with DOUBLE DOORS?"

"I don't know. So it's not easy to...escape?"

"So the air outside won't mingle with the air inside. The first one closes before the second one opens. It's a perfect system. And the same principle applies for THE TWO GATES. The golden one and the burning one. You wouldn't like the nasal-burning air of hell to get inside our air-conditioned heaven. So now you have to go through THE GATES OF HELL!" he shouts like a Serbian general high on gunpowder before he suddenly jumps at me, Jackie Chan style, crying out some karate shit and kicking me hard in the face with his right foot. My lips explode as if he just hit a balloon full of blood.

WHAT THE FUCK!

Then he comes at me from behind, hitting me in the back of my head with his brick of a hand. I fall on the floor. Blood stains the mattresses. I'm half out of this world and inside those fucking GATES, when the Bible-blaster grabs me by the ears and starts pouring his blessed acid into them:

"YOU FUCKING BALKAN SON OF A BITCH! YOU FUCKING DESERVER OF NOTHING! YOU FILTHY MUR-DERER AND MUDDY MANSWINE! YOU FILTHY SCUM OF THE EARTH! YOU DEVIL OF ALL DEVILS! YOU ASSHOLE OF THE UNIVERSE!"

He picks me up by my ears, then head-butts me down again with his biblical forehead so I'm almost KO'd, crawling in my own blood, then kicks me in the groin. He kicks me again and then throws his heavy body on top of me, like a G-string clad wrestler in Madison Square Garden. He puts his right arm around my throat and twists my head with his left one. Fuck it. I'm being whacked by a priest.

I can't let it happen.

The good old soldier from the *Hrvatska* army rises deep inside me, like Tito from his grave, and goes straight to work. In an instant my mental and physical weakness is gone. In a flash, my starved body is seized with the force of the hungry boar. I bite his hand to the bone and whip the fucker off my back with a swift turn of the spine. He lands on the floor, red with pain, and I land on top of him. I put my hands around his neck and let the grip tighten like a noose. I'm about to silence him for good when Comrade Tito suddenly appears in front of me. He's in his good old general's outfit, holding Munita's head. I close my eyes and shake my own head. I reopen them and they're still there. Head and leader. Leader and head. I fasten my grip around Torture's neck, the image becomes clearer. I let go a little, the image disappears. I fasten it again and the image reappears. It's like those plastic toys that squeak when you squeeze them. What's it supposed to mean? The head of my life with the head of my love.

Torture senses my confusion and comes to life, starts pulling my hands away from his neck. As he manages to loosen my left one, it gets tangled up in his glasses and they fly off his face. I instantly forget Tito and go back to work on my holy victim, getting back my grip on his throat. With a violent force, I manage to turn his head from red to purple, from purple to pale, from pale to white. I do not look up, I do not dare to look. But somebody keeps on bugging me: Suddenly the face of Torture becomes the face of my father. Without the glasses he looks just like him. Suddenly I'm holding my father by the neck.

The fuck.

I immediately let go, jump to my feet, and hurry into a corner, turning away from the man, catching my breath, blood dripping from my loud-breathing snot.

What the fuck.

The seven days of soul-saving have come to nothing. I finish the week of fasting by killing a boar. The born-again is dead again. Being a double priest-killer didn't look good on my application for heaven, but being a triple one will surely destroy it.

I pass a few more moments in hell before I sense some movement on the plastic covered mattresses behind me. The holy animal slowly rises.

"Tomislav Bokšić…" The voice is broken but extremely dramatic. "Tomislav Bokšić. The Balkan soldier…" He seems to have done his homework. "I cannot beat you at your own game, so we better try mine."

He grabs my shoulder and turns me around. The glasses are back on his face and his cheeks show some color, but his blood-stained gown is in great disorder. He breathes a little. I welcome the fact.

"You little son of a Croatian cunt," he says and slaps me in the face. "You little son of a crazy Croatian cunt!" He grabs me by the shoulders. "Who do you think you are, huh? You think you're something more than a lousy little louse that crawls around the kitchen floor in the kingdom of God, with a small hellish flame on its back? YOU FOOL!"

He pushes me around. I do not react. He sort of drives me backwards around the room, with his hands on my shoulders, his feet fumbling from exhaustion. He uses me as his underpants-wearing Zimmer frame. Speaking like a drunkard: "You bloody fool. You bloody son of a Serbo-Croatian fool."

"Croatian."

"SHUT THE FUCK UP!"

He stops. We stand still. Facing each other. Then he asks, in a more calm way, "How many people have you killed?"

"Eh, how many? One hundred twenty something."

"One hundred and twenty SOMETHING!?"

"Yes. I'm not totally sure."

"What do you mean? You don't count them? You don't count them like the women you've had? How many women have you had?"

"I don't know. Counting hookers?"

"Counting hookers? I don't have all day."

"Then…I'm not sure…sixty, seventy maybe…"

"Sixty, seventy? You've killed more people than you've slept with? You're worse than I thought."

"But I've never killed a hooker."

"What?"

"I mean…a woman. I've never killed woman."

"Never killed a woman?"

"No…well, yes, some people in the war were women, but that was not an issue."

"Not an issue?"

"We were just ordered to shoot. It was like shooting deer. Shoot or be shot. That was our choice."

A pause. He takes a long, loud-breathing look at me. Then:

"Do you know what you've done?"

"Yes. I do."

"Do you regret it?"

"Yes."

"You have killed people."

"Yes."

"You have taken into your hands the power of God."

"You mean…?"

"And that is a sin. The sin of all sins."

"You mean, God…kills people, or?"

"He creates and he kills, he reigns and he rules! You should obey and not betray! How does it feel?"

"How does it feel, what?"

"How does it feel TO KILL someone?"

"It…it feels like…"

"Yes?"

"It feels like…preaching."

"What?"

"Yeah. It makes you feel powerful. You're in control."

"Bullshit. You think you're in control, while you're being controlled by…Who was the first?"

"What?"

"Who was your first victim?"

"My first hit?"

"Yes. Who was your first hit?"

As quickly as a missile leaves an aircraft carrier in the Persian Gulf, my mind shoots to the bottom of my list—through concrete floors and rusty iron hatches, all the way down to my beneathest basement where the dark is smelly and the smell is dark—breaking open an old moldy coffin lying in a damp and dusty corner.

"My father," I say.

"Your father?"

"Yes."

"You killed your father?"

"Yes."

I killed my father. I probably should have mentioned this before.

"You killed your father?"

"Yes."

"You killed your own father?"

"Yes. But nobody knows."

"Nobody knows?"

"No. I didn't tell anyone. Nobody saw it."

"Nobody saw it? God sees everything! Murder is murder, no matter if…and a father…a father is always a father. *How could you do it? How in the bloody hell could you kill your own father?*"

"I…It was…"

"Yes? It was what? Your hot blood chilled with ice from the Devil's fridge?"

"It was accidental."

I've never talked about this before, and the mere thought of it, especially in the presence of this guy, is enough to bring me to my knees. I kneel before him like a semi-naked knight in front of his white-gowned queen. She lets him feel her sword.

"An accident? But you did kill him?"

"Yes. But…"

"But what?"

"It was his fault."

"His fault?"

"Yes, because…"

I'm at the end of my battery. Like a dose of poison timed to go to work some fifteen years after it was consumed, my big secret suddenly takes hold of my body and knocks me over. All of a sudden, I'm lying at the feet of Torture.

"What? Because of what?"

"Because…"

I'm taken with a coughing fit, mixed with a bawling I didn't know I had in me. I must sound like a baby seal being beaten with a baseball bat. He listens to me for a while and then brings the scene to its conclusion.

"You have killed your father. May God save your soul."

I can feel that he puts his bare foot on my quaking back, like a triumphant general on his fallen enemy. Somehow this gesture seems to calm my bawling a bit. But instead, I'm taken over with an incredibly strong feeling of hunger. An all-you-can-order, all-you-can-eat hunger. I want to run out in the church, up to the altar, and start gnawing away at the big wooden cross like a desperate horse.

With my left ear I can feel a slight and gentle man-made wind. This either came from Torture's back end, or it's a breeze from his doing the sign of the cross over my hapless body.

"May God save your soul," he repeats. "If he can."

And give me something to eat. If he can.

CHAPTER 22
FATHER'S LAND
05.31.2006

So I exit the Gates of Hell, carrying the slim body of my dear father, and ring the huge Golden Doorbell. God lets me wait a while. I guess my application has to be approved by the Committee of Die Hard Cases before it reaches his eyes.

Meanwhile Torture takes me over to his place, a huge white house on a hill close to his church, and puts me up in a window-free space in his basement, visited only by him and his wife. They tell me they have three kids. I can't see them, nor can I hear them. Apparently they spend their days in silence, reading the Bible. Just like me. Every morning the preacher-man picks three chapters I'm supposed to read that day. "Or despisest thou the riches of his goodness and forbearance and longsuffering; not knowing that the goodness of God leadeth thee to repentance?"

It's Torture Therapy: Step 3.

Torture's secret weapon is his wife, Hanna. She's just as classic-looking as him: a burly woman with soft skin, nice leathery wrinkles, a biblical bust, and a pleasant voice. She moves silently about the house, wearing colorless T-shirts and long skirts, with long graying hair like a horse tail and not a stitch of makeup. If there were a TV show called *Miss Mother Earth*, she'd be visited with lights and lenses by the all-American camera crew. One has the feeling that her hair grows a foot a day and that she cuts it every night before going to bed. And that every morning she milks her breasts, putting what the household needs in the fridge, but donating the rest to the milk fund of CWCC, Career Women with Carbon Chests. She speaks English with an accent that goes a bit deeper than the Icelandic one. As if she belonged to some hot spring nation. She's more like the mountain behind the man than "the woman behind the man." She is the Christian country of care that her husband, the eyes-on-fire ambassador, represents in his clumsy way.

Hanna's big drawback is her incredibly bad breath, which doesn't really go with her incredibly good vibes. It probably stems from the biblical amount of frustration she's had to swallow over the years. It can't be easy being married to Torture.

Still, if she was the only woman on our platoon and we were stuck in the mountains for a month, I'd start dreaming about her on day seven.

Breakfast is a slice of homemade bread that I kiss before eating. And a glass of milk that I keep hoping is homemade as well. Lunch is exactly the same, but dinner is always meat. A lamb, a calf, or a foal. Some animal that Torture has slaughtered up in his garage, I'm sure. I'm back in the Old Testament. In the care of Sarah, wife of Abraham. My room has no windows, my bed is hard, my book is the Bible, my days are simple, and my nights are getting more and more peaceful.

Therapy seems to be working.

I've done away with a hundred hits. Only one remains. Every day my glasses-wearing guardian angel comes downstairs and listens for half an hour. His lust for violence is biblical. His crazy eyes have calmed a bit though. Or I have grown accustomed to them. He informs me about his outside-the-box methods.

"I have the black belt in both judo and karate. This is where I come from. I didn't meet God until I met my wife, when I was thirty-five. I always say that I married God," the bearded man says with a gentle laugh. I think I'm starting to understand his talk about circumcising the heart. It's probably crucial when you're married to God. He laughs a little more, adding: "I was lucky." Somehow his laughter sounds a bit learned. As if he had learned it at Preaching School, to spice up his speeches with short chuckles here and there. "No. I'm only putting my knowledge and expertise to the service of the Lord. We have a saying in Icelandic that you have to fight evil with evil."

By going through the disaster of my life, calmly and carefully, I'm slowly trying to bury it. Trying to bury my father properly. It's like this artist once told me in some dingy little diner on the East Side: He only painted the picture he did not want to see ever again. "It's just takin' out the trash, man." He was going through a tough divorce, he said, and only painted his ex-wife. Big horrible nudes.

For fifteen years I have carried this thing inside me. For fifteen years my dead father has been the unborn child I've been carrying in my womb. I guess that's why I've always been on the fat side. By finally giving birth to it I can possibly stop living like an ostrich stuffed with shame. The delivery was painful as hell, but I had this great midwife: an Icelandic priest in a karate outfit. The newborn baby looks like this:

It was at the end of my first week in uniform. We'd volunteered for the big offensive out east, me, my father, and Dario, shortly after the fall of Vukovar. Our assignment was to cross the river Vuka.

But they didn't want a whole family out in the front lines so they told me to stay behind. "Keep post and shoot every sucker you see!" I spent the cold night with my virgin rifle and chattering teeth, looking after three tents and a jeep. In the distance I could hear rifles arguing like angry insects. An occasional flame would light the leafless woods. My brother and father were out there doing their national duty in the cold forest mud. I was trying hard to distinguish the noise of our rifles from the Serbian ones, hoping the former would silence the latter. But of course we were all using the same fucking weapons. Somewhere not so far away some fat fucker was sleeping his ass off on a comfy mattress made from the profits of war.

Finally it started to snow. The flakes were thick and heavy, as if they were full of dirt already. I grabbed one with the tip of my tongue and it tasted like mud.

Close to daybreak, I heard a voice followed by some rustling of bushes. I reacted instantly, firing my first "manly" shot. I was surprised by my swift and sure reaction. Met with silence, it seemed to be a success. Still, I remained on the trigger for half an hour, for safety's sake, watching the snowflakes fall on the rifle and my hand, building up a small snowdrift on the barrel, but melting away on my skin. Then I thought I heard that voice again, some low murmuring out in the bushes. I fired another shot. They did not fire back. But the faint murmuring didn't stop. I remained still for another half an hour, firing a couple of more times, but the voice kept creeping through. So I crawled like an undercover snake to the bushes. Finally, I could make out a body lying buried in the naked branches, talking to himself. He seemed to be wearing our uniform. I cried out a warning before rushing through the shrubs, rifle first.

I found my father lying there with a leaking heart. The lower part of his body was covered in snow, as if his legs were dead already. His face was pale, and his eyes were as big as eggs that instantly broke upon seeing me. He managed to whisper the first half of my name, and then he was gone.

I shot my father and let him lie like a wounded deer out in the bushes for an hour, blabbing his life away. When I finally listened to him, he had only half a word left. "Tod…" The thing I became. It was like a fucking curse.

I accidentally blew off the second half of my name. And the better half of my life.

I stood there for some minutes, staring at the face so close to my own. Snow kept on falling, and I watched as the flakes slowly stopped turning into water on my father's brow and cheeks and started building up small drifts around his screaming eyes. I was surprised how quickly his fatherly warmth turned cold. I couldn't touch him. I just walked away from his body, leaving his big eyes open for interpretation.

I didn't cry.

When they brought me the news of my father, they told me my brother Dario had also died a heroic death. As always, he was on the offensive when he met his destiny. He ran like a Jamaican sprinter towards the Serbian spear speeding towards his heart. It was pure Dario.

They said my father witnessed his death and that he instantly went nuts. He threw himself over his body and then suddenly started crying out my name, "Tomo! Tomo!" before running back to our post without his shotgun.

"Oh?" I said to my fellow soldiers, nodding a few times, as if they were telling me the results of some football games. "But, what about the battle?"

"We took the river bank. We hold the river bank now."

I have seen that fucking river bank. It fucking sucks.

CHAPTER 23
MADE IN ICELAND
06.06.2006

Hanna's big hands are incredibly white. Much paler than her arms. It's almost as if she's wearing white gloves. Her long and strong fingers move softly about in a very swift but silent way. There is hardly any noise to be heard as she gathers my empty plate and glass. My mom is the absolute opposite. When she was doing the dishes, it always felt like there was a punk band rehearsing out in the kitchen. Maybe Dad didn't give her enough sex. If that's the reason, Torture must be biblical in bed.

"Are you feeling better?" she asks me in her homely voice that is red wine to my ears, but rotten to my nose.

"Yes."

"That is good."

For some mystical reason she has 100 percent faith in me. I'll be "góður," she says half the time. It both means "good" and "to get well."

Once again I read the story of Saul, the self-made holyman from Tarsus, Turkey. It's the same story as Goodmoondoor spontaneously told his audience my first night in Iceland, and now it has become the foundation of my recovery, Torture says. I get the point. Like me, this guy also changed his name. And like me he has a bloody past. Yet he became St. Paul, "the father of the church." I'm sure to become St. Tom, father of something. Hopefully not a church, though.

Deep into my second week in Torture's basement, Hanna brings me a letter after dinner. She lays it gently on my chest, with a nodding smile that wrinkles her skin around the eyes, and says "read it" before she silently gathers empty dinnerware from my bedside table and goes back upstairs, her great horse tail swaying behind her back, above her round and solid bottom.

I open the letter. It's handwritten. No e-mails in the house of Abraham. Nice hand. Blue ink. *"Dear Thordur."* It's Father Friendly writing, from his house in Virginia, last October.

"Let me start by thanking you so much for your kind words and the invitation to visit Iceland. The thought of coming all the way up to your exotic island, which I have heard so many fascinating things about, I find very exciting, to say the least.

My good friend Rev. Carl Simonsen has informed me about your excellent work on behalf of the Lord, and I am aware of your friend Engilbertsson's TV station. I would only be happy to do some shows up there.

It is therefore with great regret that I inform you, that due to my personal situation, I cannot possibly accept your good offer. Last month, my wife Judy had a terrible car accident and will be hospitalized for the next three months at least. As you must understand, this sad situation prevents me from all traveling for the time being. I have postponed everything that includes flying until early spring next year.

Please write me again in 2006."

Professional but Friendly. The busy brother.

Poor guy. For staying at his wife's deathbed he was rewarded with his own death. How cruel of me.

The letter is accompanied by an autographed color photo showing the Friendly family standing in front of a big white house that could either be their church, their home, or both. Here is my bald victim with the white collar around his neck and his beaming blonde wife Judy by his side, the woman I was married to for two whole seconds in Goodmoondoor's car earlier this spring. She's a southern semi-beauty that could pass for Laura Dern's well-preserved mother. A Day 7 type. The couple proudly stands behind two kids, about ten and eight years old. One is black, one white. The latter sits in a wheelchair. Like only American women are capable of doing, Mrs. Friendly is smiling so hard she cannot possibly see the camera. She's blinded by bliss. Actually, they're all smiling with the same enthusiasm as if they were modeling for the brochure of the best hotel in heaven. The disabled kid has a bit of a disabled smile, though. A touch of disappointment with life in general.

I sum up my impression of Rev. David Friendly from letter and looks. He doesn't strike me as the usual southern televangelist, the con man of Christ. Somehow he seems genuine. I guess he didn't deserve to die at the age of forty. Despite all his homophobia. The soul-saver outweighs the widow-maker on any scale. Plus he has a crippled child, and another one adopted… And now the kids are orphans, fatherless, and motherless little creatures. I should probably offer to adopt them.

The day after, Hanna rubs it all in. Did I read the letter and see the photo? Yes, I did.

"He was a good man," she says with wrinkled eyes and without the slightest hint of accusation in her voice.

"And he lost his wife?"

"No," she says. "She had an accident and is para…What do you call it?"

"Paralyzed?"

"Yes. She is in a wheelchair."

"But Goodmoondoor told me she died."

"No, no. She almost died but she is getting better, I think."

"And they have two kids?"

"Yes. They have two adopted kids. The younger one is from Gambia. And the other one is in a wheelchair, also."

No shit. The crippled one is adopted as well. How fucking holy can you be? And now there are eight wheels in the family…

"You maybe want to write to them?" Mrs. Torture continues.

No.

"Yes, maybe."

"Of course you don't tell them who you are. You just say that you knew Father Friendly as a preacher and that you heard about his death, and that you are sorry."

She makes a pause. We look at each other. Me and Mother Earth.

"If you are," she adds.

"Yes, of course I'm sorry."

"That's good. You're getting better."

And here comes the good part. She strokes my cheek with her big white hand. With her strong, soft fingers. If this was a movie, I would now grab her with my Tom Cruise arms and we would kiss like two people eating their first grapefruit after a week in the desert, and then I would tear off her clothes and in one cut we'd be making biblical love on my Old Testament bed. The movie would be titled *Trinitatis*, containing a love triangle between sinner, priest, and his wife.

"I just think it could be good for *you* to write them a letter."

"OK. I'll think about it."

Actually, I should write the other sixty-six widows as well. I should write them all a standard sorry letter.

Dear Mrs. _____ ,

It is with great regret and a degree of sadness that I write to inform you that it was me who killed your husband. Of course, I know that nothing can replace the love of your life, and no matter how deep my regret will be, it can never bring him back to life.

All the same I want you to try to understand my situation. At the time of your husband's extermination I was a professional hitman for a certain national organization. Killing was my living. Between the years 2000 and 2006, I killed 67 men. Your husband was only one of many.

Mr. _____ was hit #__.

I can assure you that his death was among the most memorable on my list. Your husband was a good man. He died with great dignity and did absolutely not complain about his fate.

It is, however, with great pleasure that I inform you that I have now decided to thread a new path in the forest of life. As from May 2006, I am leaving the homicide industry. Shooting people is certainly one of the most difficult jobs you can find. The physical pressure and the psychological strain is very high. And now I have simply had enough.

Therefore I can assure you, in case you have found yourself a new partner (which I want to congratulate you on, if this is the case), that I will not kill your husband again.

Yours truly —Tomislav Bokšić.

This is the last time I will use my father's name. It's dead now. My attempt at suicide wasn't a complete flop.

The new me comes with a new name. After killing two priests, I'm baptized by two more.

"Good morning, Mister Ólafsson!" Goodmoondoor says as he suddenly appears at the end of my second week in hiding, smiling his teeth out. He hands me a brand-new Icelandic passport sporting my face and my own Icelandic social security number, called *kennitala*. I'm resurrected under the name of "Tómas Leifur Ólafsson." The two preachers have a good laugh when they watch me read it. They just can't control themselves. I don't know exactly why, but they find it extremely funny.

"Tómas Leifur Ólafsson! Congratulations! You are Icelandic now! You have to learn Icelandic!" Goodmoondoor almost shouts.

I study the passport. It looks impeccable. Even more so than the Chinese-made one for Igor.

"How did you…? Where did you get it?" I ask them.

"It's made in Iceland! Handmade!"

Goodmoondoor can hardly control his joy, nor can he hide the immense pride he feels from having been able to arrange this illegal artifact.

"I have a friend in the police," he says and winks at me with the silliest of smiles. "And another one in politic party."

I want to run outside and laugh myself to death. There is nothing more hilarious in this world than holy men doing illegal things.

They produce another round of laughs when they ask me to say my new name. "Thomas, leave her" is my first, and for me quite logical, attempt. Apparently "Toe Mash Lay Fur" is more like it. They make me say it some ten times before they're ready to wet my post-Friendly hair with the tap water that Torture makes holy with a blessing and a smile. They're having the time of their lives.

"Actually, you should have been Tómas Leifur Bogason," Torture explains. "That's the direct translation of your Croatian name, and for a long time this was the tradition here in Iceland. Immigrants were forced to take on an Icelandic name that was usually a translation or some version of the original one. But we don't want to risk anything, do we, so we came up with this one. Ólafsson means 'son of Ólaf' and that's the name of our president."

That's his first name, that is. Those guys have no use for family names. Icelanders still uphold the Viking tradition of letting their children's second names be derived from their father's first. If I had kids, they'd be honored with the cool and catchy *Tómasson* (boy) or *Tómasdóttir* (girl).

I beg my ministers for an easier version of my new name, and after some thinking they come up with *Tommy Olafs.*

CHAPTER 24
HARDWORK HOTEL
06.13.2006

To go with my illegal passport, they put me up in an illegal housing close to Torture's church. It's a pretty young building that houses a fancy furniture shop on the ground floor and some grungy immigrant workers on the first floor.

I enter the Icelandic underground. It seems we've switched roles, me and my holy friends. Goodmoondoor's man from the political party, a big-nosed guy with no neck named Good Knee, (no relation to the Wounded one) has that international Mob look in his eyes that is quite difficult to explain to the innocent reader but his colleague can't fail to notice. Those are eyes that have seen all of life and some of death.

He scuttles over to the entrance from his black and bruised SUV, a chubby unkempt man of fifty wearing a dark blue windbreaker that seems to be oversized, but on a closer look is just overweight with pockets full of keys (and guns?). He brings out a dozen and tries three of them before finding the right one.

Goodmoondoor introduces me, looking quite ridiculous, like a proud father recommending his son to a famous football coach.

Good Knee gives me a dull eye for a second and murmurs an all-Icelandic "hi" before entering the shabby entrance flooded with colorful, but footprinted, advertising brochures and unread local newspapers. We follow him up the staircase and down a long, raw looking corridor with a new door every fifteen feet, left and right. The ceiling is pretty high, rising up in the middle, but the walls, being only about eight or nine feet high, don't connect with it.

At the end of the hallway, a few red-eyed and dark-browed men with small white bits of concrete in their hair are sitting in a small kitchen clutching beers. A small TV sits on the cheap work-top, beside an ancient looking microwave. Some amateur murder thing lights the screen, but the workers are not watching. Good Knee greets them with a few inaudible words in Mobish.

One of the workers answers him in English with a thick Slavic accent and points down the corridor we just walked:

"Number three on right."

That's my cell. The president's son has to settle for storage space built for spare parts and divided into for-sleeping-only stalls by paper thin walls. The bed is a futon mounted on leftovers from the wall-building, with piled up sawlogs for legs. There is nothing else in the room except for an old, cheap office chair, a lamp lacking both bulb and shade, and a lonely silver spoon lying on the dirty floor. The wall facing the door is basically one big window with an oblong radiator beneath it. The view is a building similar to this one, with shops on the ground floor and a parking lot in front of it. Goodmoondoor throws a black plastic bag, containing some sheets, on the bed, saying, "this is good" to his friend before turning to me with his born-again smile:

"You know that you can always come to our house to eat, washing the clothes, or watching TV."

Something I never heard my father say.

The Good Knee gives me the good key plus his billion-dollar cell phone number in case there'll be an uprising in the barracks or some hostage taking. I better not tell those foreigners that they're sharing a roof with the president of Iceland's only son. I should probably ask the Good Moon to give the dump a quick blessing, but the two Goodfellas are off. My new life begins.

It starts with a small sports bag and a big Bible.

My fellow inmates are from Poland and Lithuania, plus one black-browed but thin-haired Bulgarian named Balatov who looks like a fellow hitman. It's the good old Warsaw Pact. Our only bathroom is called the Mausoleum. According to house rules, you either go there to see Lenin (the yellow thing) or Stalin (the brown thing). The camp itself they call Hardwork Hotel. They usually come home around eleven at night and are gone by seven, sighing out in the hallway and kicking themselves into their steel-toed shoes.

"I no Seven-Eleven," Balatov informs me. He stays home all day playing loud Iron Curtain Rock on his small boombox and watching TV out in the kitchen, cursing everything that appears on the screen in his native language. I have to take good care not to show him that I understand some of these words.

The Man from the Black Sea underscores his origins with a black sweater, black beard, black hair, and black brows over a pair of blackberries. He seems to be for all things black.

"Is black," he informs me in his thirty-word English when the odd black woman appears in the middle of the dental white daytime soap. "I fuck black. Is good."

I dive into the fridge, reaching for my container of white milk.

During the day, it's just me and him. Me and Balatov. Besides advertising his sexual preferences six times a day, he smells like horse manure marinated in petrol. Plus he uses every opportunity to make you his running mate. "I show picture of black. Is in room. Come." It's like being stuck with a tiger on a small boat in the middle of the Indian Ocean. You have to think about your every move. I silently smuggle my lunches out of the kitchen and only see Lenin when his boombox gives me a go, spending hours in my cell trying hard to separate the writing of the prophets from the wonderful sounds of *The Best of Bulgarian Heavy Metal*. In a way, those ambitious bands could as well be from Arkansas or Ecuador. The hairy rockers of this world seem to belong to one nation, though being spread all over the earth. The Jews of tomorrow.

But Mr. Black Sea won't take my LPP for a sign. He fucking knocks on my door. My instant reaction is to look for my gun. I miss it like the cleaner his mop.

"You have saving cream?" he asks me.

"I wish."

"What is?"

"No, I'm sorry, I don't have any."

"I will save face."

"I see. Good for you."

"You Iceland?"

"Ah, well...Partly. I'm partly Icelandic."

This country sucks me up like a volcano in reverse. Come winter and I'll wake up with a snowball face and a pebble nose.

"You no work?"

What's next? He'll ask for my passport? He asks about Good Knee and Goodmoondoor. I give short answers, with eyes fixed on the top of his skull. It shows through his black hair like the head of a baby breaking out from a thickly bushed vagina.

"Good Knee and priest is friend?" he says with a short laugh full of satisfaction, as if this was the thing he was really after, and then we're back to his favorite color. "You fuck black?"

"Eh…yes. I have."

"Is good?" he says with a disgusting smile that breaks out in a nasty laughter. "Is good!" He laughs all the way to his cell. "Black is good."

I'm going to ask Torture if his therapy allows for one last little murder.

Saturday night the Good Knee appears with a cardboard box full of vodka bottles that scream SMUGGLED! He places it on the kitchen table, looking very much like a nineteenth-century Southern landowner who knows how to treat his slaves. He doesn't open the thing, only sighs out through his big nose in his busy way and then leaves in his noisy windbreaker. I prepare myself for a sleepless night, but nothing happens until the day after. Sunday morning the Poles are up early, working on the vodka box like grasshoppers on sugar canes. By noon they're singing their polka hits out in the kitchen and shouting for Tomasz.

I pretend to be dead when they knock on the door. Dead as I wanted to be.

They find it pretty strange that an *"islandski"* guy is living in a place like this. Hardwork Hotel has always been for foreign workers only. For them I must be like an SS officer who voluntarily checks into Auschwitz. I try to tone it all down by telling them that I'm only 25 percent Icelandic, making up a long, boring story of a father from Fresno, Mr. Chuck Ólafsson, who was half Icelandic, went into the army, and died in some small war in the Caribbean during the Reagan era ("it was friendly fire, a sad story"), and a German mother who later married this Croatian priest and that they now live in Vienna.

"You know Rapid Wien?" I quickly ask them.

"Is football club, yes? They play Legia Warszawa in last year. Is your club?"

"Yes. I was ten when my dad died and then we moved to Austria. I've been living there until now."

I space out for a brief while. Why did I pick Vienna? I was only there for a weekend. But I had my BMM there, Best Massage Moment. Hungarian girl, who told me she was twenty but looked to be fifty, dragged her big breasts up and down my back, it was the most heavenly feeling, as if they were God's balls or something. I come back to my senses and finish the paragraph:

"Actually, I've never lived in Iceland before."

"But you speak Icelandic?" one of the three Poles asks. Somehow they all look like soldiers from WWII. Could be stand-ins in some black-and-white Oscar-nominated Jews-R-Us movie, sitting in the back of an army truck, about to be blown up in the next scene.

"Just a little. My mother, no, my grandmother used to speak to me in Icelandic when I was a boy."

I went a bit too far. One of them disappears for a while and comes back with a letter in Icelandic, full of crazy letters—a pregnant I, and an A making love to an E—asking me to translate it for him. I take it to my stall and make a quick call to Hanna. It takes me forever, though, to read her the unreadable words. It turns out to be a simple invitation to the inauguration of some building the guy was working on. He can't go, he says, too busy working at another construction site. The Seven Elevens are real working machines. Their bodies are so used to going to sleep at midnight and waking at six, that they're unable to sleep in Sunday morning. Therefore they can't get drunk on a Saturday night but have to do it the day after. They start at seven in the morning and finish at eleven at night.

CHAPTER 25

GRANNY'S

06.17.2006

It must be Balatov's good influence, but after a week on the Hard-work floor I can't think of much else other than sex. My Bible reading hours are crowded by memories, fantasies, and day-dreams. Sometimes they all collide into one, into one big Senka, my Split girlfriend. My great Split girlfriend. Again and again her head pops up from the dirty pool of my unconscious. I even dream about her for three nights in a row. It's kind of strange, for she hasn't really visited my mind in years, though I try googling her name every once in a while.

Senka was always big fun, and a bit crazy, with her triangular breasts pointing east and west, and her short, black hair pointing up and down. She had a big black birthmark on her left cheek that made her look a tiny bit like Brooke Shields. Her lips were full and soft, but her cheeks kind of hard, angled. Somehow you always wanted to press them with your finger. And despite the dimples they always made her look kind of boyish.

She had a much older sister and her mustached mother was old enough to be her grandmother. Her stepfather was a poet, a very serious, very unknown poet. Senka knew a lot of poems by heart and sometimes she would recite some for me. I don't know why, really, but I always remember this one, written by one of her stepfather's friends:

Svatko tko je putovao zna da se jabuke nigdje ne jedu
kao na ulici i trgu nekog stranog grada.
(Anyone who has travelled knows that apples taste /
the sweetest on a street or a square of a new city.)

Now the two lines only appeal to my dick, making him rise up from his den, trying to listen. (Mr. Crotch Dweller has a very good ear for poetry.) I spend my days between her strong, almost manly, thighs, remembering her clumsy dancing style or going through our early morning lovemaking on that beach in Brač. The still blue water, the loud white pebbles, her wicked smile…

I don't get it really. I'm held hostage by Senka. By good and solid old-fashioned pre-war sex. Yugoslavian national sex.

Senka's was the hairiest crotch of the Adriatic. (I've always been a bushman. To me the idea of a bald pussy is like steak without sauce.) She used to suffer from it, she said, but I tried my best to convince her that hairy wasn't scary, that Brazilian wax was to sex what this new French *cuisine* was to cooking. No fucking sauce.

I wake up with her on top of me and before falling asleep at night I bury my face in her bushy crotch, humming old Arsen Dedič songs. I probably just miss my country.

The good man that goes by the name of Good Knee seems to feel my frustration, and my week of Homeland Sex finds its appropriate conclusion when the good slave master decides to take all his subjects to Granny's, a strip club buried deep in an industrial zone close by.

We walk past rusty car bodies and a blue container that must be full of teddy bears stuffed with heroine. After all, this is the town of Cop War. Once past the standard heavyweight bouncer, we enter another world. The new me had thought of staying home, but after a week under Balatov's surveillance, I had welcomed the strip-trip. I'm really starting to think the Black Sea man might be something other than the stranded whale he looks to be. At least his interrogation technique smells of the FBI.

"Black is for me. OK?" he assures the two Lithuanians as we walk down the red carpet stairs.

I take a deep breath and enter the loud cave. *Again, the devil taketh him up into an exceeding high mountain and sheweth him all the sexiest women of the world, and the glory of them, and saith unto him: You can have them all tonight if you promise not to kill them after use.*

That's the Devil for me, or God, for that matter. The big sinner is allowed to sin in a small way, as the drug addict is allowed to smoke cigarettes after getting off heroine.

Although it's still pretty early (the Poles only last until midnight, remember), the club is quite crowded. The design seems to have been based on a twenty-year-old Muslim's idea of paradise. Lots of booze, half-naked babes (might not all be virgins, though), and loud sexy music. The "Thong Song" boffs the sound system, and a thonged blonde shines in the spotlight, polishing the pole with all her softest body parts. Around her a few foreign workers are sitting, fingering their half empty beer glasses that are standing on the edge of the round stage. Further away some pebble-nosed and beer-bellied locals are buried in deep armchairs, enjoying the company of pole dancers on pause, looking anxiously cool as men tend to look when they're forced to hide their inner excitement.

It's your average strip joint. Could be Miami. Could be Munich.

The Good Knee introduces us to his good friend, the owner: a round moon-faced man named August, like the month, but better known as "Goosty Granny." He could, in fact, pass for a happy grandmother as he swings his big fat belly around the place along with his great double chin that vibrates from his happy laugh like lemon Jell-O on a flying saucer. He's got some lovely dark hair, but there are no signs of any growth in his smooth cheeks. His nose is a small rosy pebble.

Granny would make a great belly dancer, no doubt.

As he goes to get the menu, our man explains the joke about his name: the phonetic translation of "Goosty Granny" would be Thin Goosty. I voice my surprise of discovering such a joint in No Ho Land and some of the Poles agree with me. Good Knee tells his friend, once he's back with the wine list, that we didn't know that places like this existed in Iceland.

"But it doesn't!" Goosty bursts out loud and shakes his sexy booty with a happy laugh. "It doesn't!"

The menu lists meat courses only. Bare or medium bare, Baltic, Czech, or Russian style. The prices are as high as the silent pole in the middle of the stage, but our fat friend offers a fifty-percent discount for all of Good Knee's men.

"Because you deserve it! Because you are building the new Iceland!" he exclaims with a set of red cheeks and beaming eyes.

"You have black?" Balatov asks.

"Black Russian?" Goosty laughs, then suddenly stops, and snaps his fingers in the air.

A slim Caribbean princess, a pearl-eyed Day 5 Girl, appears from a corner as dark as her skin, and the Black Sea man immediately orders a bottle of champagne. I settle for a big beer, standing by the bar, watching my friends scatter all over the place, each one nursing his sexual loneliness.

A new song fills the air—"Hot in Herre." It's an old Kelly hit. Or, Nelly? Belly even. I put my tongue where the missing tooth is and watch the dancer tear off her thong, and we have…a cactus crotch. The Gillette Generation has turned sex into a fucking surgery. I say a silent "skull!" to all my hairy queens, remembering Munita's pitch-black rainforest. "I have to think of the ozone layer," she used to joke.

Her look-alike appears by my side, asking me in bad English whether she can "join my drink." She calls herself Angel, a name that is at least one Atlantic away from her gypsy looks. Angel is a big-lipped, dark-skinned mother of two big tits, a small woman mounted on sky-high heels. She's a rather pathetic copy of Munita—a Day 6, my old man Toxic would have it—but at least her head's still connected to her body. I try to buy time with a little chat about her three weeks in Cop War while resting my eyes on the Day 3 Latvian beauty at the other side of the bar who looks uncomfortably much like Gun.

The story of my life.

Remembering Goosty's generous offer, I ask the dark Angel whether one can super-size one's meals in this joint. You can, she says, and winks the Latvian Gun over. She wears a blue satin dress and a lustful smile hiding a set of heavy braces, some excellent Baltic handiwork that really should call for an even deeper discount. But I have my fifty-percent off already. I put my virgin credit card, Torture's special gift to me (laden with contributions from hardworking supermarket cashiers to his church fund) on the bar table and watch the waitress, a freshly retired stripper with wrinkled cleavage, squeeze out of it the equivalent of a two month's stay at Hardwork Hotel, in exchange for a bottle filled with twenty minutes of double fantasy. This might just be the most expensive bottle in the history of mankind.

I follow the four high heels down an alley of curtains. Behind one of them, Balatov must be trying hard to save his white cream for his last sip of black champagne. The deeper we go into the cave, the darker it gets, but the music doesn't fade one bit. It's Beyoncé time now. She and Jay-Z. "Crazy in Love."

At the end of the alley, Angel opens a curtain and leads us into the thinly veiled private space, furnished with a big box of Kleenex and a very laid-back La-Z-Boy. The blonde girl, who calls herself Ina, opens the bottle and fills our glasses: three flutes' worth my mother's salary for standing ten hours a day, six days a week, for three whole months in her *hardverski* store in Split, copying keys and searching out those hard-to-get .765 caliber cartridges she keeps in the back.

I should probably tell her about this born-again thing.

I throw myself into the chair. Angel starts moving about, but Ina kneels by my side and starts rubbing my left knee. Must be an order from the Good one. The stripper seems lost without her pole, like a pole-vaulter without his tool. But who's going to criticize dancing when it comes with stripping? Not me, at least, though Crotch Dweller remains unimpressed. No standing ovation. I should be worried. I'm buying him the most expensive date of his life, and his first sandwich in years, and he better be up to it. My heart goes out to those hardworking supermarket cashiers, the donating members of the Church of Torture. I can't let their contributions be in vain.

Dweller doesn't buy my arguments.

I don't quite get it. In the past, the flag of my manhood has been successfully raised by countless soldiers of sex, but now it's turning into a fag. Must be all that Bible reading. I call out my fantasy-squad, the elite cells of my brain, and with the help of another bubbly glass I manage to fully morph the two girls into a pirate copy of Gun and Munita.

Finally, as the dark one lets out her twins and the blonde one takes off her dress, unveiling a slim and very Gun-like body dressed in some delicious underwear, I sense something that could pass for boner-building. I rise to my feet and clumsily start to slow dance with the two ladies of my life. The image of the born-again hitman dancing to Beyoncé brings a smile to their faces, and Gun lends her hand to the buildup down under. The development aid from Latvia works like magic, and now my worries are all focused on her braces. They scare me. Could cause injury. Whether it's because I want to check out their sharpness, the good feeling from the girl's hand, her close likeness to my ice-queen, or simply the bubbly wine, I get carried away for a very brief second and I try to bloody kiss her.

Like a fucking priest in a fucking brothel in some fucking century.

She immediately turns her head away from my lips and removes her hand from my pathetic crotch. It's like a slap in the face. Out of old habit, I automatically reach for my semi-automatic problem-solver, but there is none, of course, and I have no other option but to walk away.

As I rush up the alley, the curtains swing a bit open as I pass by them. I look behind me and see men lying in La-Z-Boys being nursed by half-naked women. They kneel down beside them like widows mourning their dead husbands. I walk away from it all and head for the bar. I wave the waitress over and ask her whether it's possible to get a doggy bag.

"A what?"

"A doggy bag!"

Damn. I'm fucking angry.

"For what?"

"I couldn't finish the meal I just paid for!"

"The what? The…meal?"

"I PAID FOR TWO HEADS! I WANT TWO HEADS IN A DOGGY BAG!"

I guess my voice must have cut through Beyoncé and Jay-Z's loud lovemaking, for suddenly I'm the center of everybody's attention. Even the dancer on stage stops dancing. The Good Knee appears from a nearby chair, followed by Thin Goosty. As he draws closer, he waves his hand like a football captain trying to prevent a teammate from receiving the red card. He's about to say something, but I won't hear it. I'm gone.

CHAPTER 26
THE MEAT MAN
06.21.2006

I ask Goodmoondoor to get me a job. *Please.* The Bible is OK, but I can't possibly spend ten hours a day on it. I'm not a monk. Plus I owe Torture a night at Granny's.

After a few phone calls, the TV-man finds me a job in the kitchen of Samver, a Christian catering service for the needy, that his friend runs in a nearby suburb. Every morning the chef makes three hundred meals out of three fish. I have to be there at one o'clock to do the dishes as they start returning. I even take the bus, something I haven't done since childhood. Usually I'm the only passenger aboard the big yellow bus 24 that takes me almost directly from our hotel to the industrial zone overlooking most of Reykjavik. The driver is Kosovan, and we sometimes joke that we should fill the bus with bombs and head for the Serbian embassy.

"You shouldn't take the bus, Tommy," the chef assures me. "People might see you."

"What do you mean?"

"The bus is only for old ladies and lunatics. And the new people."

"The new people?"

"The Poles and the yellow dogs…If you're Icelandic, you don't take the bus."

The chef calls himself Óli, pronounced something like "Olie," a nickname derived from Ólafur, the name of my father, the president. He's a chain smoker, pale, with a big birthmark on the left side of his chin, a small round earring in his left ear, and a great attitude towards foreigners. His English is surprisingly good. The third man in the kitchen is a small Vietnamese guy called Chien, with a virgin mustache and a hundred small teeth, and Olie reminds him ten times a day that his name means "dog" in French. The Toxic Croat is safe though, since he's twenty-percent ice and carries a local name. I try not to smile as he shouts at me from his open door smoking corner:

"Hey! Tommy! Tell the dog to empty the trash as well."

The owner, Goodmoondoor's friend Sammy, is a small guy with a potbelly and a swollen forehead who chews on gum like a cow on hay, keeping the small glasses on the tip of his nose dancing all day. He wears that born-again-for-the-fifth-time-and-definitely-not-the-last smile on his face, a smile that says his life is in God's hands and though the Old one might occasionally drop it on the floor, he'll always pick it up again. Sammy and Olie went to jail together, the chef tells me at the end of my second day. The former for stealing some forged paintings and the latter for manslaughter in the first degree. A crime of passion executed with a butcher knife, he says, pointing his weapon at me, in the middle of slicing up beef for the next day's goulash. "He was fucking my girl, the bastard. I had to do it, or she would have dumped me on the spot." Apparently they're still together. Harpa is her name. "There is nothing like the love of a woman you've killed for."

I should give it a thought.

By letting me in on his secret, Olie gains my respect. At last I have met a real man in this land of limps. I'm curious about his seven years in the pen. Whether he got raped in the shower. No, he says. Icelandic prison is more like an American college campus: endless football games and all the drugs you can dream of.

"Icelandic prison is very popular with foreigners. The Mafia guys from *Litháen* sometimes come up here just to get caught. For them it's like a spa or something."

I could love this country.

"What about your victim? You think about him when you were inside?"

"No. Not much. It was a happy murder. The days after, I was the happiest man alive. I mean, he totally deserved it. Sometimes I even wish he was alive so I could do it again."

"But, seven years…It must have been boring?"

"Yeah, a little bit. But I studied cooking and French and… Then my relationship with Harpa was never better. I mean, I didn't have to listen to her, go shopping with her, or go see her mom anymore, you know. I only got the good stuff. Sex in jail is the best, man," he says with an icy smile as he throws his cigarette out on the wet parking lot overlooking some drab industrial blocks and the rest of leafy Reykjavik.

"You never shot anybody?" I ask him.

"With a gun? No. Killing somebody with a gun is like making love with a mouse," he says, picking up his slimy knife. "You know, computer mouse."

I better be impressed with my holy benefactors, the comedy duo known as Good 'n Torture. They do have some interesting friends. Just the other day, Balatov told me the Good Knee already served in Norwegian prison for drug trafficking. He was caught fishing something fishy off the coast of Lofoten.

If society were drawn as a circle, the PC-preaching, re- and bicycling majority would be on top (all those people who never cross the street on a red light but start licking the TV screen each time Tony fucking Soprano appears on it). To the right we'd have the gun-loving old-timers who prefer beating their wives to sleeping with them, and on the left we'd have the anti-global guys, the bitter bunch who're against all the good things of this world, like meat, porn, and global warming. I would find myself at the bottom, where the extreme right meets the violent left. Where holy men and women sit next to murderers and art thieves.

It's here where the ring closes. In the kitchen for the needy. I can see how the two worlds meet in the sharp edge of Olie's knife.

It's my first "honest" job since my short stint as a waiter back in *bitte-schön* days, and I find it more than OK. Not having to think is a welcome relief; washing the brown plastic trays is my form of meditation. First I clean off most of the food (the needy of Iceland are clearly not so needy), and then I rinse them with water before placing them in the big old dishwasher, about which Sammy asks me every time he drops by, as if it were his aging mother. "How's she doing today?"

Olie sometimes drives me "home," speeding past the bus stop where *le Chien* waits along with the local loonies, and even his famous girlfriend once gave me a ride in her little white Polo. Harpa is an all-Icelandic butter-blonde with a fake tan and tribal tattoos up her sleeve, and she tells me her name means "harp." Actually, "lute" would better fit her long neck and big ass. Yet, she's kind of sexy. I'd probably start killing for her on Day 10 or 11.

It feels kind of cool to come back from work every day without having killed anybody. My warehouse sleep may not be perfect, but at least I've stopped adding new bodies to the inventory.

I'm usually back in the barracks by five or six, accompanied by the leftovers from the Samver lunch that I warm up in the prehistoric microwave and eat in the kitchen if Balatov's not around. I have to watch my budget, plus Olie's food is all right. Knowing that the chef's a convicted killer, a man who relishes cutting meat, adds an extra flavor to the meal. After I started working for a living, I realized that Iceland is the most expensive country in the world. It costs a fridge's worth to fill one. Half a kilo of cheese costs as much as half a kilo of weed. Many foreigners only eat expired food that the supermarkets leave at their back door every night, and Gun told me about a German tourist who suffered a mild heart attack after getting the check for a couple of cocktails in a trendy hotel downtown.

I always tell her that "the best country in the world" has to be like the best night club: it must be the most expensive one.

According to therapy rules, I'm not allowed out at night. Torture doesn't even allow me any books apart from the holy one, and absolutely no DVD-gazing nor Internet browsing. So, apart from the short ebony poems recited by Balatov ("I think Oprah in shower. Is good."), the Bible is my only form of entertainment. Reading was never my thing, though I did read two or three novels when Dikan had me touring the States, doing a hit in every town. Those long hotel days couldn't be spent on call girls only.

So I spend my long white nights with the big black book.

Of course there is the small TV out in the kitchen, but it's all Icelandic programming—some butter-blonde bimbos reading the small town news, followed by American dumbos eating live maggots—plus it's monopolized by Balatov who, rather than watching it, has started guarding the TV set as if it was a safe. He curses every single subtitle that appears on the screen, while scratching his armpits, the loudspeakers of smell. (If he is indeed

182

working for the Feds, his would be the best disguise in the history of the Bureau. Very far from the Michael Keaton hairdos.)

I really have to force myself through the fucking Old Testament. It's got some nice stories and everything, but most of it is just pro-Israel crap about tribal feuds and boundary conflicts. How this-and-that Mr. Pushy pushed this-and-that Palestine or Philistine off his land. Pretty similar to what we have on the TV news today. Those guys are still stuck in the Old Testament; they should at least check out the new one. Jesus is OK, though I have a pretty hard time with the concept of handing over your sins and letting him deal with them. I find it kind of cheap. Plus he must be really busy. It's like taking your trash to church and leaving it there, by the altar. Or maybe that's the idea behind it all. The church as a recycling container. In a way, it's not unlike the system we have at the Zagreb Samovar. There is this guy, Tomislav, called The Cleaner, who, every time needed, comes in to clean up our sins.

I think God made a huge mistake in showing his face, his hand, or whatever it was that Moses saw on that mountaintop. He was just writing a check of trouble for the whole fucking region. Ten thousand years of trouble.

It reminds me of that play I once saw at the HNK in Split. Senka was a big theatre fan and made me sit through all kinds of crazy things. One of them was this play from Poland where the author was sitting on stage during the performance, all the time shouting his commandments at the actors. I guess it was the first time I considered killing someone.

You can't fucking change your play after the curtain rises. And that goes for God as well.

I never thought reading the Bible would make you angry. But maybe it's meant to. At least when you think of Torture. God is like alcohol, I guess. The deeper you dive into it, the more you wonder if it was such a good idea in the first place. The more religious your country is, the more likely it is to see war. At least God never showed his face in Iceland. Olie tells me it wasn't even created by him. No wonder it's the most peaceful country in the world.

"I thought you guys were all born-agains?" I ask him the day after.

"Well, God is Sammy's friend. He's helped him a lot. He even bailed him out of prison and lent him some money to start this company and everything," he says with a grin, while emerging from the fridge with a leg of lamb. "But as for me, I don't know. After I killed this guy, for me it's all just…" He pauses while he searches for the right word, then shakes his head and places the leg on the worktop. "…meat."

"Meat?"

"Yeah. I love life and all that, but it's all just meat to me."

"OK."

"Life is very simple. It's just either dead meat or moving meat."

He picks up his knife. His favorite kitchen knife. He's talking to it now. I'm just a bystander. It's all between man and knife. Chien is out by the sink, washing the frying pans. Olie's voice turns low, the small golden earring shivering against his cold looking cheek.

"When I sliced this guy's throat, it was…it was like seeing God, or something. I saw…I saw how life is. And it's just…"

He looks up now. He looks at me.

"You know, we made love while he was still on the floor. It was crazy really, but it was like God."

I guess I picked the wrong weapon.

CHAPTER 27
LAVA OF LOVE
06.25.2006

I try to keep my life simple. After my clumsy sidestep at the strip club, I'm back on track. The power priest calls me every other day, checking up on me, giving me more reading tips, and inviting me to their great all-the-meat-you-can-eat Sunday lunch along with Goodmoondoor and Sickreader. They're all so proud of me, they can't take their eyes off of me, looking at me like the farmer at his most promising stud. I'm their guinea pig, the black rat turned white. Torture and Hanna's kids, a silent girl and two younger boys with big eyes, look at me like the David Beckham of the worshipping world.

I try to smile like the born-again blockhead I am. I'm even shaved close and sporting a short haircut done by Hanna. If I were wearing a tie and holding a Bible, nobody would open their door to me.

"It's so wonderful to know that you're working and have a place of your own and everything," Sickreader says, already sounding like my mother-in-law.

I should invite her over to give me decorating tips.

"Yes. He will be OK. He is a good man," Hanna says.

I put on the new-me smile. The others look at her in a silent surprise. She probably crossed their line with this one. She quickly adds, turning to me:

"I mean, you were just unlucky. If you were born here in Iceland, you would never have seen war and…you are a new man now. We will just hope that the Americans will not find you."

They all mumble their yeses and I assure them:

"I think, with my Icelandic passport, I'll be OK."

Again a round of nods.

"Yes, Father Friendly did not die in vain," Torture then proclaims, putting his heavy hand on my shoulder.

The phrase is too difficult for Goodmoondoor to understand. His friend has to explain the words "in vain." The simple one lights up:

"Yes, he died for Tommy's sins!"

There you have it. Mr. Christ got the day off and Mr. Friendly stepped into his shoes.

You just have to love this religion. First you shoot 125 people, and once your conscience starts getting bad (around #124), all you have to do is to find someone holy enough to carry your sins. Then you just shoot him and, *bang!*—he's off with them to heaven. You never have to see or think about them again.

I'm slowly getting used to my new name. Gun still uses Tod though. She calls a lot. I answer half the time. Wedding is inevitable, I guess, but for the time being I try to keep her at bay. I'm not ready yet. I need to get Munita out of my system, or out of my fridge at least (I sometimes see her head there, between the local milk cartoons and the Polish salami monster). I'm also not sure how well her parents will take it. Saving my life is one thing, but giving me their daughter is another altogether. Most of all, though, I need to finish this fucking therapy.

The ice-girl regularly invites herself for a visit, but I assure her that no woman has ever set foot on this floor, and the sight of a homegrown beauty would undoubtedly set off a riot in the barracks. The Jaroslaws would all burst into my room and get busy with Gun, asking me to hold the camera.

But trying to hold back love is like trying to hold back lava. Running lava that is. One day, when coming back from work, I find the Daybreak Girl sitting out in the kitchen with the Bulgarian mountain of fun. I wonder what they're talking about. He must be asking her whether any one of her forty lovers was black. I'm surprised that she hasn't been raped yet. She must be too white for him.

"I told you, you shouldn't come here. You're like a lamb in a lion's den here," I whisper to her as we walk back to my cell.

"Well, you didn't want to come and see me, so I had to come and see you," she says with an ice-cold, gum-chewing smile. She looks casually sexual or sexually casual, depending on which one is better English.

"That guy is dangerous. He's so lonely he's like a black hole. He could swallow you up in an instant. What were you talking about?"

"Nothing really. He was just telling me about his family farm. That his mother makes her own jams, and that he used to pick the berries himself or whatever."

So he's a berry-picker as well. The greatest disguise is still getting better. We enter my space and there is no more talking for the next forty minutes. For this procedure I have to bring the futon down from its rocky base. We also try to keep our body-sounds down, since, as mentioned before, the walls of my room do not travel all the way up to the ceiling. (The cell sometimes reminds me of a big toilet stall.) I don't want to risk ending up in the sexual department of Balatov's brain, being stored away on a shelf, like a jam in a jar, right next to him and Patti LaBelle in the back of her limo.

Then we lie together on the thick mattress, me and my warm Gun, and watch the neon lights and listen to the cars move about on the parking lot below. It's closing time. The Day 3 Girls in the fancy tile shop and the Indian furniture heaven across the lot are off for the day, shooting car locks with their small key-guns or being picked up by their impatient boyfriends driving black BMWs.

"How do you say Iceland in Icelandic?"

"*Ísland.*"

"Wow. Sounds like Easeland."

"Yeah. You got it right."

"But it doesn't seem right. You Easelanders never seem to be at ease."

"You can say that," says Gunnhildur. "We're very impatient people. For example, we don't know how to wait in line. We always wait in a triangle."

"Why?"

"I think it's because we're so few. We don't know how to wait because we never have to."

"But I don't get it why you're so impatient? I've never been to a more relaxing and quiet country."

"It's also because we're so few. Everybody's trying to act as if they were three different persons. We're trying our best to make Reykjavik look like New York."

"Well…you need to work a bit harder then."

"I'm doing my best. In the morning I'm a waitress, in the afternoon I'm in the office, and in the evenings I'm studying massage."

"You are? Massage?"

"Yeah. I just started last week."

I'm on the brink of proposing. We talk about massage for a while. She explains to me the difference between the Swedish and Shiatsu techniques, and I explain to her the difference between regular and full-body massage. Then we lay silent for a bit, until I say:

"Yes, I don't think I'd like to be a hitman in Iceland."

"Why not?"

"Because you're so few. I don't think I could bring myself to shoot."

She laughs her husky tobacco laughter that evolves into a series of small coughs. They call for a cigarette.

"But how come you're so few? I mean, you never had any wars."

"No, but some say that the weather is our war. Ice can be just as deadly as fire."

The small size of the Icelandic nation is explained by the past, she says, while she fills my room with Gunsmoke. Volcanic eruptions, plagues, and freezing cold winters almost managed to rid the land of its people. The Easelanders didn't really start flourishing until they got hold of electricity and central heating. In the last fifty years they've increased their numbers by 150,000. That's about as many as got killed in our war. We could have solved the thing by sending them all to Iceland, a land that could easily carry a population of ten or twenty million people. But they would never have allowed them all inside the country, Gunnhildur says.

The hitman bows to his fellow men, who would rather see people die than allow them to camp on their lawns.

We talk about the war and Gun continues her cigarette. She asks me about by brother Dario.

"How old was he when he died?"

"He was three years older than me. Twenty-three."

"Wow. What was he like? Was he like you?"

"No. He was our hero. The favorite son. He was much more fit, looked like a Greek god, was in sports and...He was on the national team in pole vault."

"What's that?"

"It's jumping on a stick. You know Sergei Bubka?"

"No."

"You don't? The greatest athlete of all time. Ukrainian guy. He won the gold in Seoul. Dario trained with him for a while. He was his big hero. And it was kind of strange, really, for the same night that Dario was killed, Bubka set a world record. His twelfth or something world record. Six-point-oh-eight meters. In some Russian town. It was like my brother's soul was helping him out, lifting him up a few more inches. Soul vaulting."

Fuck. I'm getting too sentimental for this frosty girl.

"Wow. That's amazing. Did your brother ever go to the Olympics?"

"No. But he would have gone to Atlanta in ninety-six, if..."

I open my eyes as much as I can. Hanging them out to dry, hoping she doesn't notice. No. She only watches the smoke rise from her übermouth.

"Wow. So he was like, a star?"

"Well, maybe not. Pole vaulting is not that big in Croatia. He was like a shooting star or something."

I always sound like a lame old lady when I speak of my dead brother. Therefore I never do.

"So it must have been hard for you, to..."

"Actually, it was kind of strange. The death of my brother numbed the fact that I killed my father. Our father."

"Why? How?"

"It's like when you accidentally set fire to your house, it's a bit soothing, or it kind of makes it less bad, to see your neighbor's house go up in flames as well."

"But your own brother is more important to you than your neighbor's ugly house?"

"Of course. Or you can say that the thing with my father blocked me from the blow that the death of my brother would have been to me. You can't have two MHMs in your life."

"MHM?"

"Most Horrible Moment."

"Aha. So the murder of your girlfriend and your road accident was not as horrible?"

"No. But when you rejected me because you thought I was a priest...that was pretty horrible."

She smiles, before saying:

"But then I found out that you were a serial killer and fell in love with you."

She laughs. I keep the word "love" between my ears, letting my brain fondle it like a newborn puppy.

"You're sick," I say.

"Yes. Lovesick," she says and then puts out her cigarette in the half empty Gatorade bottle standing on the floor beside the futon and grabs my face. I smile my broken smile. She puts her index finger up to my mouth and replaces the missing tooth with its tip.

Eye for an eye, finger for a tooth. She holds it there for a while, smiling, before removing it for a kiss.

She kisses me like an island girl who finds an ugly ship-wrecker on the shore. He's all bruised and battered, trout-red in the face from a salty sunburn, stiff like a huge piece of meat, and can barely move his tongue. She helps him out.

Between my ears, John Lennon screams out an old Beatles' number. The one about the warm gun.

CHAPTER 28
BED OF ROSES, BED OF MOSS

06.25.2006 — 08.05.2006

According to local wisdom, the Icelandic summer only lasts six weeks. From the last weekend in June till the first one in August. It is also said that this is the time it takes to fall in love. The only problem is that during this period the ice country is lighted up like Madison Square Garden at a Knicks game, 24-7. There are no shadows, no dark corners. It's pretty impossible to hide things, like a car or a kiss.

We decided that Gun better not come to the hotel again. We wanted to keep her parents out of it until we had set the date. The Seven Elevens are not the problem, but Balatov may be, and Good Knee definitely is. But my genius girl finds a way. She realizes that one of her girlfriends actually works at Mahabharata, the Indian furniture shop across the parking lot. All I have to do is to sneak out around midnight and take a stroll around our deserted neighborhood, saying hi to the team of seagulls responsible for keeping it clean, before ending up at the back door of the Indian store, where Gun waits in her little red Fabia, fresh from massage class or a night out with the Tarantino Fan Club. She's got the key as well as the security code she types into the thing on the wall next to the entrance. We make our way through the office and out into the store. In back there are three king size beds on display, all made in India by twelve-year-old carpenter whiz-kids. We've tried them all, but the one behind the Kama Sutra room divider is the safest. It can't be seen from the screaming bright window out front. So after all, we manage to find a semi-dark corner in the bright and shining land. And by making the Hindu handiwork squeak, I can honor the memory of my lost love. Still the bed holds up to all our freaky gymnastics. Those Indian kids really know their craft.

Our nights in the Mahabharata must count as one of the best products of globalization. The Croat celebrates his Indian summer in Iceland with French champagne, Japanese sushi, and muscle-relaxing Thai music. (Gun brings this all, the music bit from her class.) Condoms come from Manchester, England, and cigarettes from Richmond, Virginia, the hometown of our Friendly Father. No, she doesn't smoke inside the shop. And we have to be careful not to leave any stains or bras behind.

Bit by bit Gun manages to move the rest of Munita's stuff (head included) out of my brain and redecorates it with her own. Indian rugs and lamps. And bit by bit the summer of sex becomes the summer of something else. The secrecy adds a deeper dimension to it, and I try everything I can to make her ice melt, while her newly-learned carnal tricks easily turn my blood into running lava. I could die happy and be buried in Icelandic soil with a tombstone marked: *Tommy Olafs, dishwasher (1971–2007)*. At the end of each session, Gun sprays the bed with some Indian aroma she found in the office. By the end of the month it smells like the best little whorehouse in Bombay.

"It's OK, really," she says. "Nobody buys beds during the summer."

"Why not?"

"They're too busy using the old one."

Apparently Icelanders are a different people during the bright season. They stop doing things they use to do in wintertime, like watching TV, dressing up, and bathing. Until recently TV was even shut down in July. Summer is so short that people really need to focus on it. If the temperature reaches fifteen degrees Celsius (happens three times a year), all the shops and banks close two minutes later, so the employees can go outside and enjoy the heat wave. It's called "sun-break," Gun explains. You have to feel for these people. Those six weeks wouldn't qualify as summer any-where else. "The Land of the Ten Degrees" is no joke; the aver-age temperature in July is exactly that. Icelandic summer is like a fridge that you leave open for six weeks. The light is on and all ice thaws away, but it can never get really warm. After all, it's only a fridge.

But one Saturday night in early August, all the beds vanish from the store. Gun calls her friend. They're getting ready for autumn, she explains. The Sweet Karma line, from the elemen-tary factory in Bombay, is bound to arrive any day now. We break the rules of Torture, and she takes me for a ride outside the city.

It's a beautiful night, with fancy clouds out west participating in the golden sunset across the bay, and all the winds have gone abroad for the weekend. We drive east and I get that fresh-out-of-prison feeling. Finally I get to see something other than Balatov and bus line 24, Olie's mole, and Indian furniture. The road takes us past the former home of a famous dead writer. Apparently this is the only house in Iceland that comes with a swimming pool. It was part of his Nobel Prize, Gun explains, though he had to provide the water himself. It's a museum now. You can see the water he swam in, hoping to eye his strokes of genius, I guess. She's taking me to the most famous place in the land, Thing Valley, the site of the world's first outdoor parliament. Actually, I don't think there have been any others.

But midway through, we realize that our Czech-made car is pretty low on gas. We decide to stop and go for a little picnic instead. We take a short walk in the lunar park and sit down on a bed of stiff gray moss. Unfortunately there are no trees and no Indian room dividers to shelter a hot game of lovemaking from the small but steady traffic, plus the temperature is more fitting for a game of ice hockey. We settle for a kiss and a sip of Kaldi beer, admiring our small red car parked on the roadside, framed by a deep blue mountain under a lone pink cloud. Above it, the sky is almost white. Some long-beaked bird flies-walks-and-flies around us, at a distance he considers safe (well within gun-reach, though), screaming his lungs out. Apparently we're in his backyard. The conversation turns a bit serious, as it should, I guess, when most of the fucking has been done.

"So, you think you can live in Iceland?" she asks me.

"Well, I guess I have to."

Silence, punctuated with bird screams.

"So, that's the only reason?"

"No. I don't know."

She looks at me. Her Gatorade eyes are two blue-green hot springs in the rocky field that surrounds us, just like the ones I saw in the photos of the in-flight magazine on my way up here. She's still looking at me. Does she really want to waste her life on Toxic waste?

"You want me to?" I finally continue.

"I don't know. I'm just asking."

She brings out a cigarette. It falls from her shaky hands. She picks it up and places it between her stern lips. Lights it.

"I mean, I guess I have to. For the time being," I say.

"For the time being?"

Her words come with a lot of smoke. Actually, the smell is kind of nice, out here in the crisp cold air.

"Yeah, I mean…"

"You like it?"

"Iceland? Yeah, sure. I mean, how can you not like this?" I ask, gesturing at the scenery fit for any lunar love story.

"But you wouldn't want to live here?"

"You mean, for good?"

She nods. My apartment on Wooster and Spring appears in a flash, my flat screen full of Hajduk games, the barbecue restaurant down the street, and my beautiful black Heckler & Koch that I keep under the loose tile in the corner of my bathroom. I wring my right hand with the left, while murmuring:

"I don't know. I haven't really thought about that."

She takes to her feet, leaving the half empty beer bottle lying in the moss, and heads for the car.

"Hey!" I say.

I catch her climbing the roadside, with two beers in my hand. The bird takes to his wings and hurries across a small pond on the other side of the road. He seems to have rented the whole fucking area.

"Hey, Gun. What's the matter?"

Her eyes are wet when she turns around. We're standing in the roadside, beside the car.

"You haven't thought about that?" she asks.

"No, I mean, you have to think of my situation. I only take one day at a time."

"What about MY SITUATION?" she says in a rather harsh way and then takes a quick draw from her half-burned cigarette, with shaking lips.

I have nothing to say. I didn't know this girl could cry. The bird is back, screaming at us. At me.

"I'm sorry, Gun…Gunnhildur."

"What do you think this is?"

"You and me? It's been the hottest summer of my life."

My shoulders shake from the cold.

"Really?"

"Yes. The best summer I've…"

"What's the matter then? You're still not sure?"

"I mean, Gun. You're a nice girl and I'm a…"

"You're a great guy."

I am?

"You're a fucking great guy. And now you're telling me that…"

She can't finish. Only her cigarette. That she throws away before walking over to the driver's side of the car.

"So you want to…?" I try to say.

"YES!" she screams, opens the car, gets inside, and slams the door.

I'm left standing alone between the car and Iceland, holding two half empty beer bottles. She seems to be serious about us.

Am I?

A brand new looking SUV approaches from the east. It slows down as it passes by. I'm faced with a Talian looking couple in their fifties. Some gray haired lovers with a heavy tan, wearing dark blue windbreakers over yellow polo shirts. Dead happy bastards. They're smiling so hard that you have to suspect that the site of the world's first outdoor parliament must be hosting an outdoors senior group sex festival this weekend. The woman in the passenger's seat even has her arm around her partner who, come to think of it, looks a bit like a retired hitman.

CHAPTER 29

THE KAUNAS
CONNECTION

08.06.2006

We drive back in silence. Even the radio is quiet. I gaze out the window thinking about my two NY bags that now have been circling the baggage carousel in Zagreb for eighty days in a row. The midnight sunset is mostly over, but a few clouds maintain their red glow out on the horizon, hovering like a flock of zeppelins over the glacier that tips the peninsula called Snow Fall's Ness or something similar to that. Closer, the city of Reykjavik spreads in front of us like a desperate lady begging me to love her. It kind of reminds you of LA at night: flat, vast, and full of lights. The tower of the impossibly named church that stands on the hill in the middle of town is the only thing that rises above the horizon, a dark dildo against the pink sky.

Gun drives into my dead neighborhood of furniture stores and fugee camps and stops the car at an empty traffic circle close to my cell. I tell her I'll call her. She answers by making her lips disappear inside her mouth. It makes her look a bit like her mother.

It's about three in the morning when I check into the hotel. The Seven Elevens are fast asleep, as well as their dirty steel-toed shoes at the top of the staircase. From the end of the hallway, I hear the low murmur of TV. Balatov's out in the kitchen, sitting at the table, wearing only his dingy underpants and still-white undershirt, plus a pair of black socks. He's as hairy as a gorilla. It's even hard to see were his socks come to an end and leg hair takes over. He'd need a truckload of "saving cream" for a full body shave. On the screen some stupid actor pretends to be a gunman, holding his weapon like an amateur, looking very much like the pope with a plunger.

"Fuck white night. I want black," murmurs the voice between the two hairy shoulders.

For the first time since meeting him, I almost don't dislike him. I grab a beer from the fridge and join him at the kitchen table. I need a friend.

"What about the Icelandic girls? You don't like them?" I ask him.

"No Iceland girl in Granny Club."

New friend has limitation.

We watch for a while. It's one of those "Everybody freeze!" films. I guess every second movie made on this planet has someone like me for a main character, or the main character spends the whole fucking movie going after a guy like me, and always succeeds just before the credits start rising like spirits from the bad guy's grave. The Mafia hitman is one of the most popular heroes of our time. Then why can't I live like the actor who plays me, in a Hollywood mansion with a Nobel prize-swimming pool and palm trees all around it? A handful of servants arguing in

Spanish out in the kitchen and a bunch of small time celebrities with big time boobs wailing outside my front door, hungry for sex. Fuck it. I should have all that instead of idling up here in the arctic nowhere, a born-again dishwasher with an ugly name and a jumpy girlfriend, sipping on stolen Polish beer and discussing philosophy with the grandson of King Kong.

"What do you think of movies about the Mafia written by some wimps high on soy lattes. Some unshaven campus kids who've never even seen a gun in their lives?"

"What is?"

"Aw, nothing."

We go back to the movie and Balatov does a round of Bulgarian swearing. Our part of the world is the true home of colorful language. Croatia holds the world record in men's cursing. I'm only a word away from coming back at him with: "You look like you just fucked a porcupine!" Or: "I just fucked your dead mother's rotten body in the hole where her left tit used to be!"

"You girl is good," the bastard then suddenly says.

"My girl?"

"I see you and girl in shop," he says with the slimiest smile and a very hairy thumbs-up. "Is good."

"You mean…?"

"I see you make sex in shop. Is daughter priest, yes?"

There you have it. He's been spying on me. So he's working for the Fucking Bureau of Impotents after all.

"So why don't you call them? Why don't you just arrest me then?"

"What is?"

No. After a quick interrogation I have to conclude that he's not an agent undercover. He's too genuinely stupid. But then what is he doing up here? Why the hell is he staying in this horrible country of sunny nights and Sanskrit subtitles if he hates it so much?

"I work in housing build. I no pay. I wait money."

Of course it's quite possible that this man is a genius acting stupid and that he is really undercover. But then the cover would be so thick that he would never be able to get any information through.

The next day we're woken up by the usual Polish Sunday morning prayer. Some altar wine and a sermon on modern day slavery in Western society. But the drunken brawl is soon overshadowed by an uproar in the Lithuanian camp. Some hefty arguing goes on at their end of the floor, for a good hour, until one of them rushes out, slamming doors behind him. Somehow the Lits all have the same look: flat dark hair and a pale face full of birthmarks.

Outside my cell, Balatov informs me that we have a dead man on our floor. The small guy who only joined our little society last week passed away. After flying up here with a kilo of cocaine in his stomach, he came down with constipation. He's been lying in the cell down the hallway for five days now, the blackbeard says. He couldn't shit, not for his life.

"I see him. Belly was balloon."

Balatov offered his help, he says, but they didn't accept it. For some reason, he seems to think quite highly of himself when it comes to the inner workings of the human body.

Somehow the Poles have heard the sad news and come flying out of the kitchen like drunken crows. They want to call their beloved master, the Good Knee, at once. Some even want the White Hats. But the Lits won't have any of it. It's a pretty funny scene, actually. A shouting match in English between Poland and Lithuania.

"No call police!"

"No! Call! Please!" The argument swiftly ends when one of the Lit guys brings out a gun. It's a small German model, similar to the one the Hanover Polizei uses. The Poles look dumbfounded then immediately shut their mouths and return to their bottles of Wyborowa. Balatov plays the wise old man, telling the gunman to cool it.

Seeing the gun makes me all warm inside. It's like seeing an old friend. I stand for a while, dizzy from gunsickness, watching him walk down the hall, before retreating to my cell.

It's a long Sunday. I lay in bed, with the Bible open to "The Raising of Lazarus," while my heart plays the theme from *The Twilight Zone*. I try to call Gun three times. She doesn't answer. I could try to sneak out of the barracks and crawl back into Torture's basement, but I guess it's better to stay cool. I guess I should be more afraid of my Lithuanian colleagues than the White Hats. I reach for Tommy's overcoat, search out his Icelandic passport, and put it in the pocket of my pants. Just in case.

Every half an hour I hear the dead man's friends rush up and down the hallway, up and down the stairs, talking loudly on the phone in their even-weirder-than-Icelandic language. Actually, I didn't know Nokia phones supported Lithuanian. I go to the bathroom and see one of the pale ones disappear inside the dead man's room. Out in the kitchen, the vodka party has settled for a game in the Icelandic premier league. From a distance you might think it was women playing. Icelandic soccer is pretty close to regular soccer except the players are all on heavy tranquilizers. The minute they run onto a football field, those fast-forward Icelanders switch to slow motion. It would take kilos of cocaine to fix these games.

When the zero-everything match is over, we're all in the mood for pizza. Tommy is kindly asked to show off his Icelandic by ordering five pepperonis and six liters of Coke. I manage to say *"Gouda dying"* (good day) before leaving the kitchen and do the rest in low-pitch English down the hall. Forty minutes later the delivery boy arrives. He turns out to be a Serbo-Croat and does a round of *dobro veče* for the laughing Poles. Then, for a brief moment he turns his Serbian eye on me and puts on a quirky smile, as if he spotted the national emblem tattooed on my soul.

The pizza party brings us all together, and this is probably the best hour of my lager life. Even Balatov is smiling, showing off his yellowed teeth. But in the middle of our happy meal, one of the pale skins comes asking for a word with the Bulgarian. We watch in silence as he wipes his mouth with the bushy back of his hand, gets up, and follows the Lithuanian down the corridor. Some minutes later he returns to the kitchen and holds up his hand like a routine surgeon talking to his nurses:

"Knife."

I lend him mine, and the smell of pizza is soon replaced by the most gut-clearing smell ever to hit my nose. And that's coming from a man who once had to open a three-week-old mass grave in ADV because Javor had lost his glasses and ordered me to find him some new ones.

It sounds crazy, but the black-loving Bulgarian tells us he has a doctor's "B-gree" from some university in Sofia. I guess a B-gree in medicine allows you to operate on dead people only. We watch him walk down the hall, knife in hand, his legs like two parentheses, looking more like a killer than a physician. But apparently he knows his craft. He performs the autopsy with great skill: The goldmining procedure is a success. The Lits stop mourning their friend the moment Dr. Balatov hands them the slimy condoms full of white gold. His own cut is a hundred grams. Not being a fan of white, he immediately offers to sell me some, but I have to say no.

I guess it's all part of my therapy. Torture is still testing me, or else he would have set me up in his mother's basement full of mobiles and cuckoo clocks instead of in this loft space charged with strip-trips and fresh-from-inside-the-dealer drugs.

After dinner the Poles go back to drinking. As soon as the vodka starts working, they begin singing slow funeral songs from the Karpaty Mountains or whatever. I hold my breath and make my way to the Lithuanian corner to retrieve my Swiss army knife. The smell is overwhelming, but I manage to knock on the dead man's door. It's quickly opened, but barely so. The gap is only wide enough for the word "knife" to cut through. Still, I manage to see that the room is full of some exciting items while waiting for my instrument. It comes with a warning. Two Litheads emerge from the cell to assure me that the Kaunas version of a certain organization will do me in if I ever tell anyone about the bloody mess. I count the birthmarks in their faces (as many as the capitals on the map of Europe) while I restrain from asking who their hitman is, how many he's done, how he would kill me, the details that matter.

At midnight, the smell still fills the floor like an invisible fog. I hear some heavy breathing out in the hallway, accompanied by the sound of a heavy suitcase being dragged across a sandy floor and bumping down the stairs. I look out the giant window to see my Baltic colleagues put it in the back of a rundown white van and drive away.

This is my cue.

I patiently wait until the house doctor is in the bathroom and all the Seven Elevens are in bed. With my heart on techno, I dive down the hallway, accompanied by the longest log from my bed stand. I place it upside down beside the dead man's door, step on top of it, and climb the wall. It goes smoothly, though I get tangled up in a brightly colored basketball banner on the way down. The stall is filled with plastic bags and cardboard boxes full of Apples. Five virgin flat screens are stored away in a corner. I search all the right places, and wrapped inside a yellow plastic bag from Bónus, the food store, I find a small German army pistol, a Walther P99, similar to the one I saw earlier today. Fair enough. I feel like a free man at last, holding a gun in my hand. I'm fucking Toxic again. It's even loaded. The magazine holds twelve bullets. I'm ready for two six-packs.

I must be beside myself with joy, for I don't even fucking notice that there is a police car in the parking lot. The White Hats are already inside the building. I can hear them coming down the hallway, heading my way.

CHAPTER 30
SCHMAU-WAYISH
08.07.2006 – 08.08.2006

I'm Catman. I'm crouching on top of the wall between the dead man's cell and the next one, holding on to the thick overhead ceiling beam touching the back of my head. I have a fly's view of the whole floor. Some six stalls on this side and another six on the other. A narrow hallway between. In the far end, the kitchen.

I can hear the officers talking down the corridor. They speak in Icelandic between themselves and in English to one of the Poles, who sounds both drunk and as if he just woke up.

"Are you Polish?"

"No, you police!"

There are two cells between the wall I'm crouching on top of and my space. The closer one is empty. I wonder about the other. My heart skips from trash metal to speed metal when I hear the policemen try to open the door to the closest cell. But after shaking the handle for a second, I hear the Polish guy murmur no, no, and soon they're at the dead man's door. I just hope my saw log will keep quiet.

I wait until they start hammering loudly on the door and working on it with a crowbar. Then I gently slide myself down the wall, Catman style, and onto the windowsill in the cell next to the one I just robbed. The white police car outside is empty. No hat to be seen, though the night is still bright enough for reading. The police continue their carpentry and I climb the next wall, carefully peeking into the cell behind it. It belongs to one of the Poles, probably the squealer, because the bed is empty and the door is open.

I turn down the music in my heart before gliding down from wall to windowsill and then move across it, soundless, with my eyes on the open door. Nobody sees me, and then I'm in my room. Speed metal gives way to power ballad. It almost has me singing "With Arms Wide Open." My favorite Creed song.

I spend the next fifteen minutes thinking where to hide the gun—THE GUN!—but I still haven't made up my mind when the White Hats knock on my door. There are two of them standing out in the hallway, two round pebble-nosed snowballs in uniform, and suddenly I'm dead convinced that they're the same guys who had a small chat with Tadeusz, the Polish housepainter, that fateful night last May. Some of Tadeusz's vodka-weary countrymen are standing behind the two policemen, and one of them explains to them that I'm a local.

"You are Icelandic?" the police asks me in Icelandic.

"*Schmau-wayish,*" I answer with a lot of nods and a smile.

This means "a tiny bit," a magical word Gun taught me this summer that turns out to be a real ass-saver here. I then bring out my mountain-blue passport, and my heart plays the drum 'n' base version of the Icelandic national anthem while they ponder the impeccable craftsmanship. They read my name aloud, examining my Slavic face, with a stern look.

"Tómas Leifur Ólafsson?" they say.

"*Jau. Tommy!*" I hit back with an acting-stupid smile and tell my right hand to stay the hell out of my right pocket.

"Where do you work?" they ask me in their cold language.

I switch to English (explaining that my father was half American and all that shit), and tell them about Samver. Their faces instantly light up.

"Do you know Sammy?"

The Good Samaritan's name works like a hair dryer on the frosty situation, and we talk for a while about the small man with the dancing glasses. The two policemen know him from work. One of the most fun guys to arrest, they assure me. Then they get serious again and ask me whether I've any connections with the Kaunas guys. I tell them no.

"Did you notice something spacious in the house today or tonight?"

"Suspicious, you mean?"

I've got the upper hand now. I can relax.

"Yes," they say.

Without thinking or blinking, I decide to be a good sport, forgetting all about the Lithuanian threats. Must be the gun. Or a belated show of gratitude towards the White Hats for giving me the summer of my life.

"Yes. I saw them take the dead man's body outside, just some twenty minutes ago. I saw it from my window," I say, inviting them inside my cell. "They had it in a big suitcase. It looked quite heavy. They put it in the back of a white van and drove away."

"Did you see the number of it?"

"The license number? Yes. It was SV seven-four-one."

I'm not kidding. I remember the fucking license number. The two officers look at me as if they want to invite me on a Caribbean cruise. First class. Next summer. Just the three of us. They then come to their senses.

"And where was the car?"

"Just…right here below. Outside the entrance."

We're by the window and one of them leans over to my side to have a better look outside. In doing so, he accidentally touches the hard little thing in my pocket with his left hip. The policeman automatically turns his face towards me and says in the most polite way:

"*Afsaky.*"

This is Icelandic for: "Sorry, I didn't mean to touch your gun."

The day after, when I come home from work, I see three white police SUVs parked outside our beloved hotel. Some yellow police tape rattles in the freezing summer breeze, and a White Hat guards the entrance. I keep walking past the building, at a good distance, once again taking on the role of the odd stroller on the empty sidewalks of Iceland.

An hour later I ring Gunnhildur's bell. She opens the door and soon we're up in her messy kitchen, kissing like a pair of desperate lovers. I completely forget myself and hug her too hard: she feels the hard thing in my pants.

"What's that?"

"German steel."

CHAPTER 31
ICE-ROCK
08.08.2006 – 09.08.2006

Torture talks, Tomo walks.

The great man takes me back to Hardwork Hotel to pick up my things and has a word with the police, using his powers of persuasion and invaluable TV fame to explain my case. Tommy Olafs is his protégé, a real sensitive guy who only wanted to get to know the country of his origin and can't bear living with cruel and reckless criminals. I say goodbye to my Polish friends, and to my surprise I lean into Balatov's cheek for a quick hug. Exile is a hairy sea.

I spend the night in my Old Testament room in Torture and Hanna's house. At work the day after, I have a crucial talk with Olie, and in the evening he greets me and Torture, at his doorstep, on the third floor of an old concrete building close to Gun's house. Harpa is out for the night shift at her solarium, and me and Olie act out a little scripted scene for our beloved Torture: pretending that I'm renting a room at his place. Apparently Bible Man knows Meat Man, through Sammy, and they chat about the underestimated role of violence in teaching the Gospel while I examine

Olie's great collection of kitchen knives that he has hanging over his fancy gas stove. Despite being aware of the chef's violent past, Torture has perfect faith in him as my landlord.

"As long as you pay the rent, he won't kill you," he said in the car, with a hearty laugh.

Some minutes after the preacher has left in his holy SUV, I'm over at Gun's place, asking her where to put my things. She looks stressed, taking the cigarette into her bedroom (something she normally doesn't do) and points at two empty shelves in her large wardrobe with a shaky finger.

"Something's wrong?" I ask.

"No. Why?"

"You maybe think we're not ready to start living together?"

"No, no. It's just…"

"I thought you wanted this. Is it Truster?"

A heavy sigh, then: "Yes."

"You're afraid he'll tell your parents about us?"

"No, it's not that. I don't mind."

It's not that. It's something else. But what it is, she won't say. I offer to sleep upstairs, in the attic, but she says no, and soon we're in her bed, trying to cheer ourselves up with some cheerless sex. Afterward, she picks up her cell and has a long and visibly difficult talk with her brother, who doesn't seem to fancy living with a hitman. Shortly before midnight he shows up, pale and gloomy. Without even saying "hi," he retreats into his small room out by the entrance and plays loud ice rock until two o'clock in the morning. Gunnhildur is shaken and smokes a whole packet before brushing her teeth for twenty long minutes.

We lie in her bed, cast in marble, locked in a silent embrace, like ancient lovers in a museum. This not my favorite really, to lie together like this, but I put my preferences on hold for the special occasion: my first night living together with a person I've had sex with, plus we're not getting any sleep anyway with the ice-rock blasting through the wall. I'm missing Balatov already. Thirty more minutes of musical torture and his name has acquired the distinction of a famous classical composer. Then the poor guy puts the same song on repeat for the next half an hour. The singer screams as if he were stuck at the bottom of a glacial canyon, with a broken thigh.

"What's he singing?"

"*Sódóma,*" she answers in a weak voice.

"What does that mean?"

"Just…you know…Sodom…"

"Like in Sodom and Gomorrah?"

"Yeah. I guess."

Bible-reading is paying off. And the priest's son across the wall knows how to get his message through. Gunnhildur clings to me like a dying mouse. Finally Truster has exhausted his sibling jealousy, and the two sodomites get their sleep.

Luckily the crane bird spends even less time around the house now than back in springtime days, when yours truly was a freshman fugitive and everything was a bit more exciting. I slowly adapt to the Icelandic every day. I spend the mornings on the Internet, googling my various names along with the "FBI," "David Friendly," or "Lithuanian Mafia" without much success, writing emails to people who could possibly know where my good old Senka might be found, or writing letters to my mother, which Gunnhildur's friend brings with her to London and posts at some royal post office. Noon has me standing at the main square again, waiting for bus 6 along with the local loonies. The month of August finishes with a more traditional timing of sunset. I welcome the dark.

Torture Therapy fades out in the form of a few check-up calls from the master, plus regular visits to the crazy masses at his sweaty church. At my first visit he welcomes me with bravado and introduces Tommy to his desperate we-take-the-bus crowd as "a good Icelander and a dear friend! A man who spent most of his life in Hotel Hell but has now checked out and rented a room in heaven, God bless his soul! Hallelujah!"

The congregation takes to its feet (in fact they hardly ever sit), and the hairy ladies throw their hands in the air, repeating Torture's hallelujah. It's like Harlem without the choreography. Before I know it, I'm hugging a skinny disabled man with a very cold cheek. *"Velkominn,"* he says, in a weak voice. Then the preacher switches back to Icelandic, and to my surprise I understand most of it.

"You should know your enemies! You should know that Sin is your worst enemy! And you should never invite Sin to your house! Never invite Sin over for dinner! YOU SHOULD NOT EVEN BUY SIN A CUP OF COFFEE!" he screams in his manly baritone, sounding more like a Hell's Angel than God's mouthpiece. "For Sin will ask for cream in its coffee. And Sin will ask for sugar. And Sin will ask for WHISKEY in the coffee. So before you know, Sin will be drinking IRISH COFFEE! And soon YOU will be drinking with her. You'll be drinking with Sin, singing with Sin, and dancing with Sin, to all her favorite songs! So let me tell you one more time: DON'T YOU EVER BUY SIN A CUP OF COFFEE! HALLELUJAH!"

I hear myself echo the last word, along with the crowd, while feeling the form of my old new gun with the sole of my right foot. The small piece fits just right in my size forty-six shoe. I bought myself a pair of sneakers, the ones with the thickest sole in the shop, and did a little surgery on the right one, removing enough of the layers in its sole to fit the PP9 right into it. So now I'm "walking on God's road" as Goodmoondoor says, with a gun in my shoe. It's pretty uncomfortable, but when the time comes, I will be prepared.

I don't think the Pearly Gates come with a metal detector anyway.

My warm Gun doesn't know about the cold one. This is not her problem; we have enough already. Don't get me wrong. Gunnhildur is great. The real problem is me. I haven't shared an apartment with anyone since good old Niko back in our Hanover days. Living with him gave me a bachelor's degree in tolerance, but Gunnhildur's endless smoking, and her habit of throwing jeans, sweaters, underpants, empty bottles, ashtrays, and pizza boxes around the house, finally get on my nerves. I may be a sociopath, but I like my place in order.

"I just don't fucking understand how you can be the daughter of your parents. I mean, their house is like the White House while yours is a complete Shit House."

"OK, so let's get some house help."

"We already talked about that. We can't afford it."

"We don't have to. You just kill her after she's finished her first cleaning. And then we hire another one, and you kill her as well. I mean, you're a fucking professional aren't you?"

This is how all our arguments end. My ex-job is always there, like some psycho ex-girlfriend. When you've killed more than a hundred people, you have no right to complain about a dirty floor or a messy room. That's just the way it is. She's almost made it into an art. Every time she finds herself in a corner, she bursts out with: "You're probably more used to dealing with dead people, aren't you?" or "You can't stand people who do boring things like *breathing* and *talking,* can you?" or simply "Why don't you just kill me?"

Apart from that things are OK.

We go to our jobs and then team up for dinner before I drag her with me to see the latest Spiderman movie, or I let her drag me to one of the countless concerts this small city has to offer. I must have quite a crush on her for I don't mind standing for two whole hours, nodding to worthless indie bands like Earplugs and The Sleeping Pills, while Creed plays inside my head to the fire-blooming invasion of Knin.

The only real downer is Truster, who doesn't seem to be even *searching* for a place to live. His silent presence can easily break your brand new self to pieces and allow the old one to shine through. For the first two weeks, he used no more than two fucking words. "Hi" and "bye." When I hand him his fucking dinner, a killer of a goulash that I held in my lap for some twenty minutes on a bus full of rainmen and rape victims, he doesn't even say a single *"takk."* Luckily he's at work most of the time. One of the Seven Elevens recently worked with Truster on a construction site. Apparently the silent bird is a star in the concrete world.

"Is genius with crane. From hundred meter can pick up small money, in very big wind."

Well, good for him. If he only could use his crane to pick up girls…

I manage to keep my demons at the door, but at night they come creeping through our bedroom window. Gunnhildur prefers to leave it open.

As soon as I fall asleep, the Serbian tanks come rolling in, with treads made of screaming heads—the bloodied and muddied heads of Croatian villagers, old men, women, and children. The Chetnik panzers break through my sleeping defense, speeding across the dark fields of my soul like worked-up rhinos, followed by a platoon of sixty-six American businessmen, armed with cell

217

phones and briefcases, who're being cheered on by an equal number of widows, yelling out all the way from the deep blue forests of New Jersey to the flat hot roofs of the Manitoban prairie, the whole of it backed by the blessing of a bald priest with a Southern accent dressed in a white karate outfit, sporting a black Bulgarian belt marked: YO BITCH!

They attack us from all sides. They've surrounded us: me, my dad, and Dario.

We work our fingers off on the machine guns, turning our small fort into a sprinkler of bullets, but to no avail. We're overwhelmed. Pretty soon we can hear the horrible shrieks of our own women and children, rolling with the caterpillar tread of the fast approaching tanks, through the super-loud gun sounds.

I suddenly sense that my father is wounded. He's been shot in the right shoulder. I look behind me and watch him turn slowly towards me. But I can't do anything about it, for I have to face the enemy, I have to continue shooting. But a second later I can feel his hands on my neck, around my neck. He's got his ten strong fingers around my neck. I feel he's about to strangle me when I wake up and see Truster's red face in the blue morning light that fills the bedroom.

Truster is trying to strangle me. The fucker. I grab his arms and try pushing him away, but he's strong as a rib-eyed bull. Gunnhildur wakes up and starts screaming his name. This weakens him enough so that I'm able to loosen his grip on my neck: soon we're fighting on the floor beside the bed, creating a whirlwind of magazines, earrings, condoms, and a lamp. It doesn't last for long though. The Croatian soldier and Manhattan hitman, worked up by the Word of God, easily defeats the son of a preacher man.

Only to find out that he is *not* the son of a preacher man. Truster is *not* Gunnhildur's brother. He is, or rather, he *was* her BOYFRIEND.

This is news to me.

For three whole months I've been under the impression that he was her brother, that he was Goodmoondoor and Sickreader's son. And, as a matter of fact, they told me so, right in the very beginning, when I was still playing Friendly and everything was complicated in a more uncomplicated way. They told me he was their son, but their accent made "son-in-law" sound like "son in love" to me. It appeared strange to me at the time, their boasting about their son's love life, but now I get it.

And now I can see that the ice-girl cheated on him with me. Up in the attic. I was their love-buster. Shortly after, they must have broken up, but the poor bastard didn't move out of her place, not even after I moved in! The Icelandic male must be one of the most uncomplaining animals on the planet. But of course his blood was boiling under the lid of silence. It had to come out, sooner or later.

And of course he had to move out sooner or later. He does so now.

CHAPTER 32
DETOXED
09.10.2006

"How could you NOT know he was my boyfriend? I mean, we were living together, sleeping in the same bed."

We're on our way to Silence Grove. The son-in-law-thing has to be settled. I have to face the saviors of my soul and tell them that on top of everything else I'm taking their daughter as well. But I guess her father won't mind. We're "living the last days" anyway.

As always, she does the driving. Tommy has a passport but no driver's license. We drive past the downtown domestic airport. Rain beats the windshield. Radio plays Shakira. "Hips Don't Lie." Me and Munita once saw her enter a fancy restaurant on Theatre Row at one of our many pre-foreplay dinners. We both had our eyes on her great Colombian butt, and once it was out of sight, Munita declared it too big. I didn't want to tell my Bonita that it looked pretty tight compared to her Aztec Temple, so I quickly added the third Latin treasure to the conversation: J-Lo's biggest asset, concluding that South America was big on behinds in every meaning of the word. It made her laugh all the way to my bed.

I need all my mental strength to lift the three great butts off my mind and register the fact I'm sitting next to my new blonde girlfriend in a car in Iceland.

"Sorry. What did you say?"

"How on earth could you think we were brother and sister?"

"I didn't think he was your brother. I thought he was your *dog*."

She drives for a while. It's a rainy Reykjavik Sunday. Everybody's on the move. In their car. Waving to each other with windscreen wipers. We pass The Pearl, the rooftop restaurant. It's a dome of glass and steel built on top of some volcano-water tanks. I'd take her there some day if my job involved some money.

"We'd been together for too long," she says.

"How long?"

"Since high school. But with, you know, some good pauses."

Very good indeed. Having slept with four football teams (goalies not included).

"OK. And when did you split up?"

"What do you mean?"

"When did you tell him about us?"

"Just, you know, when we started getting serious."

"And when was that?"

"When you moved in, for example."

She sounds pissed. I'm holy pissed.

"When I moved in? You only told him then?!"

"Yes, about that time."

"So for a month he was like…All our nights in the furniture shop…He thought you were still together?!"

"Well, I guess he had his suspicions."

"So you lied to him, and you lied to me?"

"I didn't lie to you. You never asked."

"I never asked? I mean, how could I? I thought we were together! I didn't know you had *a boyfriend!*"

"I didn't know you had A GIRLFRIEND!"

"But she was dead!"

"Not the first time we..."

"No, I know. That was not good. That's why I left."

"Bullshit. You left because you found out she was dead and you were in a state of shock."

"Can you stop the car?"

"What?"

"I want to get out. It's over."

"It's over? Why?"

"I have to be able to trust you completely."

"But you can."

"No. You lied to me."

"I didn't lie! You never asked!"

"You lied to him and you will lie to me. I'll never be able to trust you."

"Jesus, Tod. Why don't you just shoot me and then you'll have trust!"

Silence. She steps on the gas, I step on the gun. The one inside my shoe. We both look ahead. Through the foggy rain you can make out the red-lighted butt of a white Nissan Pathfinder driving ahead of us. The wipers work the windshield, going from my side to her side, from her side to my side.

"I'm pregnant."

Obviously, that's her talking. And I can only repeat after her, like the first imbecile member of mankind did, when he found out his wife was knocked up.

"Pregnant?"

"Yes."

"Wow. When did you find out?"

"This morning."

"And...?"

"And...?"

"Is it mine?"

"YES, OF COURSE IT'S YOURS! WHAT DO YOU THINK I AM! IT'S FUCKING YOURS! I'M HAVING YOUR FUCKING BABY!!!"

She starts crying. Tears outside, tears inside. Difficult driving conditions. She pulls over at the next gas station. I try to tell her how sorry I am. How wonderful it is that she's having my child. MY CHILD! It must be the best news I've heard since Suker sacked the Germans in France '98. I offer her my arms, and she unfastens her seatbelt before falling into my lap. She cries for a while. I guess half of it comes from the fact that she's pregnant. Munita once told me pregnant women cry a lot. It's something about water building up in the womb and adding to the water supply, causing overflow at times. I stare out the windshield. The brand new gas station also houses a fast food joint. I watch a young father pass under the bright red Kentucky Fried sign, holding the hand of his small son. She cries a bit longer. My crotch is getting wet. It's precipitation returning to the source. Cycle of life.

Our emotional outbursts put steam on the windows, turning the car into some kind of a cocoon. She then finally rises with a tear-torn face. I repeat my sorries.

"I'm sorry. I didn't mean to make you upset. I'm very happy about it."

"You are?"

"Yes. Of course. I'm thrilled."

"So you think you can like, trust me?"

"Can you trust me?"

I feel the gun's texture with my foot.

"Yes."

"But you know who I am, Gunnhildur. You know what I've done. I don't get it. How can you trust me? How can you start a family with someone like me?"

"I love you."

"Me…me, too."

It might not be grammatically perfect, but she gets the meaning and we kiss. I've come a pretty long way. I've come all the way from pulling a gun out of a guy's rectum in a forty-fifth-floor hotel room in midtown Manhattan, to embracing a butter-blonde girl in a Red Cross–red Škoda at some shitty suburban gas station in Iceland and telling her I love her. And I'm not lying. I guess.

Feels fucking good.

To put things in the most absolute perspective, the radio DJ decides that this is the perfect moment to play Britney Spears' "Toxic." Quite incredible really. Back in NYC it used to be "my song" of course. The boys would tease me with it. I kind of liked it, actually, and even ended up buying the bloody CD and used to play it, loud, on my way to a gun-job. It made me powerful, got me into the mood for a good killing. Hearing it now can only appeal to the old self that the new one has swallowed up, the former small as a bullet, the latter big as love.

I'm detoxed.

Gunnhildur doesn't notice the song, and after a prolonged moment of hardcore happiness, we drive on. The two-lane highway takes us through a tunnel, down a slope and up another, then under a flyover. Fancy SUVs speed past us, stirring up "dust" made of water. She makes the turn into Garðabær, the sleepy town where her parents live. Then, out of the blue, she says:

"So you want to live in Iceland, then?"

"Yeah. But only while you're alive. As soon as you're dead, I'm off."

"So you'll probably kill me?"

"Not if you marry me."

"Is that a proposal?"

"No, it's a threat."

She looks at me with a grin I could kill for. Sorry, no. With a grin I could let myself be killed for.

We're two happy hamsters expecting the third as we pull up in front of her parents' house. I give her a quick and serious look, asking:

"Should we also tell them about the baby?"

Her face is almost back to normal, though her eyes are still a bit red.

"No, not now. I'm not sure if I want to keep it."

"What? Gunnhildur? No!"

She looks at me for a while, cultivating a smile on her juicy lips.

"Relax. It was just a test."

CHAPTER 33
TJ TIME
05.12.2007

It's May 2007. A year has passed since my incidental arrival in Iceland. Since my early retirement from the homicide industry. A winter full of dim days and snowy nights has entered my soul. And now it's bright again. Spring is here, cold as ever, with endless light and Eurovision, the annual orgy of gorgeous women and gay men.

It's tonight.

We go to Gunnhildur's parents for the traditional *fjölsky-lduboð* (family gathering). The big Croatian baby inside her is due any moment now, and she looks like the snake who ate the basketball. Gun says I stroke the belly as if I were expecting a million dollars instead of a baby. Sickreader greets us, kissing her daughter and son-in-law on the cheek, the latter for the first time, actually. It's taken her a whole dark season to accept the fact that her daughter is expecting a future gangster.

"I want you to know that if you let us down, I will go to the phone and call the American embassy at once," she told me at Christmas Eve, when we accidentally found ourselves alone in her kitchen.

Well-trained in Icelandic customs, I take off my sneakers and put them away in a corner. Gunnhildur is allowed to keep on her almost-Pradas. (According to Icelandic house rules, you're allowed to enter in your shoes if they cost more than two hundred dollars.) She marches through the living room and out on to the veranda to give her father a kiss. Goodmoondoor is out there fiddling with the *gas-grill*, the pride of every Icelandic household; a black four-legged creature with a bright yellow udder that silently endures the long winter, loitering out in the icy gardens like an arctic mammal. Originally designed for Texas BBQ parties, I've seen the Easelanders dust snow off its back before lighting its flame. Sometimes the well-done steak returns half frozen from the blizzard. These people are true masters of self-deception.

Gunnhildur's brother, Ari, is next to arrive. He's home for a few weeks from his computersomething studies in Boston. A blonde guy with red cheeks and glasses, he looks like an updated version of his father. We're meeting for the first time.

"Hi, I'm Tómas."

"Hi."

"We call him Tommy!" Goodmoondoor happily shouts out from the veranda, now wearing a BBQ glove and holding grill pliers. I sometimes call him Goondy.

I chat with Ari about the Westin Copley Place Hotel in Boston where he recently attended his friend's thirtieth birthday party (and I carried out hit #30 a few years back). Then I watch Gunnhildur open the front door to Olie and Harpa who greet her with a smile, a bottle, and a bouquet. They look a bit like an interracial couple: the lute girl is tanned to the max, but the Meat Man is as white as a chef's toque.

Soon after, Torture and Hanna arrive with their silent kids. As usual his handshake is straight out of the Bible and her natural breath unspoiled by fluoride or mouthwash. They bring their own meat, probably from the lamb that Torture slaughtered himself in his garage. He brings it to Goodmoondoor, and the two men chat for a while out by the smoking grill, looking like tribal chieftains.

"How is it going with the letter?" Hanna asks.

"It's going OK."

She's referring to the Friendly letter.

"That's good to hear. And are you going to send it?"

"I don't know. Maybe."

We eat early, since the live broadcast starts at 7:00 in this part of the world. Goodmoondoor wears his pink tie over his shoulder as he brings the warm meat in from the cold veranda. Ari asks me about work. It sounds like they didn't inform him of my bloody past. I tell him about my jobs, plural, because by now I uphold the national tradition of having two of them. In the morning I work in the cafeteria at the National Library, and four times a week I'm an usher, a best boy, or whatever you call it, at Torture's church. This includes mopping the floors of revelation sweat and occasionally comforting the lone woman who stays behind to talk about her losses. In between, I do my Icelandic lessons and work on my letter. This last thing involves research that I usually do in the library on Hanna's daughter's old laptop, a twentieth-century brick full of tricks, but devoid of any latter-day luxuries. From time to time I also take karate lessons from Torture in the mattress room.

Olie and Harpa are a bit shy around all the famous people. Olie concentrates on eating, his small earring dancing by his jaw like Sammy's glasses as he relentlessly chews on the heavenly lamb, but Harpa hardly touches her portion. Torture looks at their bottle of red as if it were filled with the blood of Satan. Olie offers to pour me some but I silently decline. A brief moment of suspense arrives when Gunnhildur asks me to pass the sauce and calls me "Tod." She bites her lip, but Olie and Harpa are too stressed to notice, and Ari is talking to Hanna.

The conversation turns to the war in Iraq and Iceland's participation in it. Somehow the no-army nation managed to come up with a single soldier and then sent him down to Baghdad to help out with the big mess. But now he's being sent back home. It took a whole platoon of Americans to protect the poor bastard.

"They didn't want to risk a wipeout of the whole Icelandic army," Ari says in his American accent, and then laughs a certain nerdish laughter I haven't heard for years, but remember from the university cafeteria in Hanover. Niko's brother studied computer science and his friends used to laugh like that all the time. Intelligent boys laughing at other people's stupidity, the "other people" including *all the people in the world* except the ones who were studying computer science at Hanover University.

Olie laughs with him, but Torture looks at them both from under a set of heavy brows, as if he were contemplating arming his whole congregation and sending it down to Iraq to teach those Muslims how to circumcise their hearts. But instead of saying it, the Bible-boomer turns to me and says this will be the first time he has ever watched the Eurovision Song Contest. He's doing it for me, he says.

"And you're looking at a man who once told his people that devoting your time to this festival of fools was a form of devil worship. *Ha ha.* It was the year we sent a sodomite dressed up as Lucifer himself. No. It's nothing but vanity and vexation of the spirit. But I will bite my tongue this evening. *Ha ha.*"

Some heavy biting it will be. Since the monsters from Finland won last year, this year's contest is being held in Helsinki. The broadcast begins with them playing the winning song, "Hard

Rock Hallelujah." It's everything but torture to watch Torture's reaction. Yet, I suspect he admires those religious rockers a bit. It's his own preaching style, taken to the heavy-metal max.

The Icelandic entry is number five on the list. One weather-beaten leather-wearing rocker with red hair cries out about his "Valentine Lost." Gunnhildur likes him, so I do, too. I watch her sitting next to her brother on the sofa, stretching her long white legs out on the floor, from beneath the short, black, belly-stretching dress. My Daybreak darling. Red lips and thighs that are one inch thicker than last year. Her behind is almost Latinal by now, and her breasts have risen to the occasion. On the whole her figure is much juicier, apart from the hard basketball-belly. It stems from the water buildup. I haven't given her any reasons to cry this past winter.

I then take another good look at Torture. My new boss. The Icelandic Dikan. If he had a soft spot for the hallelujah-monsters, he's back to his hard-rock self by now. The fluttering bright flames of "vanity and vexation of the spirit" are reflected in his glasses, while his contempt is expressed by his lips, moving about in his beard like two worms in the grass. It's way more entertaining watching him watch this song contest than watching the thing itself. He reminds me of Dikan watching his Dynamo Zagreb lose to my Hajduk.

Like Iceland, Croatia goes for an old-timer this year. It's the one and only Dado Topić, playing with some kids I haven't seen before. Dado is the king of Croatian rock. He wrote the soundtrack to my youth. He was even there the night I lost my virginity.

Now he sings: *"Vjerujem u ljubav"* (I believe in love) in his deep scratchy voice, still sporting his long hair and cowboy boots. The song is pretty good, actually, but Torture says the girl singing with him is out of tune. Bite your tongue, man.

Before the song is over, the doorbell rings. Goodmoondoor goes to the door. He comes back saying it's for me. I take a quick look at the mother of my child and head for the door. It's halfway open—the incredible chill of the Icelandic spring comes rushing in my face like some sort of an odorless gas that makes you shiver to the bone—but I can't see anyone out there. I step on the famous golden threshold and look about. Someone grabs my arm and I can feel the barrel of a gun piercing my left side. My brain may have been washed in the river of Jordan, but my nervous system is still that of a soldier. I sense a gun when I sense it.

It's Niko.

Of all the guys in the world, it's fucking Niko.

My heart instantly skips a beat before the needle lands on Britney's "Toxic." In one instant my new life is blown away by the old one.

"Nice to see you," he says in Croatian, with the customary grin, and asks me to join him for a ride, pointing to a black Audi idling out on the street. "I think we have to talk."

It's nice to hear my mother's tongue again.

I tell him I need to get my shoes. Clearly, he wasn't prepared for this one, and is thrown off guard as he watches me turn back inside the house.

The shoes are behind the door. I should probably call on Olie to jump into the kitchen for a sharp knife or ask Torture to roll out his fiery tongue. But I only bow over my thick-soled sneakers, feeling Niko's sharp gaze stab me in the back, listening to the final chords of Dado's song echo from the entrails of the house followed by the crowd's crazy applause. I put on my shoes and straighten up. When I reach for my black leather jacket, Niko shakes his head.

"But it's fucking cold," I say.

"We won't be long."

Gunnhildur shouts something from the living room and I hesitate a moment, looking my old friend in the eye, before closing the door behind me.

Once we're outside, he quickly searches me, looking for an automatic rifle in my armpits, in my pockets, or in my crotch. I'm wearing a thin black sweater over a white T-shirt and some cool jeans that Gun helped me pick out. As I get inside the car, I think I notice some movement in the living room window of my in-laws. As if someone had seen us. I shouldn't worry, really. The holy men will have their SWAT team of angels come to my rescue.

So for the second year in a row I'm prevented from watching all of Eurovision. I was really looking forward to the Serbian entry. Rumor had it they were entering a lesbian dwarf, who looks like Milošević's illegitimate daughter, praying for love, peace, a piece of our land, or whatever.

Niko looks the same. His goatee has turned a bit gray though, and his skin shows signs of the cold. But the long nose and the hard black eyeballs are there—this gaze of his that clearly says *"Don't fucking fuck with me!"* He throws himself into the seat beside me and the driver darts off. The car smells of leather and luxury. It looks to be about two hours old.

I recognize the driver. It's the New York Neck-backer. Good old Radovan. Shaved to the skull. He's even wearing the same fucking sunglasses he wore my last day in America.

So it's reunion time. *Ponovni susret.* We must be heading for a fancy restaurant where Don Dikan waits at the end of the table, surrounded by Gun lookalikes and sucking on the fat Havana cigar he's been trying to light for the past thirty years.

Niko has his eyes on me, keeping his gun LPP, though always pointed at me. It's his Desert Eagle, a pitch-black semi-automatic made in Israel. I remember when he first got it. He blushed like a boy. He just had to have one after he saw the first *Matrix* movie. Typical Niko. His black eyeballs resemble the opening of the barrel. Three black holes stare at me. *"Don't fucking fuck with me!"* So this is how my victims must have felt when they were faced with the loaded gun and the willing finger. Except I have God on my side. *The eyes of the Lord are in every place, beholding the evil and the good (Proverbs 15:3).*

Radovan seems to have spent a week in Reykjavik. He drives like a local already, with great confidence and great speed. The streets are deserted. Everybody's watching the Serbian lesbian.

"So you waited for the right moment?" I ask.

"We've been waiting for this moment," Niko says.

"Me too," I say. "It took you longer than I thought."

"You maybe thought you'd escaped us, 'Tomaš Leivur'?"

I must admire his research.

"Who's your man? Truster?"

"Truster? Who's that?"

"Never mind. What's happening in New York?"

"You messed up, Toxic."

Radovan drives the empty road. He seems to be heading for the airport. They're bringing me back. The only question is whether I'll be traveling business or cargo.

"What happened?" I ask.

No answer. I try again:

"How did I mess up? I followed orders. I only did what Dikan asked me to do."

"You messed up, Toxic. Ivo is dead. Zoran is dead. Branko Brown is dead. And Branko Karlovać as well."

"And Dikan?"

"Boss is OK."

Radovan breaks in, smiling from the driver's seat, talking into the rearview mirror:

"Dikan told me to kiss you. When you're dead! Ha ha."

"Shut up and drive!" Niko shouts.

So cargo it'll be. My final fifteen minutes have started ticking. Heart switches from Britney pop to funeral fugue. The black Audi takes us past the long aluminum factory, on the outskirts of town. The soft radio delivers Louis Armstrong, blowing his trumpet "Cheek to Cheek" and telling us he's in heaven.

"Who killed them? The Feds?" I ask, casually bringing my left foot behind my right.

Being able to speak my language again this close to the end is like a former chain-smoker being offered one last cig before the big event. Croatian words exit my mouth like lustful smoke rings. Actually, seeing Niko's face again, makes me want to smoke.

"You killed them, Toxic."

I killed them. The dumpsite hit must have triggered a series of TJs. But the Feds don't kill people. At least not until they've heard their life story through the dirty underwear placed over their heads, encouraged by the crazy police dog barking at their naked genitals. I don't get it. I was just a hitman. I didn't want to hurt anybody. And now I'm to blame? I focus on simpler things. I have to keep talking.

"You kill Munita?" I ask my old friend and former roommate, while discretely pushing the tip of my left shoe against the heel of my right.

"Munita?" Niko repeats with a smile and a short nasal blow.

"She had a great body," Radovan says. "But an ugly head."

Niko laughs. Niko laughs and this is the right moment. I push the bottom of my right heel with my left toe, quite hard, until the sole breaks loose from the heel: I manage to "open" the shoe at the back, and by raising the foot, and shaking it a bit, the small gun gently rolls out from the back of my shoe. It's on the floor now. I step on it with my left leg. I've done this a hundred times. Been practicing hard all winter. Niko doesn't notice a thing. He's still laughing.

"Ugly head," the meatloaf repeats.

He then turns off the main road and heads down a dirt road in the direction of the mountains. The snowdrifts are almost gone. The moss on the lava is green. The *nothingness* around us is absolute. No trees, no birds, no nothing. Just some scruffy rocks and splashes of moss here and there. This lunar landscape is pretty far from the white cliffs, decorated with cypresses and olive trees, that I know from the hills around Split. I've started to appreciate the ice cold emptiness now, but I have to admit that I still miss my Adriatic spring. Suddenly I start humming our *Lijepa naša*, the national anthem of Croatia:

"Drava, Sava, keep on flowing,
Danube, you know where you're going."

Niko pricks up his ears, but he can't make out the song, nor the words. I hum a little louder. My eyes get warm. Every time you hear this song, some twenty thousand Croats appear in front of your eyes, all dressed in the red-and-white national jersey, roaring in the stands and crying their lungs out before our last game in France '98.

"Tell the sea and tell the sand
That a Croat loves his fatherland."

"SHUT UP!" Niko shouts. "SHUT THE FUCK UP!"

"OK," I say. "Can I have a cigarette before you kill me?"

"You started smoking again?" Niko asks.

"Don't worry. It won't kill me."

He looks at me as if he wants to shoot me immediately. He probably would, if the Audi were more than two hours old.

CHAPTER 34
BOK
05.12.2007

Radovan parks the car in a rough parking area next to the road and the silence of the land takes over. I try to keep my cool as Niko gets out of the car, leaving the door open. He makes some quick modern dance moves, showing the surroundings to his great gun. Yeah, man. You better watch out for those White Hats. I casually bend forward and manage to pick the small gun up from the floor, without the driver noticing. I mean to do him right away, but when Niko shouts for me to get the hell out of the car, I fucking hesitate. Discretely, I pocket the piece and exit the car with my heart playing all kinds of music, like a radio gone haywire.

I'm fucked.

The bright spring night is freezing cold. Niko orders me to walk ahead of him, away from the road, and then shouts at Radovan, still inside the car. I make my way across the harsh, uneven lava surface. Here and there are patches of light green and gray moss, and we have to step over some oblong, narrow openings in the lava floor, which look like miniatures of the Grand Canyon. Clefts, you might call them. I try hard to walk naturally while doing my best to conceal the loose sole of my right shoe. I hear Radovan get out of the car. The car door slams, filling my ears with sound. The last door of my life…I could just as well turn around now, grab the gun, and ice them in a flash.

No. Won't do. Niko is fast enough.

Finally he tells me to stop. I get it. They've really done their homework. We stop at the edge of a lava cleft that's big enough to serve as my coffin. Iceland will swallow me up like an unlucky tourist.

I turn around to face my friends and executioners. We all shiver with cold. It must be around two degrees Celsius. Not a car, a bird, or a plane can be heard, and the air is completely still. The silence is absolute. I think about Gunnhildur. She must be in the car by now, driving around aimlessly, desperately. Or maybe they're still at the house, held hostage in the sofa by the Ukranian entry, thinking I must have gone out with an old buddy from Mob School.

Niko orders Radovan to give me a cigarette. Actually, I'd almost forgotten about it. The blockhead brings out the packet and throws me one. It's a Pall Mall. There is absolutely no limit to the strangeness of this guy. Though he looks like a white Hulk in a suit, his favorite artist is Celine Dion. He's watched *Titanic* thirty times, he once told me. I ask for a light, and the bald one searches his pockets without success. Niko keeps his Desert Eagle pointed at me. I keep my eyes glued on the barrel, while he uses his free hand to fish a lighter from his pants. He throws it at me. I pretend to catch it, while allowing it to escape my hands. It lands on the lava floor. I excuse myself before bowing to get it. It's from the Zagreb Samovar. I hesitate a moment before picking up the lighter, giving Niko a quick look. He's as tense as a bound eagle. *"Don't fucking fuck with me!"* Obviously, he can't wait to bomb my face with a long bullet from his big black gun. Still, he promised I could have a final smoke. For old times' sake.

This could be my moment, I say to myself as I grab the lighter. But no. I hesitate again. Without doing anything, I get up and light the cigarette. It shakes in my mouth like a tractor's gearshift. My heart repeats the same beat over and over again, with the sound of a CD stuck on a scratch.

I remove the cigarette from my lips and give it a good look, those 3.5 inches of paper and tobacco. I'm 3.5 inches from the grave. I've got 3.5 inches to work from. Now, 3.41, to be exact.

I started smoking in the war. In those crazy days, every cigarette you could get your lips on represented seven minutes of cease-fire, a glimpse of heaven in the midst of hell. After the war it became the opposite: every cigarette brought back seven minutes of shooting and bombing. So I quit. This one here can only bring back my scattered memories: my mother cursing in the kitchen, Hanover fucking *Hauptbahnhof,* the Winnipeg guy and his bloody wallet, Gunnhildur's stick-red smile. I smoke it as slowly as possible.

"But why kill me? What's the purpose?"

"Shut up."

"I've quit. I don't even travel anymore. I'm just…"

"Shut the fuck up!"

"Sorry. Let me just finish this and then you can…"

As before, we speak in Croatian. You have to picture bright white subtitles flickering across our dark chests.

Once again I inhale, watching the low blue mountains ahead. They must have witnessed a thing like this before. The sky is empty. No cloud, no plain. Somewhere behind me, Reykjavik spreads out in the distance, the fourth city of my life, and further out, at sea, the bright spring sunset must be well underway. Goodbye world. *Doviđenja svijete.* I exhale and look at the butt. There is about one puff left; less than 1 inch left of my life. My two visiting friends are getting restless. I lift the small cigarette up to my lips and inhale.

Here we go.

I bend forward, pretending to put the cigarette out in the stiff moss with my left hand while reaching into my pocket with my right. Niko immediately shouts and steps forward, pointing his gun downwards, toward my head. Quick as a fox on fire, I dive to my right, rolling on the harsh lava floor, and he shoots. The bullet bouncing off lava rings in our ears. And before he even realizes I'm holding a gun, its bullet is buried in his upper right arm. His scream is muffled. Radovan immediately reaches for his tool, but receives a bullet instead, in his right wrist. He screams out loud. As Niko grabs his gun from the wounded arm with his left one, I'm back on my feet, pointing the pistol at them and screaming:

"DROP IT! DROP THE FUCKING GUN!"

Niko looks at me with bewildered eyes. *"What the fucking fuck?"* He now has the piece in his left hand.

"I SAID DROP IT!"

Blood drips from their wounded arms. Radovan is still wearing his sunglasses, looking quite ridiculous, like some wannabe mobster in a Russian B movie.

"DROP THE FUCKING GUN!"

For some mystical reason I use the English word "gun" here, instead of the Croatian *pistolj*. It makes me think of Gunnhildur. The thought distracts me and Naughty Niko sniffs out the weakness expertly. Before I know it, he has raised the gun against me. We strike simultaneously, like the spiritual twins we used to be. My bullet lands in his gun-holding left arm. His scream is less muffled now. I try to swallow mine. A streak of strange warmth shoots down my groin, in the direction of my left thigh.

The warmth then turns into fire. It's like when a match is being lighted. First there is the strike and then there is fire.

It's a typical left-hander. He aimed for my heart but got the bladder. But mine was on target. He's as good as armless. As well as Radovan, after another one from the PP9. Suddenly I'm aiming for arms only. I've fired fucking four shots and still no one's dead.

My friends' faces are tormented by pain, as mine must be too. Their hands hang lifelessly beside them, freshly slaughtered piglets, blood dripping from their hoofs. I have my small gun aimed at their heads now and after some more shouting, Niko drops his big Desert Eagle. I order him to give it a kick and then quickly bow to pick it up. It seems to take me forever to get back up, though. The pain in my groin is of groundbreaking proportions. Holy shit.

I put Niko's gun in my pocket.

I order Radovan to come closer and open his jacket for me, but he can't, of course, with his hands. I carefully approach him, my eyes going between him and Niko every two seconds, and open his black Armani jacket with my left hand. His weapon rests in the inner pocket. A silver Smith & Wesson. But as I grab it, the stupid Hulk tries to push me away with his elbow. Niko uses the opportunity for coming at me, head first, like some crazy hornless ram. I put him out with a simple "elblow," something I perfected in Torture training this winter. With Niko down, Radovan doesn't risk any more tricks, and soon I have two guns in my pocket and the third one in my hand.

I fish the car key out of Radovan's pocket and then silently wait for Niko to come back to his senses. I order them both to crawl down into the mini-canyon. This takes some time. Still wearing the sunglasses, Radovan looks more and more ridiculous, heading for a comic death. I tell them to lie down, facedown, biting my lips from the pain. Something is leaking down my left thigh. Feels like I'm peeing with my balls.

This is wartime all over again. Shouting at people in Croatian with a gun in my hand and a leaking leg. The driver's bulky torso takes up most of the space in the lava coffin. Next to him, Niko looks like a slim virgin wife about to be buried with her husband, eyes screaming: "Please, fuck me instead!"

"FACE THE FUCKING EARTH!" I shout, sounding a bit too nervous.

I lower my gun. I've got two asses in sight. Two rectums screaming for lead. There is nothing else to do. Munita's killers will have to face the fridge. On fucking Fridge Island. I'm about to pull the trigger when there is a sudden breeze in the otherwise still spring night. I swiftly look around but see nothing. Nothing coming, nothing going. There's just this sudden breeze, blowing across the lunar lava field, pushing up the good moon door…

Amen.

I take a long good look at my former buddies, lying face down in the cleft, like two gentlemen overdressed for a mass grave. I then nod a few times before telling them goodbye with a short little Croatian word:

"*Bok.*"

I turn away and start limping towards the car. My groin cries, my heart shakes, but my soul says hallelujah.

CHAPTER 35
THE SERBIAN ENTRY
05.12.2007

Driving an Audi you think you should be happy. Success has rewarded you with soft leather seats and a pilot's dashboard. Luckily it's an automatic, since I'm losing all feeling in my left leg, as well as the lower half of my torso. My pants are soaked in blood, urine, or some other inner liquid that is about to fill my left shoe. I wonder if the bullet is still inside me somewhere. Feels like it's resting on the bottom of my bladder, working as a plug in a bathtub.

When I had walked some sixty painful feet away from the two idiots, I turned around and looked them in the eye. They were peeking out of their lava-grave with dumbstruck eyes, looking very much like two sheep stuck in a hole. *Why didn't you kill us?* I even sensed a touch of disappointment in their eyes. I turned my back on them and continue towards the car. I threw their guns in the trunk, put mine in my pocket, and managed to pack my pain into the driver's seat.

I'm driving back the same way we came. I can already see the aluminum factory down by the coast. Some cars drive past it, on the Reykjavik-Keflavik highway. The song contest must be over.

Senka was Serbian, a way-too-beautiful Serbian, a fact I hid from my parents. Her real name was Dragana, the Serbian equivalent of Sickreader, so we decided on Senka, that indicated a Bosnian, even Muslim, background. We went out together for over a year. But then came war and she had to move away with her family.

After our capture of Knin, we were focusing on the region around it, and I was ordered to search some German-looking villas. One of them had a bombed-out roof and broken windows, with scorched walls. It was a huge house on three floors, and I took my rifle from room to room. They were all empty, but when I came down to the basement, I heard some noise. I rushed into a side room, screaming at the Serbian soldier hiding under an ugly old bed. After I'd spread some bullets around the room, he came crawling out. Except he was a she. It was Senka. Dragana Avramovič. She was still too beautiful. Even more so, wearing that awful uniform. Her hair had been cut even shorter, making her look even more boyish. But the mole was there, and those tempting lips, eyes full of poetry...I wanted to stroke her hard cheek with my finger. We were both dumbstruck. I noticed an ugly scar across her neck.

"Senka?"

"Tomo?"

Before we knew it, we were kissing each other. Two soldiers in enemy uniforms. But then she suddenly stopped kissing and stepped back, holding a gun in her hand, a Serbian made Zastava, pointing it at me with serious eyes. She didn't trust me? I tried to keep my cool, my AK-47 hanging at my back, strapped around my shoulder.

"You want to shoot me?" I asked her in a very calm way.

"I always wanted to."

"Why?"

"Because you're such an asshole."

"I loved you."

"Liar."

"No. I really did."

"I missed you," she said with shaking lips.

"I missed you too."

"You never wrote me back."

"I did. You didn't get it? I wrote you to Belgrade. To your aunt's place."

"Liar."

"Senka..." I said with a smile. "You're still crazy. I remember...You always said you wanted to kill me."

"Yes. And now I can."

I suddenly felt like we were back together, arguing in her stepfather's funky basement in the heart of Split, and without thinking I reached out and touched her army gun with my index finger. I put the finger inside the barrel, as far as it could go, while telling her in the most relaxed voice that kissing was better than killing. I kept on playing with her gun, doing the international sign for "make love, not war" (making my finger enter and exit the barrel a couple of times) until her juicy lips gave birth to the smile I'd been missing for five long years.

And soon we were kissing again. Me and my crazy girl. Me and my Serbian girl.

In a short while we were on the bed, our thirsty hands trying to find their way through five lost years and heavy outfits. Bombs went off outside. The whole house shook like from a bulldozer and there was the sound of broken glass. It only added fuel to our fire. Nothing makes love more exciting than war. We were breathing heavily and I had my fingers on her firm army breasts when two of my fellow soldiers suddenly appeared inside the room, laughing and cheering me on. It had the opposite effect. They noticed and pushed me aside, putting their dirty hands over Senka's mouth.

I had to watch them. I tried closing my eyes, but it was only worse. I had to fucking watch them. I didn't want them to kill her so I had to wait until they were done.

You can have two MHMs.

For years I tried to contact her. Every single one of my months in New York, I googled her name and wrote to her family and friends without much success. One of her Split girlfriends wrote me from Italy, telling me she got a postcard from Senka some years back, from Belgrade. Other than that, nothing. Not even our great national cemetery files seemed to contain her name. Only her stepfather's. He was buried in Novi Sad in 2002. She was probably living outside the reach of the Internet, in a mountain village or some faraway land. I hadn't typed her name for over three months when this past winter I fucking ran into her.

In Reykjavik.

Of all the places in the world, I bumped into her in the Kringlan Mall, just outside the Penninn bookstore, next to the crazy souvenir shop. It was right before Christmas. The place was buzzing with overstressed Easelanders, and we literally bumped into each other. There was no denying it was her. I'd recognize that birthmark in any mass grave. It took her a few seconds to recognize me. People rushed by as we just stood there frozen, looking at each other without saying much. I'd gone to the mall in search

245

of a Christmas present for Gunnhildur and found Senka. She hid her big scar with a scarf. Her cheeks were still kind of hard and her lips looked soft and juicy, but her beauty had faded. She'd also turned a bit fat. I could tell that she thought the same of me. We sat down for a coffee, and she added some tears to her latte.

"You should have killed me in that basement," I said in our beloved language.

"No. Then your friends would have killed me."

"They almost killed me for letting you go."

"I guess we all died a little in that war. It's like mother used to say. War kills everybody, including the ones who live."

The two of them had been in Iceland for more than three years, coming up here after a decade of living all over the place, including a Red Cross refugee camp for over a year, where Senka's stepfather, the poet, had passed away. Her sister had died in the war, along with her family. Finally they decided to join a group of thirty Serbs and start a new life in a new country. In the beginning of 2003, the group settled down in a small village in the west part of Iceland. There mother and daughter stayed for two years, in a brand-new apartment furnished by the locals.

"The people are really nice up there. But it was like living in a closet, with steep blue mountains all around us. During wintertime you don't see the sun for almost three months." Her mother stayed at home gazing out the window, at the ocean—"You could see all the way to Greenland"—while Senka worked in the fish factory. "The most boring job of my life." But when the old one needed more nursing, they moved to the city down south. At first she worked as a cashier in one of the Bónus's stores, but just recently she fulfilled her lifelong dream when she landed a job as a "stagehand" at the City Theatre.

How freaky was it all? Of all the cities in the world, we both ended up in this one.

Now the old woman had gone senile, Senka said. "She doesn't talk about anything other than Greenland. That she has to go to Greenland." Her mother found the best way to deal with her losses, through Alzheimer's disease. Me and Senka found a different way.

She's expecting my baby.

I know. My Torture School degree didn't come with a minor in sainthood.

I make my way into Garðabær. The black Audi seems to find its way all by itself. Soon I have parked it outside the house of my Icelandic in-laws.

The bullet has made my bladder swell to the size of a Desert Eagle egg. It takes me about four minutes to exit the car. Why did I come here anyway? I should have gone straight to the morgue. That way I'd have saved a lot of people's time and money. I just wanted to give Gunnhildur Senka's number so they can have my babies meet.

The groin-pain grows with each step, as I make my way to the front door, leaving behind me a trail of blood. With the sound of silent church bells, I open the door and step over the golden threshold. I'm greeted with music, some flutes and stuff, coming from the living room. As I enter (in my shoes) I can see that they're all still there, gathered around the loud TV: Goodmoondoor and Sickreader, Torture and Hanna, Ari and Gunnhildur, Olie and Harpa. They seem surprised to see me, staring at me with big eyes, small noses, and open mouths. Eight good snowballs facing a man on fire.

"I didn't." I manage to say before I collapse on the floor. "I didn't kill them."

They rush to my rescue. Olie's small golden earring flicks above me like a halo thrown at me from a thousand feet. Torture gets all red in the face, turning his glasses into two half moons. Gunnhildur's bright face hovers over me like a large sun over a troubled land. She says something, but I can't hear it. And then more faces appear. Hanna, Harpa, Sickreader...And they all say something, but I can't hear it for the room is filled with music. I don't recognize the song, but I can make out some of the words.

"Al Bogu ne mogu..."

"What's the song?" I manage to whisper.

"It's the winning song. From Serbia. Serbia's the winner," Gunnhildur says.

"Oh? They won? Good for them." I say.

Then I'm not sure what happens.

ABOUT THE AUTHOR

Hallgrimur Helgason began as an artist, showing his work in galleries in New York and Paris. He made his debut as a novelist in 1990 and gained international attention with his third novel, *101 Reykjavik*, with praise including an apt description by novelist/critic Tim Sandlin: "Imagine if Henry Miller had written *Tropic of Cancer* on crack instead of wine." It was subsequently made into a film starring Victoria Abril. In 2001 he received the Icelandic Literary Prize for *The Author of Iceland* and has twice been nominated for the Nordic Council Literature Prize: first with *101 Reykjavik* in 1999 and then *Stormland* in 2007. A film based on the latter was released in early 2011. *The Hitman's Guide to Housecleaning* is his only novel written in English. The author's own translation was published in Iceland in 2008 and became a bestseller in Germany in 2010. A father of three, Hallgrimur divides his time between Reykjavik and Hrísey Island.

18630625R00148

Made in the USA
Charleston, SC
13 April 2013